THE TWO WEDDINGS OF ZHAO PING

Patricia A. W

ISBN: **1539138291**
ISBN 13: **9781539138297**

FOR CHUCK

*My wonderful and patient husband who allowed
Ping to live with us for over eight years.*

PART ONE

"Women must obey their fathers when they are not married, their husbands when in wedlock, their sons in widowhood."

—Confucius

CHAPTER ONE

Chongqing, October 1984
In the gloomy haze of early morning, dressed in khaki slacks and a black top, Lei Lei flitted through the horde of pedestrians on the main thoroughfare in Chongqing. Gasping for breath, she paused to inhale the tainted city air and wipe the perspiration from her brow. She thought of her visit the day before to the obstetrician. The visit when she'd learned she was carrying a daughter. The visit that had prompted her husband to tell her she must abort. "We can have only one child," Zhao Jiang said, eyes black and hard as coal. "And that child will be a son."

Lei Lei resumed her flight, nearly colliding with a vendor, whose wares, held in two baskets, dangled from opposite ends of a rod across his shoulders. Sidestepping the peddler, she raced down a street lined with small open-front shops. Her frantic eyes focused on the path before her. She dodged past vendors selling containers of nuts. She ran by stalls heaped with produce and flowers. Sweet fragrances of jasmine and peonies filled the air. As Lei Lei traveled farther, pungent aromas from sizzling woks in nearby eateries overpowered the more delicate floral scents. At the end of the street, she sped past ladies on makeshift benches weaving large spade-shaped fans to sell to tourists.

Leaving the hustle-bustle of the marketplace, Lei Lei scrambled down the stone steps of a narrow alley, ebony tresses floating behind her. Exhausted, she leaned against the entryway of a small cinderblock house. While one hand cradled her expanded belly, the other pounded on the wooden door.

The door opened. Yi Ma appeared. At the sight of her younger sister, she gasped. "What's wrong?" Lei Lei collapsed into her outstretched arms.

Yi Ma helped her inside the house, supporting her as they walked toward a rumpled sofa in the living room. Once seated, palms on her stomach, Lei Lei turned a tear-stained face to Yi Ma. "I am carrying a girl. Zhao Jiang told me I must abort."

Yi Ma left the room and returned with a box of tissues. Lei Lei took one and dabbed at her eyes. Then she lifted her head, jaw set, chin firm. "I cannot kill my baby." She placed Yi Ma's hand on her protruding belly. "Touch her little head. Put your ear on my stomach and listen to her heartbeat. She's alive. She's moving. I will never abandon her."

CHAPTER TWO

Chongqing, twenty years later

Zhao Ping's fingers caressed the red silk *cheongsam* hanging in her closet. The day after tomorrow, she would be married in this dress. Never had she felt so miserable.

She glanced at Auntie Yi Ma, sitting on her cot in their small shared bedroom. Her aunt looked at her, an expression of concern on her wrinkled face. "What are you doing?" Yi Ma asked.

"Packing."

"Are you so eager to leave us?"

"Of course not."

She couldn't tell Auntie Yi Ma that packing kept her mind off unpleasant things—like her approaching nuptials.

Ping took a pair of dark slacks and a slim black skirt from the closet, carefully folded them, and placed the items in the backpack on her bed. She trudged over to the worn wooden chest that she shared with Auntie Yi Ma. Ping's belongings were in the two bottom drawers. Opening one of them, she sifted through her underwear and selected the dingiest set to pack. The other she would wear at her wedding. She removed the remaining clothes, three tops and a black cardigan, and placed them in the backpack.

Returning to the chest, she knelt on the floor and pulled open the bottom drawer. Here, Ping kept her treasures: a silk folding fan with cherry blossoms that had been her mother's; a woven staircase bracelet from her friend Meihui; two rollerball pens, one red, the other silver; several filled notebooks from her classes at the university; and three dog-eared English paperbacks, *Wuthering Heights*, *Emma*, and *Jane Eyre*.

Sitting cross-legged on the floor, she reached for the books. Through downcast eyes, she perused them. She had room in her backpack for only one. She selected *Emma*, identifying with the Jane Austen heroine. Like Emma, she was twenty years old. Like Emma, she had lost her mother at a young age. And like Emma, she did not want to marry.

Ping wanted a career like her two best friends, Meihui and Zhilan. The three had performed well on the *Gaokao*, the national examination needed to enter college. Meihui was studying to become an accountant; Zhilan, an engineer. Attracted to languages, Ping's dream was to teach English at a university. She had just completed her second year of college. Marriage and a move to Beijing, where her future husband worked, meant abandoning her studies.

She had told this to her father, Zhao Jiang, when he informed her of the arranged wedding. "Please let me finish my studies," she had pleaded, but to no avail. Baba was old-fashioned.

"Why do you want to become a professor? Your duty is to marry and bear a son. How will you be able to raise my grandchild if you work?"

When Ping told Auntie Yi Ma of the arrangement, she shook her head. "Don't be angry with your father. He is concerned about supporting our family. It is expensive to have a university student living at home."

Ping frowned. She could not argue this point. Most of her friends from senior high school had jobs. Only a privileged few attended university.

She closed the drawer containing her treasures and put the novel in her backpack. She zipped it shut and placed it on the floor. Then she sat on her bed across from her aunt's, shoulders hunched forward, hands folded in her lap, eyes cast downward.

"What's the matter?" Auntie Yi Ma asked.

Ping brushed a tear from her cheek. "I'm frightened."

"Of what?"

"I have never even kissed a boy, and now I must sleep with a stranger. What if he is unkind? What if he beats me?"

Yi Ma stood up, put on her purple slippers, padded over to Ping, and sat beside her. "Don't be afraid. The marriage broker assured us that Wang Jianbo comes from a respectable family. Your father consulted a feng shui expert to select the best date for the wedding. And tomorrow night the good luck lady is coming to comb your hair."

"I don't want to go to Beijing and give up my studies at the university. Besides, I'll miss you and Baba."

"You are like the newborn sea turtle who only knows the hole in the sand in which she is born. She has not yet ventured out to make the trek from the nest to the ocean. There are many wonderful things awaiting you in Beijing. Perhaps you can continue your studies there. And as for seeing us, Chongqing isn't that far from where you'll be living. Wang Jianbo's parents are here, and he is their only child. You'll probably be returning often to visit your in-laws. When you do, you'll come see Baba and me."

Ping's lips widened into a reluctant smile. "You always make me feel better."

Auntie Yi Ma rose and walked over to the chest. Reaching into the top drawer, she pulled out a small, framed picture.

"Take this," she said. "This way I'll always be with you."

Ping looked at the photo of her aunt taken at Pipa Shan, a nearby park, and thanked her. Opening her backpack, she placed it between two sweaters for protection. "I wish I had a picture of Baba, too."

"Why don't you ask him?"

Ping wandered into the living room. A worn brown sofa sat against a wall yellowed from tobacco smoke. Sheer white curtains pirouetted at the open window; a shaft of sunlight shone through and fell on the frayed carpet. In a green chair on the opposite side of the room, Ping's father dozed, sleep noises whistling through parted lips.

"Baba," she said, gently shaking his shoulder.

Zhao Jiang sat up and rubbed his eyes. "You couldn't let your old father sleep?"

"I'm sorry I woke you, but I'm packing for Beijing. Auntie Yi Ma gave me one of her photos. She thought you might have one of you I could take."

Mumbling under his breath, Zhao Jiang slowly pulled himself up from the chair and shuffled toward his bedroom. "Wait here."

"Does he have a picture?" Yi Ma asked, joining her niece on the living room couch.

"I don't know. He went to look."

Zhao Jiang reappeared clutching a wallet-size photograph. He handed it to Ping. She studied the faded snapshot of two children, a boy and a girl, around ten or eleven years old. Yi Ma glanced at the photo and turned her head away.

"Who are the children?" Ping asked.

Her father repositioned himself in his chair before responding. "Me and my little sister, your auntie Yangmei."

"I didn't know I had an auntie Yangmei."

"She is no longer with us. She died many years ago."

"Why have I never heard of her?"

Zhao Jiang closed his eyes, hands folded over his chest. "We do not speak of Yangmei. She is a reminder of the poverty and shame of my family—the victim of an act of desperation."

Ping sat in silence waiting to hear her father's story. The old man opened his eyes—eyes filled with sadness and regret.

"You are older and will soon be married. I think it is time you knew my sister's story. We were happy when that photo was taken," Zhao Jiang began. "We lived on a farm in the countryside. My father was part of a production team that worked the soil from dawn to dusk."

Zhao Jiang paused to light a partially smoked cigarette retrieved from a tin ashtray on the small table next to his chair. "Everything was good," he continued, "until the winter of '59. The weather was very bad that year. My father's production team could not meet its quota. We were forced to subsist on less food. The next year, it was worse. There was nothing to eat."

Zhao Jiang recounted how he would go into the woods with his father to hunt for squirrels and other small animals. His mother and Yangmei looked for berries and nuts. But since everyone else was doing the same, even that source of food became scarce. Many people in the village died—some from starvation, others from diseases that invaded weakened bodies. His father knew that his family—the four of them—could not all survive on what they were able to find in the woods.

Zhao Jiang took a drag on his cigarette and coughed uncontrollably. Ping rushed to the kitchen and returned with a glass of water. After drinking, Zhao Jiang continued. "My father, your grandfather, decided if any of us were to live, a sacrifice must be made."

Zhao Jiang's voice broke; his chin trembled. Inhaling deeply, he continued. "Yangmei would receive no more food. Her portion would go to my parents and me."

He paused to take another sip of water. "I loved my little sister and would sneak food to her. When my father found out, he beat me. After that, Yangmei no longer accepted my offerings. She knew she was dying. I sat next to her, holding her hand when she passed away."

Ping sat transfixed, filled with sadness for this aunt she never knew. After a pause, Zhao Jiang told of his mother's death, brought about by the sorrow of Yangmei's passing. Lack of food and the shame of not providing for his family caused his father to become ill. Unable to care for his son, he sent Zhao Jiang to live with a brother in Chongqing. "I saw my father only a few times," he said, "before he, too, died."

Leaning his head back against the chair, Zhao Jiang closed his eyes. Ping studied his weathered face, deep creases a remnant of his sorrow. Her heart ached for her father. She knew his parents had died when he was young but had never been told the circumstances of their death. Poor Baba. Fate had indeed been cruel to him, and yet no complaints ever left his lips. She glanced down at the snapshot. "I will take very good care of this photo."

"There is more to take away from this than just a picture," Zhao Jiang said, eyes now focused on his daughter. "Your future husband, Wang Jianbo, is ambitious. It is why I arranged this marriage. He has plans. He wants to become wealthy. You must do whatever is necessary to make this happen. Remember: those who have money never go hungry."

CHAPTER THREE

It was lunch hour in Chongqing. Unlike in other large Chinese cities, no bicycles competed for space on its roads. Perched on steep hills, the city overlooked the confluence of the Yangtze and Jialing Rivers. The precipitous terrain made bike riding impossible.

Wang Jianbo and Li Feng sat at a table in front of a food stall on a major thoroughfare. The stall was the last in a series of small restaurants. From their vantage point, they could observe the throng of pedestrians, motorbikes, and cars on the bustling street.

The young men were as dissimilar as a horse and a pig. A pair of vertical parallel creases formed by years of introspection and brooding separated Jianbo's dark eyebrows. Slender and flexible as a reed, he appeared stylish in his aviator sunglasses and white shirt rolled up at the sleeves and opened at the neck. Feng, the more outgoing of the two, was shorter and more thickset than Jianbo. Beads of sweat trickled down his round, flat face due to both the food and the burning noonday sun.

"The hot pots are spicier here than in Beijing," Jianbo said, washing down a mouthful of the fiery stew with a swig of beer.

"If my bride isn't worth the long train ride here, the hot pot definitely is."

"It's too bad your parents are so old-fashioned," Feng replied. "Hardly anyone has an arranged marriage anymore."

"My father lives in the past. His marriage was set up through a broker, so he thinks mine should be as well. My mother's no help. She's afraid I'll end up with someone unsuitable now that I'm living in Beijing."

"Didn't the marriage broker show you a picture of your bride-to-be?"

"Yes, but the photo was too dark. I couldn't really tell what she looked like." Jianbo chugged the rest of his beer. "At this point I'm stuck. I'm twenty-seven, an only child. My father's health is not good. He wants to make sure that he has a grandson to carry on the family name. I cannot disregard his wishes. But, I'll tell you this," he added, lowering his voice and moving closer to Feng. "If I find tomorrow that my bride's ugly or in any way not to my liking, I'll go immediately back to Beijing after the wedding—alone. Let her live with my parents in Chongqing."

"You sound serious," Feng said.

"I am. I have plans, and they don't include a homely wife."

Jianbo signaled the waitress for another drink. The young girl brought two beers to the table. Feng ordered a second bowl of stew. He coughed deeply, disgorging a thick wad of phlegm that he spat onto the sidewalk. The small globule of yellow slime glistened briefly before disappearing beneath the rubber-soled shoes of passersby.

It had been almost two years since Jianbo had left for Beijing. He savored the familiar sights, smells, and sounds of his native city. Meat, fish, and stuffed dumplings sizzled in large pots in the food stalls lining the street. Off to the side, down the alley, there was the continuous clicking of mahjong tiles as players shook them up in tablecloths to prepare for another game. When the weather was nice, as it was on this day in early May, families left their cramped dwellings and took their activities to the street. Halfway down the alley, Jianbo watched as a woman cleaned out the ears of an elderly gentleman with an instrument resembling a chopstick. On a bench near the mahjong tables, a young girl received a pedicure. The steady whir of sewing machines moved to outside porches added to the alley sounds. Seamstresses preferred the sunlight to dim interiors. An old man sat snoring, hunched over in a wheelchair. From his position, it was difficult to tell if he was crippled or just using the chair for a nap.

"How do you like working in Beijing?" Feng asked.

"Can't complain."

"Is the China Palace as luxurious as they say?"

"Even more so. A chambermaid let me into one of the unoccupied rooms. I've never seen anything so grand. The bathroom was twice as large as the bedroom I had in my parents' home."

"It must be expensive to stay there."

"It is. I'm told guests pay more for one night than you and I make in six months. They're mostly dignitaries and foreigners."

"I'm not surprised. All foreigners are rich. Even those who come to the humble restaurant where I work—and where you used to work—are wealthy."

Jianbo smiled at the jab from his friend.

"Have they made you head chef yet?" Feng asked.

"Very funny. For dinner, I'm back in the kitchen helping the pastry chef. But in the morning I work at an omelet station. The guests—they speak mostly English—can order anything, from fried eggs to a cheese and mushroom omelet. I make it right in front of them."

"Your English must be pretty good by now."

"Not really. All I know how to say is 'How do you want your eggs?' Most of the time, I don't understand the guests when they answer. Then we resort to sign language and pointing."

Foreign voices at a nearby table caused Jianbo to turn around. "Look," he said, nudging Feng. "Some tourists are ordering a hot pot. They're speaking English; I think they're Americans. Let's make a bet. How many spoonfuls do you think they'll take before they realize the stew's too hot for their tender palates?"

"I don't know. You always win these bets."

"I have ten renminbis that say it's three bites or less for the four of them." Jianbo pulled a ten-yuan note from his pocket and slapped it down on the table.

"I'll take the bet." Feng reached into his wallet and extracted a similar note. "With four of them eating, it's got to be more than three bites."

They watched as the waitress placed the spicy dish before two middle-aged couples at the next table. Save for a bald spot on one of the gentlemen, there was little to distinguish one diner from another. They dressed similarly: Bermuda shorts, T-shirts, and sandals. The clothes hung loosely on pear-shaped bodies; large dark glasses were prominent on pasty faces. Unable to decipher the Chinese characters on the menu, the group had ordered by pointing to the hot pots in front of Jianbo and Feng.

After examining the dish in front of him, the balding man was the first to gingerly taste the hot pot. After the second mouthful, he dropped his chopsticks and grabbed his throat.

"Water," he gasped, the word barely audible. The waitress produced a bottle that the foreigner gulped greedily.

"It's like eating fire," he warned the others at the table. The Americans decided to forgo the foreign cuisine, dropped some bills on the table, and left.

"Culinary cowards," Jianbo said laughing, pocketing the twenty yuans from the bet with Feng. "They can't take our spicy food."

Feng appeared less amused. "I can't believe you beat me again. You have all the luck."

Jianbo smiled smugly, winking at the waitress as she passed their table.

"It's not only our wagers," Feng said, "but I'm stuck in Chongqing while you're working in Beijing."

"You should come back with me. I'm learning a lot. Enough to one day open my own restaurant."

"Then you can hire me."

"Only if you want to come to the United States. That's my plan. I'm going to open a Chinese restaurant in America. Americans love Chinese food."

"Except for hot pot."

Ignoring Feng's comment, Jianbo continued. "When I open my restaurant, I'll become rich, like the uncle of one of my friends in Beijing. This man started with one restaurant in America and now has three. He's very wealthy."

"How will you get a permit to stay in the United States? It's not easy."

"I'll find some way. My friend's uncle was lucky. He married a Chinese woman who had become an American citizen. I heard that if you marry an American, you automatically become a citizen."

"That's one option you won't have," Feng said. "In case you've forgotten, tomorrow you're marrying a Chinese woman."

"Yes, but you know me. When I decide to do something, I generally pull it off."

"You're right. You told me two years ago that you'd be cooking in a grand hotel in Beijing, and now you are."

Jianbo pulled out two cigarettes from the pack in his shirt pocket and handed one to Feng.

"Thanks," he said, lighting the cigarette. They leaned back in their chairs, mouths producing a smoky haze, and watched as a young woman self-consciously passed their table. Feng emitted a low whistle. The girl quickened her step.

The thinning crowd and the angle of the sun indicated that it was well past the lunch hour. Jianbo asked a passerby for the time. "One forty-five. I need to get going."

"I'll see you tomorrow," Feng said and stood up. "I can't wait to see your mystery bride."

"Neither can I," said Jianbo as he paid the bill over Feng's protest. "Neither can I."

CHAPTER FOUR

On the eve of her wedding, Ping sat in pajamas and slippers on a bench in her bedroom facing an open window. Behind her stood the good luck lady, a wide-toothed alabaster comb in her hand. Carefully, she slid it through Ping's long tresses. Her gnarled fingers followed the course of the comb. "Your hair is like fine silk. You will be a beautiful bride."

Seated a few feet away on her bed, Yi Ma watched. "You seem a million miles away," she said to Ping.

Ping stared at the crescent moon. Its curved shape beckoned. She wished she could grab hold of it and hide in the dark night sky surrounded by necklaces of stars. Only when the jilted groom returned to Beijing would she descend from the heavens.

"I'm just looking at the moon," she replied.

"And that you must do until I finish," said the good luck lady. "I will comb your hair four times. The first time is for harmony, the second for many sons and grandsons, the third for wealth, and the fourth for a long-lasting marriage."

"Why do you wish me to have many sons?" Ping asked. "That would violate the law."

The good luck lady clicked her tongue in disapproval. "That law is not good. When I was married, we could have as many children as we wanted. But," she added, "you are right. The second time I comb your hair will be for a son."

Yi Ma folded her hands together and shook her head. "The one-child mandate caused my younger sister Lei Lei great pain."

"Why?" asked the good luck lady.

Ping sighed knowing the story that was to follow, the story Auntie Yi Ma always told when this subject was mentioned, the story that always made her sad.

"My sister Lei Lei was Ping's mother," Yi Ma began. "She wed Zhao Jiang in an arranged marriage. A few months after the wedding, Lei Lei announced she was with child. Our family was overjoyed. But she learned from the doctor that the baby she was carrying was a girl."

The old woman shook her head slowly from side to side and clucked her tongue; Ping lowered her eyes.

"Zhao Jiang only wanted a boy," Yi Ma continued. "He demanded my sister abort the child."

Finished with Ping's hair, the good luck lady placed her comb in its jewel-encrusted case. She sat down on the cot next to Yi Ma to listen to the rest of the story.

"My sister would not abort the child. She sought refuge in our parents' home and refused to leave when her husband came to fetch her. He returned to collect her every day for three days but to no avail. My father told him of Lei Lei's decision. If Zhao Jiang insisted on an abortion, Lei Lei would never return. On the fourth day, Zhao Jiang relented. His love for her was too great. When he told Lei Lei that she could have her baby, she finally accompanied him home."

Ping turned around in her chair, eyes moist. "Poor Baba. Not only was he the father of a girl, but my mother died giving birth to me. Luckily, Auntie Yi Ma came to live with us."

Yi Ma smiled at her niece, creases appearing around her weary eyes.

"You are fortunate," said the good luck lady. "Not only do you have an auntie who loves you like a daughter, but you had a very courageous mother. A woman is taught long before her marriage that she must always obey her husband."

Yi Ma nodded in agreement. "My sister had the strength to defy her husband's wishes."

The good luck lady glanced at Ping. "Perhaps your niece will be as brave as her mother."

"She will be," Yi Ma said.

⊫⊰ ⊱⊨

Zhao Jiang joined Ping and Yi Ma in the living room to say good-bye to the good luck lady. After she left, he turned to Ping. "Come sit beside me on the couch."

Ping sat down. Yi Ma walked back into the bedroom. Zhao Jiang took a seat next to his daughter. He took Ping's hand in his. "I will miss you very much."

Eyes tear-filled, lips trembling, Ping turned to face her father. Her heart ached. From his pocket Zhao Jiang produced a small box and handed it to Ping. "This is for you."

Lifting the lid, she pulled out a gold-plated necklace with a charm on which the words *mother-daughter* were written in Mandarin characters. She glanced at her father, a quizzical look on her face.

"I bought the necklace for your mother on the day of your birth to show my gratitude for the gift she had given me—you. But then..." Zhao Jiang's voice broke. He paused for a moment before continuing. "If she were here, I know she would want you to have it."

Ping ran her fingers over the gold charm on the necklace. "Thank you."

"Let me put it on you," Baba said. Ping turned away and lifted the hair from her neck.

As he snapped the chain closed, Ping felt the presence of another in the room. She looked around expecting to see Yi Ma. But no one was there.

CHAPTER FIVE

Hands shaking, Ping removed the crimson *cheongsam* from its hanger. "Please help me get this on. I'm too nervous."

Ping's bridesmaids, Meihui and Zhilan, rushed to her side. Meihui buzzed around Ping like a bee. Her eyes sparkled as she fingered the silk wedding dress. "The brocade is so soft."

Zhilan moved in front of Ping, tall and commanding as an oak. "Hold up your arms and bend forward, and we'll slide the dress over your head."

Ping did as instructed. She trembled as the silk brocade slid over her shoulders and hips. The *cheongsam*, a long, thigh-length slit on either side, clung to her body.

"You look beautiful," Zhilan said after she adjusted the dress. Meihui nodded in agreement. Ping stared at her image in the mirror that hung lopsidedly on the closet door of the bedroom. Slowly she turned around, looking at herself from every angle. The dress caressed her slender form, emphasizing her long waist, slim hips, and small, rounded breasts.

"I'll get the *qi pau*," Zhilan said, removing a matching brocade jacket from a hanger.

Just as her attendants finished helping her into the jacket, Yi Ma entered the room. "What a lovely bride you are," she said, looking approvingly at her niece. "But you must finish dressing quickly. Wang Jianbo and his escorts will be here shortly."

In one hand, Yi Ma held the flat, red shoes that Ping would wear. In the other, was the red veil that would conceal her niece's face during and after the ceremony. Ping held her aunt's arm for balance as she slipped into the shoes. After covering Ping's face with the red veil, Yi Ma led her and the attendants into the living room, where family members and friends waited.

Ping tried to hold the slits on the sides of her dress together as she walked. She was unaccustomed to such a revealing outfit. Through the red veil, the room took on a crimson hue. The yellowed, tobacco-stained walls appeared rose-tinged. The neighbors and relatives crammed into the small living room were bathed in an ethereal glow.

Approving whispers and smiles greeted Ping as she entered the room. Her face covered, the guests could not see the panic that gripped the bride-to-be. An elderly woman informed those around her that she was pleased Ping was wearing a traditional red dress and not a white Western gown. "Red is the color of happiness," she said. "White is for funerals."

"Come here, my child," said Zhao Jiang. Ping crossed the crowded room to stand before her father. "Today, you are leaving our home to begin a new life. Just as you have brought honor to our family, you will do so in your new one."

Zhao Jiang coughed. He lowered his head. When he lifted it, Ping thought she saw a teardrop glisten on his cheek. Clearing his throat, he continued. "You must obey and respect your husband, Wang Jianbo. He is now the most important person in your life. You must honor him and bear him a son. In this way, you will carry on his good family name."

"Oh, Baba," Ping said, her voice trembling. "I will miss you and Auntie Yi Ma so much."

As the father and daughter separated, the women gathered around the bride to offer suggestions on how to be a good wife. The men moved to the other side of the room with Zhao Jiang to smoke and chat.

"They're here," Meihui said, peering through the curtained window. "The groom and his escorts have arrived."

Ping walked to the window and cautiously lifted the side of the lace curtain. She watched, chin trembling, as a large black sedan pulled up before the family home. "Jianbo's parents rented a car and driver for today," said Yi Ma, standing beside her niece.

The car stopped. A chill swept through Ping's body. Three men and a young boy about five or six years old exited the vehicle. The child represented Jianbo's expectation to have a son with his new bride. The man holding the hand of the young boy was probably his father. A second, heavyset man, looked toward the house. His face was moonlike—round and flat—with large lips. He wiped his brow with a handkerchief. The third man was turned toward the car talking to the driver.

"Which one is to be my husband?" Ping asked Yi Ma.

"He's the one by the car."

Ping held her breath as Jianbo turned around. Her heart pounded; her knees felt weak. She exhaled slowly and smiled, pleased with what she saw.

"He's very handsome," Yi Ma said.

"Yes, he is," Ping replied, her eyes focused on the slender figure in the dark suit with a red and gold wedding insignia affixed to his jacket. He laughed and joked with his attendants. He did not look like someone who would be unkind to his wife.

Accompanied by his entourage, Jianbo walked to the Zhao's dwelling. The freshly painted red Chinese character on the yellow door distinguished the home from similar apartments on the street. "*Shuangxi*," Feng said, pointing to the red character. "See, you will have good fortune and a happy future."

Resplendent in his wedding suit, Jianbo beamed. In spite of his reservations about the arranged marriage, his dark eyes glowed in anticipation of the day's events. Gaining entry to his bride's home would be the most difficult challenge. It was customary for the bride's friends and relatives to guard the residence and not allow the groom to enter until he had successfully completed certain tasks.

There was no response to their initial knocking. Jianbo's escorts became louder and more boisterous. Finally, from behind the closed door, a voice was heard demanding an acceptable bride price from the groom's entourage. Much bantering and bargaining ensued between the two groups. Red envelopes stuffed with money were slipped inside the door.

"This is not sufficient," a female voice said from inside. "The groom must pledge his devotion and eternal love to his bride."

Accompanied by laughter from both those inside and outside the house, Jianbo stood before the front window with his right palm over his heart. "I pledge to my bride-to-be, Zhao Ping, my love and devotion for all eternity."

Watching from the window, Ping felt faint. She placed her hand on Yi Ma's arm to steady herself. The bridesmaids consulted to see if the groom had successfully completed his trial. "I think we should let him in," Meihui said. Those inside unanimously agreed.

Yi Ma led Ping back to the bedroom and shut the door. The front door opened. The groom entered his future father-in-law's home for the first time. The mood was festive as Jianbo and his party were introduced to Zhao Jiang and Auntie Yi Ma. The two groups exchanged pleasantries, handshakes, and greetings. Confident and charming, Jianbo met and chatted with other family members and friends of his bride. Suddenly, the steady din of conversation punctuated by occasional laughter subsided.

Ping reentered the room. A pathway was cleared between the bride and groom. Jianbo turned to look at his future wife. She stood solemnly between her two bridesmaids, head lowered, fingers preoccupied with the slits of her dress.

Jianbo was mesmerized by the graceful figure before him. Apparently giving up on closing the slits, Ping's hands fell to her side, revealing a well-formed slender leg. Jianbo's heart beat rapidly as he envisioned his hand touching his bride's thigh. His reverie was soon broken by the pushes and shoves of his escorts. They thrust him forward toward Ping. Shouts, laughter, and applause once again erupted from the crowd as the couple stood a few feet apart in the middle of the room.

"Repeat your pledge," someone yelled to Jianbo.

"Yes, but this time on bended knee," said another.

To the satisfaction of the onlookers, Jianbo knelt before Ping. He gazed at the red veil, hoping that her face would be as lovely as her body. He cleared his throat. "Zhao Ping, I promise to love you for all eternity. I will take care of you and protect you. I will do everything in my power to make you happy."

To a chorus of *ooh*s and *ahh*s, Jianbo lifted himself up and took Ping's hands in his. "I, too," Ping said softly, "promise to always love you and to bring honor to your family name."

"Don't forget obedience," said an elderly matron from the other side of the room.

The crowd laughed. Ping was silent.

CHAPTER SIX

The red veil. That was all that prevented Jianbo from seeing the face of his bride. He had tried to lift it in front of his parents' house, but Ping had pulled back. "Not now," she said. "Let's wait until we are alone.

Her sweet voice reminded him of the ehru, the instrument his uncle played—an instrument whose melodic tones dispelled sorrow and promised fulfillment. And so he would wait. He would abide by Ping's request. He wanted their wedding night to be perfect.

Inside his parents' home, a relative led Ping and Jianbo to the family altar. Kneeling side by side, they paid tribute to his ancestors. White flowers adorned the altar. Jianbo found the sweet scents of incense intertwined with the jasmine perfume of his bride intoxicating.

Following the wedding vows, there was the traditional tea ceremony. Ping poured the liquid into two cups. The cups contained lotus seeds and two red dates to ensure sweet relations between the bride and her new family. Ping and Jianbo carried the cups in both hands and presented them to his parents. They were seated among other honored family members on one side of the living room.

Later at the wedding banquet, Jianbo escorted Ping to the bridal table on the raised platform in the restaurant. The feel of his wife's hand in his sent a tremor through his body. They took their seats before a backdrop of a phoenix and a dragon, symbols of harmony and a balanced relationship. The flaming crested phoenix with its long tail represented the bride. The wingless male dragon symbolized the groom.

Jianbo watched as Ping lifted her veil slightly to sip the shark fin soup. He was entranced as ruby lips sucked out the meat from crab claws and the knuckle of the lobster. He was captivated when his bride turned to him while eating the roast suckling pig, the symbol of virginity, and smiled.

Hours later, they sat alone on the bridal bed in his parents' home, thighs touching. New red sheets covered the bed. In the center lay dried longan fruit, lotus seeds, red dates, and sprigs of pomegranate leaves. A pair of bedside lamps symbolizing the addition of sons to the family illuminated the room.

"It is time to remove the veil."

Ping obediently turned her covered face toward Jianbo. His fingers shook with anticipation as he slowly lifted the silk veil like a curtain. First to appear were the delicate chin and mouth he had already seen at the banquet. The rising veil next revealed a well-shaped nose and cheeks brushstroked a tawny pink. As he lifted it farther, he was greeted by luminous dark eyes outlined by long, black lashes—eyes filled with a combination of apprehension and expectation.

"You are beautiful," he whispered.

Jianbo strutted around the room leaving Ping to sit alone on the bed. He removed the fruit and nuts from atop the sheets. While she waited, Ping fussed with her clothes, crossed and uncrossed her ankles, and pushed unruly wisps of hair from her face. At last

Jianbo stopped pacing and unbuttoned his jacket. "It is time to go to bed. You can undress behind the screen. I'll remove my clothes out here."

Ping looked in the direction he had indicated. In the corner of the room a few feet from the wall stood a four-panel elm wood screen. A watercolor painting of various birds among lotus blossoms adorned the center of each panel.

Rubbing her forehead, a confused look on her face, Ping rose and obediently headed toward the screen. Once behind it she removed her dress and jacket and folded them neatly on the floor. She took off the veil and shoes and added them to the pile. Was this what newlyweds did? She had never come across anything like this in her books.

Emerging from behind the screen, Ping stumbled in the darkness. Jianbo had turned off the lights. A trail of moonbeams shining through the window illuminated the wedding bed, where he waited. As she crept toward him, he held out his arm palm facing her. "Wait. You need to remove your underwear."

Ping felt her chest tighten. Should she have known this? She turned her back to Jianbo and removed her bra and panties.

"Turn around. Let me look at you."

Ping slowly turned to face him, arms hanging limply by her sides, a tear forming in the corner of her eye. She had never been naked in front of a man before. Jianbo held up the red bedsheet and beckoned to Ping. Slowly, she moved toward the bed and climbed in.

"You are so tense."

Ping forced a smile and inhaled in a vain attempt to relax. Jianbo took her hand and placed it on his penis. "See how much I desire you?"

Repulsed as he moved her hand up and down his organ, Ping wanted to flee. But instead she let Jianbo push her back on the bed, force her legs apart, and climb on top of her.

She cringed, her face contorted in pain. She wanted to scream as he forced himself inside her. Just as she thought she would surely die, he groaned and pulled out, leaving a stream of wetness on her thighs and stomach.

Jianbo rolled over onto his back, a satisfied look on his face. Ping lay immobile, overcome by a feeling of nausea. Where was the "flutter of pleasure" that Emma experienced as she found her arm pressed against Mr. Knightley's heart? Where was the tremulous feeling when Jane Eyre stood in a thin nightgown alone in a room with Rochester? Why didn't Jianbo clasp her to his breast, like Heathcliff with Catherine? Ping closed her eyes and fought back tears. She felt betrayed by the authors she adored.

CHAPTER SEVEN

"You're late," Feng said to Jianbo as he greeted his friend the following day.

Jianbo paused to catch his breath. "Sorry. I overslept."

"It's eleven thirty. I doubt that you and Ping were sleeping."

Jianbo stood taller, shoulders back, chest thrust out, a knowing grin on his face.

"So, how is married life?" Feng asked as he signaled the waitress to bring two hot pots.

"Better than I ever dreamed," Jianbo replied, pulling up a chair.

"I take it you're not going to leave Ping with your parents when you go back to Beijing tomorrow."

"No, she's coming with me."

"It looks like the matchmaker did a good job."

They paused as the waitress placed two bowls of hot pot on the table. "What will Ping do in Beijing?" Feng asked.

"I might be able to get her a job at the hotel's business center. I called yesterday. There's a position available, and they want to interview her."

"What will she do there?"

"She'll greet the guests and help them. Something like a secretary."

"If the hotel is as international as you say, the guests probably won't speak Mandarin."

Jianbo leaned back in his chair, relishing the opportunity to boast about his wife. "The hostesses in the business center are required to know English. And Ping does. I found out she studied it for many years in school. Her Auntie Yi Ma told me at the wedding that if she hadn't married me she would have returned to the university to continue her English studies."

Feng shook his head, forcing a smile. "You are truly fortunate. Your wife is not only beautiful but smart. I hope you paid the marriage broker well."

The two ate in silence diluting the spicy food with occasional swigs of beer. Feng registered his enjoyment of the meal with a loud belch. They took out cigarettes, ordered more beer, and sat contentedly enjoying another late spring day. "So, when are you going to take the big step, my friend? You're a year older than I am."

"I have time. Twenty-eight isn't that old," Feng said, exhaling ovals of cigarette smoke from pursed lips. "Let me see what happens with you and your new bride."

"I know what will happen."

"Oh, so now you're a fortune-teller?"

"No, but our signs are compatible. Ping was born in the year of the Rat, and, as you know, I was born in the year of the Monkey."

"I didn't know. I never pay much attention to that nonsense. It's all crap."

Jianbo appeared disappointed by Feng's response. "OK, tell me. What are people born under these two signs supposed to be like?"

"The Rat is a good sign," Jianbo said. "My wife is friendly, sociable, and has deep emotions. She will be devoted to our family and will always stand by me."

"Sounds good," Feng said, rolling his eyes.

"It's true. She's even agreed to take my family name to show her commitment to our marriage."

"That's unusual." Feng ogled a group of giggling young girls parading by the restaurant. He crushed the remains of his cigarette in the metal ashtray on the table. "And the Monkey?" he asked Jianbo.

"Not so nice. We're intelligent and accomplish our goals. We're usually very successful, and if there are obstacles, we're not above playing tricks to get what we want."

"That describes you very well, my friend."

CHAPTER EIGHT

Beijing, China, July 2004

David Bennington stood in front of the receptionist in the lobby of the China Palace Hotel, hands pressed down firmly on the marble countertop. He squinted to read her name tag. "I don't understand, Miss Wu. How could my package not be here? It was sent overnight delivery several days ago."

"I am very sorry, Mr. Bennington. I have called the mailroom. Nothing has arrived from the United States for you."

He felt a flush of irritation inch across his neck and face. He rubbed his chin, his fingers encountering a day's growth of stubble. Weary eyes reflected annoyance as well as fatigue.

"Patience," one of his colleagues had advised him. "When you make a request in China, even for something as simple as changing a plane flight, the initial response is always that it can't be done. As frustrating as it is, don't get angry. If you stay calm, the person you're dealing with will posture for a few minutes—consult a document, talk with a supervisor, or make a phone call. But in the end, some way will be found to solve your problem."

Pulling himself up to his full height, David repeated his disbelief. "But I've never had FedEx not deliver a package on time. And I've shipped things all over the world. Are you sure you checked every possible place it could be?"

"Yes, several times. The package did not arrive," Miss Wu said. "It could be," she added, "that it did not clear customs. This sometimes happens. If I may ask, what was in the package?"

"Copies of material for a presentation I'll be making tomorrow morning."

"Do you have the originals with you?"

David nodded.

"We have copy machines in our business center on the mezzanine level. The material can be duplicated for you there."

"But, it's late. Is the center still open?"

"Generally it closes at ten, but I'll check."

As David watched, Miss Wu phoned the business center. He did not understand what she said, but the tone of her voice suggested that she had accomplished her mission.

"Everything is OK. They are waiting for you."

"How do you say thank you? '*Xie xie*'?"

"*Bu xie*, you're welcome," she replied. "You can either take the elevator or the center staircase to the mezzanine. The business center is behind the double doors at the end of the open walkway. You can see them from here."

David turned to where she was pointing.

"Yes. I see them. *Xie xie* again."

"Oh, Mr. Bennington, I nearly forgot," Miss Wu produced a yellow piece of paper. "This phone message came for you from the States."

David took the slip of paper and read the message.

Sharon's Store is on the fourth floor of the Pearl Market. It's called the Hongqiao Market or something like that. Surprise me.

—Alexis

Just like Alexis, David thought, *trying to turn a business trip into a shopping expedition.* He crumpled up the note and stuffed it into the pocket of his jeans. He made his way toward the elevators. Normally he would have taken the stairs to get exercise, but he felt too tired and groggy from the fifteen-hour flight plus the twelve-hour time change. Besides, he needed to conserve what energy he had left to prepare tonight for tomorrow's meeting. It would be his first as a newly appointed VP, and already he'd been thrown into the thick of things. The assignment wasn't easy. He had to convince representatives from a Chinese company that it was in their best interest to do a joint venture with his client. If he failed, there'd be no bonus this year, and he'd most likely be out of the running to head up the new Shanghai office. Tomorrow's meeting could make or break his career.

Just breathe, he thought as he took in the large, open lobby of the China Palace. Red pillars trimmed with gold filigree stretched several stories high; marble floors shone to such a degree he could almost make out his reflection. He'd stayed in top hotels all over the world and had heard horror stories about accommodations in Beijing, but the China Palace impressed him.

As he approached the bank of elevators, a hotel employee dressed in what looked like a long traditional gown held a door open for him. "*Huanying,* welcome to the China Palace," the man said, accompanied by a smile that took up more than its share of his face.

Even the elevator was impressive, tastefully decorated with mirrors and polished dark wood. David stood on a carpet on which was entwined "Wednesday" in English. He assumed the Chinese characters woven into the fabric below the day was the Mandarin translation. Evidently, the hotel changed the carpets in the elevators daily.

When the doors opened at the mezzanine level, a hotel employee in a dark, Western-style suit greeted David and pointed the way to the business center. As he walked along the carpeted path toward the double doors, David glanced at the lobby below. To the left of the main entrance were several lounges where guests sat in rich leather armchairs sipping drinks while a pianist played Western tunes on a grand piano. Dressed in a tux, back ramrod straight, the pianist's fingers stretched across the keys. David listened as the familiar refrain of "Some Enchanted Evening" floated up from the floor below.

Two slender Chinese employees in black skirts topped with hip-length ecru fitted jackets passed him and smiled shyly. His friends would definitely give China high marks for feminine pulchritude. The young Chinese women David had seen working in the hotel were beautiful. Were they mass-produced for the China Palace? Was there an assembly line somewhere rolling out these perfect creatures? They needed no adornments, unlike the women he knew back in New York. They were dressed in simple but elegant uniforms and flat shoes, dark hair pulled tightly back into a bun. They wore no jewelry, no makeup, no artificial nails. There were no visible tattoos or piercings. *Maybe it's just the jet lag*, David thought as he pushed open the double doors of the business center, *but I don't think it gets much better than this.*

"*Huanying.* Welcome, Mr. Bennington. We were expecting you. How may I help?"

David turned to see the owner of the melodious voice speaking to him in slow, studied English. He stood transfixed, staring through bleary eyes. All the young Chinese women he had seen before in the hotel were just a prelude, handmaidens to this beautiful princess standing before him.

Apparently concerned that he did not understand her English, she repeated her greeting, "Welcome to the business center, Mr. Bennington. My name is Ping. How may I help you?"

CHAPTER NINE

S hortly after 11:00 p.m., Ping emerged from a back room with fifteen copies of David Bennington's documents in her arms. "Let me help you with those," David said, rushing forward. He stacked them on the counter.

"I'll be right back with the originals," Ping said. As she walked to the copy room, she glanced at the clock. She hoped Jianbo wouldn't be upset waiting for her for nearly an hour. But rather than annoyance at being detained by the American, she felt a rush of excitement. Mr. Bennington had been very nice, complimenting her often on her English.

Ping placed the originals in a manila folder and returned them to Mr. Bennington. "I'll send for a porter," she said, picking up the phone. "He'll take the copies to your room."

"*Xie, xie.*"

"So, you speak Mandarin," Ping said.

"Not really. That's all I can say, but I wouldn't mind learning more expressions. Perhaps you can teach me?"

Ping could feel her cheeks redden; she lowered her head. David smiled, seeming to enjoy her discomfort. "I was wondering," he said, haltingly. "Could I take you somewhere for a drink?"

Taken aback, Ping could only stare.

"Just to show my appreciation. You've been really helpful."

"The hotel doesn't allow us to go anywhere with guests."

Just then, a porter entered pushing a luggage rack to transport the documents. Ping was grateful for the interruption. Although Mr. Bennington's invitation seemed strange, she was nonetheless flattered that he would want to spend time with her. After instructing the porter in Mandarin on where to take the documents, she said goodnight to Mr. Bennington, shut off the lights, and left to meet Jianbo.

On her way out, she realized Mr. Bennington was the only American she had ever had a conversation with. She had always been wary of Americans. In school, her teachers had referred to the United States as imperialistic and as supporters of Taiwan, China's enemy. They portrayed Americans as arrogant and bullying. Yet she found Mr. Bennington very polite and gracious.

⇥ ⇤

Sitting astride the rear rack of the bicycle, Ping wrapped her arms around Jianbo's waist as they zigzagged between buses, cars, and pedestrians on the busy thoroughfare. The rain that had been a drizzle when they left the hotel was now a downpour. "It's really raining hard," Ping said, wisps of long black hair plastered against her face.

"I'll pull over to the curb," Jianbo replied, nearly colliding with a pedestrian about to get on a bus. Once stopped, he lifted the back of his yellow plastic poncho. "Here, get under. You won't be able to see, but at least this should keep you dry."

Ping covered her head and shoulders with the poncho. Satisfied that she was protected, Jianbo reentered the flow of traffic on the roadway. Although rush hour had long since passed, the traffic along Chang'an Avenue was still heavy. It was almost midnight. It would be a struggle for the two of them to get up early the next morning and return to the hotel. But Jianbo couldn't complain. He and Ping were fortunate. They both had jobs at the China Palace. Their managers even tried to give them similar schedules so they could come and go together.

Turning off the main thoroughfare, Jianbo pedaled through the narrow alleyways of the *hutong* district. This area of Beijing consisted of groups of tiny, centuries-old dwellings with a common courtyard. Although less crowded than the main roads, many of the streets were unpaved, making it difficult for Jianbo to avoid the rain-filled potholes. Mud splashed on their shoes and up their legs.

"Here we are," Jianbo said. He pulled into a courtyard and jumped off the bike, exposing Ping once again to the heavy rain. He walked the bicycle with his wife still astride across the cobblestones. To avoid the deep puddles, he lifted her from the seat and carried her to the door.

"I'll make a pot of tea," Ping said, removing her shoes before entering their one-room dwelling. They had sublet the studio apartment from Jianbo's cousin, who was working for the year in the western part of the country. He considered himself fortunate not to have to share a flat with relatives like so many of his friends did.

After locking up the bicycle Jianbo stuck his head in the doorway. "I'll be right back."

He trudged through a mud-covered path to a squat concrete building with two wooden doors. Upon pushing one open, he gagged on the stench held captive by the humidity and fog. Pulling down his trousers, he crouched over a hole in the center of the small tiled area. As he positioned himself, he felt something brush against his leg. Rats scurried across the floor. Jianbo clapped his hands to keep the vermin at bay. Finished, he stepped out of the tiled area and yanked on a chain. Water swirled over the grimy porcelain squares whisking away cigarette butts, tissue paper, and accumulated waste.

CHAPTER TEN

Dripping wet, Ping padded across the apartment careful not to slip on the linoleum floor. As she passed the armoire with the top half of its mirrored front missing, she glanced at her image; her clothes and body were covered with the residue of the ride. She grabbed a towel and dried herself, wiping the mud from her legs and uniform. In the tiny kitchen area, she filled an electric teapot from the tap in the sink and plugged in the cord.

Waiting for the water to boil, she straightened up the double bed. That morning, they had lingered longer than usual under the covers. She fluffed up Jianbo's pillow and pressed it to her nose. It smelled of cigarette smoke and hair tonic.

Ping cared for Jianbo and tolerated their lovemaking, but she couldn't say she was "in love" with him. Her feelings for him were not those of Emma's for Knightley or Jane's for Rochester.

Some of Jianbo's habits annoyed Ping. He wasn't always forthcoming. She was never sure what he was thinking. His obsession with America and becoming wealthy bothered her, too. Their life in Beijing was good; they both had jobs and were happy. Why would Jianbo want to change it? Eventually, she'd like to visit the United

States or England to see the places she had only read about, but to live there as immigrants, so far from China? She wasn't ready for that yet.

Continuing her studies at the university, he told her, was out of the question. She understood. They could not live on his salary alone. But what she did not understand was why Jianbo insisted she turn over all her wages to him. After all, she had earned the money; she should be permitted to keep some of it. Now, whenever she needed cash, even for something as simple as bus fare, she had to ask him for it like a beggar.

Back in the apartment, Jianbo washed his hands in the basin of the kitchen sink under the light of a single bulb hanging from the ceiling. "When you use the outhouse, be careful; the rats are back."

Ping grimaced. "I think I miss the bathroom in my father's home almost as much as I miss him and Auntie Yi Ma. We're lucky that we can at least take showers at the hotel."

Auntie Yi Ma had been right; living in Beijing as a newlywed was exciting. On their day off, Jianbo promised they would visit the Forbidden City and maybe see the embalmed body of Chairman Mao. Her guidebook to Beijing consisted of a series of dog-eared pages marking sites she wanted to see. With its sense of history and culture, how different this city was from Chongqing.

Ping enjoyed the tiny apartment. Yes, it was old. Yes, there was no indoor bathroom. Yes, there was no phone. But she was proud to have a home where just she and her husband lived. She felt very grown-up.

While the tea steeped, Ping lit incense and candles in a futile effort to erase the musty and dank odor permeating their residence. She removed her wet clothes and replaced them with a faded silk robe. She hung her work uniform, a black skirt and red jacket, on hangers to dry. Tomorrow she would have to request a clean one. She hoped the hotel wouldn't charge her for the additional cleaning. Pulling off the net covering her chignon, she shook her hair loose, releasing a spray of raindrops across the room.

"Hey," Jianbo said, "you're getting me wet."

"So sorry," Ping replied playfully as she prepared the tea.

The two sat on the small sofa against the wall opposite their bed. For the past few months, ever since Ping had started working at the hotel, they would drink a cup of jasmine tea in the evening before going to bed.

"You didn't tell me why you were so late tonight," Jianbo said.

"A guest, an American, arrived about ten o'clock. He wanted me to make fifteen copies of a large document."

"Did he know he was holding you up, making your husband wait?"

"No, I couldn't say anything. But he was very nice, very apologetic. He even offered to take me out for a drink after work."

"Oh, really?" Jianbo replied, raising an eyebrow. "What did you say?"

"I told him no, of course."

Jianbo was silent. Ping planned on always being up front and honest with her husband, but perhaps she shouldn't have mentioned the invitation. Was he jealous? Did he think she wanted to have a drink with the American?

"Did you tell him you were married?"

"No. I just said the hotel doesn't want the staff to mingle with the guests. He doesn't need to know my personal life."

"Was he old?"

"A little older than you, I think. It's hard for me to tell the age of Westerners."

"Did he flirt with you?"

Ping's eyes narrowed. "Of course not."

"Strange then that he'd ask you to go with him for a drink?"

Ping wished she had never mentioned the incident. Did Jianbo think she had been flirtatious, leading the American on? "He was just grateful that I stayed after hours to help him. That's all."

⟨⟩

The first rays of dawn filtered through the solitary window in the apartment. Ping slept soundly, her back toward Jianbo. She did not awaken when he pulled back wisps of black hair from her cheek. Carefully, so as not to disturb her, he fumbled in the early morning light for the packet of cigarettes and matches on the bedside table. Propped up on the bed, he remained deep in thought, the acrid smoke from the cigarette mingling with the musty odors of the dwelling.

Three years ago, he and Feng had talked one evening after work about going to Beijing to find employment. The city's economy was booming; millionaires were being minted overnight. Opportunity was everywhere. They agreed this could be the chance of a lifetime and decided to leave at the end of the month. Although eager at first, as their departure neared, Feng found more and more excuses not to go. His parents, he finally said, needed him. Besides, an acquaintance had just returned from Beijing unable to find work. It was too risky. Jianbo reminded Feng of the Chinese proverb *Life can never give security; it can only provide opportunity.* And that it did. While Feng languished in Chongqing, Jianbo was earning more money and coming closer to achieving his dream.

He took a long drag on the cigarette producing ashes that floated onto the blanket. Could Ping's American be the next step toward opening a restaurant in the United States? The guy was obviously attracted to her. Instead of being jealous, Jianbo realized, he should take advantage of the situation. He reminded himself that there are four things that don't come back: the spoken word, the spent arrow, the past life, and the neglected opportunity.

He shook Ping with his free hand.

"Wha…? Ping rolled over trying to focus her eyes in the semi-darkness of the flat.

"The American—the one you helped last night—did he say how long he would be staying at the hotel?"

"Did you wake me just to ask me that?"

Jianbo nodded. Ping could not completely conceal a hint of annoyance. "No, he didn't say."

"Do you think he'll come by the center today?"

"I really don't know." She turned away and pulled the frayed blanket over her shoulders.

Jianbo shook Ping again. "Don't go back to sleep. We need to talk."

Reluctantly, Ping pulled herself up to a sitting position, propping her pillow behind her against the wall.

"If the American asks you to go out for a drink again," Jianbo said, "I want you to say yes."

Ping stared at her husband, eyes wide in disbelief.

"Don't worry. I'll go with you. We'll say—we'll say I'm your brother."

"But you're not my brother. You're my husband."

"We'll pretend."

"Why?"

"This could be our chance. If we befriend the American, he might help us get to the United States."

"But why do we have to lie?"

Jianbo sighed, impatient. "Don't you see? The American is obviously attracted to you or else he wouldn't have offered to buy you a drink. He might not be so interested in helping you if he thinks you're married."

"But I am married."

"This could be the opportunity we've been waiting for. Brother, husband—for the moment it's not that important."

"I don't want to leave China."

"I don't either, but the way I see it, we have no choice. China is changing. Soon there will be only two classes, the very wealthy and the very poor. I don't want to spend the rest of my life struggling as a cook in a hotel kitchen."

He paused to take another drag on his cigarette. "In America there are many opportunities. I could open a restaurant there, and we'd become wealthy."

"But it's so far away, and we don't know how they'd treat us."

"I've made a decision. If the American sponsors us, we will go."

"But…"

Jianbo held up his hand and glared at Ping. "Enough talk. I am your husband; you will do as I say."

CHAPTER ELEVEN

David Bennington slid his card key into the wall pocket just inside the door to his room, automatically turning on the lights and air-conditioning. Exhausted, he lay down on the king-size bed. He had spent more than two days with the officers of the Chinese firm trying to convince them to enter into a joint venture with his client. More than two days negotiating and renegotiating the terms. *Tough bastards,* he thought. *Polite as hell, constantly bowing and nodding—but in the end, hard as nails.* He sat up and opened his briefcase, pulling out the signed agreement. He hadn't done as well as he had hoped, but his client seemed satisfied with the faxed results.

Grabbing the remote from the nightstand, David flipped on CNN. Life was good. He had just finished negotiating a multimillion-dollar deal. He was on the fast track at his firm. And in a little less than a year, he would marry Alexis. His mother seemed pleased with his choice. He and Alexis came from similar backgrounds. Her parents even belonged to the same country club as his mother.

His fiancée certainly had it all over Christy, his father's so-called trophy wife. With her teased blond hair, boob job, and clingy, revealing tops, she looked trashier than usual next to his elegant bride-to-be. *But with all this good fortune,* David wondered, *why do I feel so down?*

It certainly wasn't China. David enjoyed this part of his job—traveling to foreign cities, learning about different cultures. His father, a Wall Street executive, had been right. The world of commerce was not only lucrative but also exciting.

As a young man, he had resisted his father's efforts to push him into business. "I don't want to be just another suit making the daily trek to Wall Street," David had told him. In reality, he didn't want to become like his father—ignoring his family, spending most of his time at the office or on business trips, cheating on his wife, and divorcing her when David was a sophomore in high school.

In college David majored in archaeology, spending summers on digs in Peru and Bolivia. His father was not pleased with his choice of career. "Archaeology's not a profession," he told David repeatedly. "It's a hobby."

David remained undeterred. However, after rejecting a number of low-paying offers when he graduated college, he begrudgingly followed his father's advice and went to Harvard for an MBA.

He plucked an apple from a basket on a small table, a gift from the hotel. As he bit into the fruit he glanced out his window overlooking Beijing. The last rays of sun struggled to penetrate the smog blanketing the city. He studied the cranes that peppered the landscape. No wonder his boss referred to these machines as the new national bird of China. They were in motion when he rose in the morning and were still operating late at night in the construction of yet another hotel, apartment, or office building.

He lowered his gaze to watch the steady stream of traffic parading in front of the hotel—cyclists, buses, automobiles. Most of the people were probably heading home to dinner with family or to a restaurant with friends. He wished he had somewhere to go, someone to talk to about the day's events.

David glanced at his watch. Six thirty. With the twelve-hour time difference it was early morning in New Jersey. Alexis would still be in bed. *What the heck.* She'd be pleased to learn how well everything was going. David picked up the receiver and dialed her number.

"Hi, honey."

"David, is that you?" Alexis asked.

"Did I wake you?"

"It's six thirty in the morning. Of course you woke me. What are you doing calling so early?"

"I thought you'd be pleased to hear my voice. After all, we haven't talked for a couple of days."

"But, David, six thirty in the morning?"

"We just finished the negotiations."

"How did they go?" Alexis asked, sounding more awake.

"All finished—signed, sealed, and delivered."

"That's wonderful, darling. Do you think you'll be able to come home earlier?"

"That depends. Do you want your pearls?"

"OK, don't change your plans."

"You know; we could always come here for our honeymoon instead of Hawaii. You could get your pearls then."

"Honeymoon in a third-world country? I don't think so."

David cringed. He didn't get the impression she was joking. "Well, I've got to go. I want to run by the hotel's business center before my massage."

"A massage? Unfair. All I have to look forward to is a morning with my mom and the wedding planner."

"I'll think of you while I'm at the spa."

"As long as you don't forget my pearls."

CHAPTER TWELVE

Ping didn't notice David until he was standing before the counter in front of her. Too late to hide, she felt a mixture of panic and pleasure.

"What? No 'Welcome to the business center'?" David asked.

"Oh, I am so sorry, Mr. Bennington. You startled me."

"Don't worry, I'm not here to have you make more copies. I just want to check my e-mail."

"Certainly, sir. Follow me, please."

Ping led him down a hallway to a cubicle, her heart racing. What if he asked her to go out with him for a drink? What if he were attracted to her as Jianbo thought? She stopped before a cubicle containing a computer, fax machine, and telephone. "Will this do?"

"Perfect."

Ping slipped by David into the room, close enough for her to smell his musk-scented cologne, close enough to accidentally brush his arm. Shaken, she turned her face away from his so he couldn't see her blush.

Once logged on, Ping entered the code that would allow David to use the computer.

"Everything is ready," she said, handing him a card with a schedule of fees. "Should I charge this to your room?"

"That will be fine."

The trip to the business center wasn't really necessary. David could have used the Internet connection in his room, but he had been hoping to see Ping again.

There were only two e-mails, one from his boss congratulating him on the joint-venture agreement, the other from Alexis reminding him of the pearls. He spent another few minutes checking his investments, the latest news, and the weather forecast in New York City before leaving the cubicle.

In the reception area, Ping was helping another guest. David picked up a *Wall Street Journal* from the newspaper rack and sat down in a black leather armchair. He pretended to read even though the paper was several days old.

It wasn't the jet lag, David decided as his eyes shifted from the newspaper to the young woman at the counter. She was beautiful. David had known and dated many women, but there was something about this girl that was special. It wasn't just her beauty. Although striking, he had been with women just as attractive. He would soon be married to one. No, there was something else, something visceral, something that excited him. He was entranced by her shyness, her modesty, her apparent lack of guile. Every emotion revealed itself on her exquisite face, either through a lowering of her eyes, a sweet, shy smile, or the blush of her cheeks. He reminded himself that he was engaged, but he could not help admiring Ping.

⤛+ +⤜

When the man Ping was helping left, David took his place at the counter. "Is there anything else I can assist you with, Mr. Bennington?" she asked.

"Actually, yes. I need your help with something tomorrow."

"I'm so sorry, but tomorrow is my day off. I won't be at the hotel."

"Even better. I need to go to this place," David paused as he pulled a crumpled piece of paper from his pocket and straightened it on the counter. "Do you know where this is?"

"I don't recognize it," Ping said. "I've only been in Beijing a few months. I'm afraid I can't help you."

"I'm really desperate. I promised to buy my fiancée pearls from this shop. I don't speak Mandarin, so even if I do locate the place, I'll have difficulty with the purchase. If you could help me, I'll make it worth your while."

"Your fiancée?"

"Yes, I'm engaged to be married."

"Congratulations," Ping said, relieved. Jianbo was wrong. Mr. Bennington wasn't interested in her. His offer to have a drink was as she had first thought—a thank you gesture. She saw a way to make everyone happy. She and Jianbo could take the American to the Pearl Market. She'd even go along with his crazy plan to present him as her brother. Mr. Bennington wouldn't care one way or the other. This would be—how did Americans say it?—a win-win situation.

"You don't have to give me anything. Jianbo—he's my brother—and I would be happy to help you buy the pearls for your fiancée," Ping said. "Jianbo has been in Beijing several years. I'm sure he would know the shop. He also negotiates very well. He can make sure you don't pay too much for the necklace."

They agreed to meet at the entrance to the Pearl Market the following morning. David told Ping his company had hired a car and driver for him for his stay in Beijing.

"Does your driver speak English?"

"Not too badly."

Ping wrote the name of the Hongqiao Market in Mandarin. "Show this to your driver, just in case."

"*Xie, xie*," David said, reaching for the card with both hands as he had seen the Chinese businessmen do at his meetings. "How do you say, 'until tomorrow'?"

"*Dao mingtian.*"

Ping suppressed a grin at David's attempt to say the phrase.

That evening when she told Jianbo of the arrangement, he held her tightly. "Thank you," he said. "You are a good wife."

CHAPTER THIRTEEN

In front of the China Palace Hotel, a line of taxis, chauffeured cars, and limousines dropped off and picked up passengers. Zheng Bai stood beside his black four-door Maple Marindo, right hand shading his eyes, searching for David Bennington. He waved as he saw him leaving the hotel.

"I hope you haven't been waiting long," David said as the broad-shouldered, muscular driver held the door open for him.

"I here not long," Zheng Bai replied, bowing slightly.

Once settled, David pulled out the card that Ping had given him and handed it to Zheng Bai. "Do you know where this is?"

"Yes. Near Temple of Heaven. Big market."

While they drove, David continued to make small talk with the driver. Although he spoke in halting English, they were able to communicate. During the few days that he had been driven around Beijing, David learned that before becoming a chauffeur, Zheng Bai had been a boxer. He had been forced to retire after several severe blows to the head. Proud of the recent advancement of the sport, Zheng Bai told him that a Chinese boxer had won the country's first medal—a bronze—at the summer Olympics. In the 2008 Olympics to be held in Beijing, China's boxers would be even more competitive.

As the car made its way up Tiantan Road, David noticed an imposing triple-gabled circular building. "What is that magnificent building?"

"That is Hall of Prayer for Good Harvests, part of Temple of Heaven," Zheng Bai responded. "Would you like to stop?"

He checked his watch. "No, unfortunately, that will have to wait until my next trip." Shaking his head, David scowled. How unfortunate that he had to spend his time in a marketplace instead of visiting the Temple of Heaven.

Zheng Bai pulled the car up in front of an imposing, long white building with a decorative red tile roof floating above it. On the wide steps leading up to the Hongqiao market, vendors sat displaying their wares. They sprang into action as David exited the car. "Mister, beautiful silk scarves. For you special price." Waiting at the entrance, Ping and Jianbo hastened to meet him. They yelled at the vendors, who scowled and wandered off.

"Hello, Mr. Bennington. This is Jianbo."

"Ping brother," Jianbo filled in, bowing to acknowledge the introduction.

"So pleased to meet you," David replied.

"I pleased also."

David followed Ping and Jianbo up the steps to the entrance of the market surrounded by a chorus of "special price," "real Rolex," "pure cashmere."

"Don't look at their wares," Ping cautioned, "or you won't be able to get rid of them."

The entrance to the building was covered with a row of vertical two-inch strips of soiled plastic. Ping watched David gingerly push the strips apart to enter. Once inside, he looked confused as counter after counter of electronic gadgets greeted him. Hordes of shoppers and vendors circulated in the aisles shouting loudly as they haggled over prices. "Are you sure this is the Pearl Market?" David asked. "I don't see anything here that my fiancée would want."

Ping related to Jianbo in Mandarin David's concern. After stopping to ask a merchant the location of Sharon's Store, Jianbo pointed to a higher level. David and Ping followed him up the escalator to the second floor, filled with leather goods and clothing. They continued on to the third floor. Open stalls with vendors selling pearls, jade, and other jewelry appeared before them.

"Tell him this isn't it," Jianbo said to Ping, as David stopped to examine the pearls. He led the two through another doorway of plastic strips and up a set of stairs to the fourth floor. David appeared relieved to see the small stalls replaced by American-style showrooms. They entered the shop over which a sign said "Sharon's Store" in English.

Glass cases contained the more expensive items while carefully arranged necklaces of all styles, quality, and price hung from display hooks on side panels. Large framed photos of a young Chinese woman with various world dignitaries adorned the walls. "Who is the woman with Bill Clinton, Barbara Bush, and Colin Powell?" David asked Ping, pointing to three poster-size photos by the entrance to the shop.

"That is Sharon," said a petite Chinese girl in English. She was dressed in jeans and a T-shirt. "She is the owner of the store. My name is Lisa. May I help you?"

"Yes," said David. "I'd like to buy a string of pearls for my fiancée."

"What do you have in mind? We have all types and colors."

David looked at Ping.

"So sorry, Mr. Bennington, but I do not know anything about pearls."

"Let me help you," Lisa said, pointing to a table. "Please sit down here. Would you care for anything to drink? We have beer, soda, water."

She asked her assistant to bring two beers for the gentlemen and a bottled water for the lady. While David, Jianbo, and Ping settled in at the table, Lisa went behind a case to get some samples.

She returned, placing three strands of white pearls on the table in front of David. "There are three main types of pearls: freshwater; saltwater, also called Akoya; and South Sea pearls,"

"Which one is the best?" David asked.

"The South Sea."

"That's the one I want then," he said as the assistant placed the beverages on the table.

Lisa held up one of the necklaces. "Would you like a strand with this size pearl?"

David shook his head. "I knew this seemed too easy. Bring me the best of the South Sea pearls."

"Do you have a color preference? In addition to white we have champagne, black, mauve…"

"Let's keep it simple. White is fine."

David winked at Ping and Jianbo. Ping reached for her husband's hand under the table. At her touch, he pulled away and grabbed his beer.

Lisa returned with several strands of larger white beads with silver and aqua overtones. "What makes these of higher quality?" David asked, examining the pearls.

"First, the luster. Notice they are not dull but iridescent with subtle variations on the surface. You can see your reflection if you look carefully. Then look at the shape. The rounder, the more valuable the pearl. You also want to make sure there are no bumps or cracks on the surface."

David fingered the pearls, turning them over in his hand, checking for imperfections. "Finally," Lisa continued, "the size. If everything else is the same, the larger the pearl, the better the quality. These pearls are almost fourteen millimeters."

"Which one of these is the best?" David asked.

"They are about the same. It depends on the color you want."

"They all look white to me."

"Is your fiancée's complexion light or dark?"

"She's fair. Since she usually has a tan, she's not as fair-skinned as this young lady," David said, nodding toward Ping, "but she is blond."

Lisa paused and picked up one of the strands. "This one would probably work best. The rose overtones look very nice on fair skin."

"Can I see it on the young lady?"

"May I?" Lisa asked as she placed the pearls around Ping's neck.

"Lovely," said David, seemingly enthralled as the stones took on a life of their own. Jianbo turned to look at his wife. Lisa placed a mirror in front of Ping.

"They are so beautiful," Ping said, gingerly touching the lustrous beads.

"How much are they?" David asked Lisa.

"This necklace is eighteen inches. Is that the size you want?"

"Looks fine to me."

"For this length and quality, the price is twelve thousand US dollars."

"How much?" Ping asked, uncertain that she had heard correctly. Could a necklace possibly cost that much?

"Twelve thousand US dollars," Lisa repeated.

Twelve thousand US dollars. Roughly one hundred thousand yuan. With that much money Ping could buy a small apartment in Chongqing. For her father, that represented twelve years of work. Ping carefully removed the pearls, fearful of damaging something so valuable.

David turned to his companions. "Is that a good price?"

Jianbo asked Ping whether he had correctly understood the cost. When Ping nodded that he had, he inhaled deeply in preparation for negotiations. With most vendors, Jianbo generally offered no more than 40 percent of the first price given. But this shop was different. The customers were wealthy foreigners.

David watched seemingly amused as Jianbo and Lisa haggled over the price. Crossed arms, scowls, shakes of the head. Finally, a softening of the features of both contenders as they reached agreement.

"You can have the necklace for ten thousand five hundred dollars," Ping announced to David.

"Great job," David said, slapping Jianbo on the back.

Ping looked at her husband, filled with pride.

"What kind of clasp would you like on the necklace?" Lisa asked.

"I thought the decisions were over," David said wearily. "Choose whatever you think works best."

Lisa picked up a gold clasp and the necklace and headed toward the back of the shop. "Everything will be ready in about twenty minutes."

"You saved me a lot of money," David said to Ping and Jianbo. "I want you to pick out something for yourselves."

"What did he say?" Jianbo asked his wife.

She repeated David's offer in Mandarin. "I'm going to tell him no thanks," Ping said before her husband could respond.

"Oh no, Mr. Bennington, it was a pleasure to be of service," she replied receiving a kick from Jianbo under the table.

"Please, I insist. You've given up your day off to help me."

A half hour later, the couple said good-bye to David in front of the Hongqiao Market. The afternoon sun reflected off the new silver watch on Jianbo's wrist. Ping held a bag from Sharon's Store. Inside was a silver chain from which were suspended three perfect South Sea pearls, one white, one champagne, and one black.

"I would take you to dinner, only I have to pack. I leave early tomorrow morning," David said.

"You've done enough for us, Mr. Bennington. Thank you so much," Ping replied.

"I plan on coming back in a few months with my fiancée. The four of us will go out to dinner then."

"Jianbo knows many good restaurants," Ping said as Jianbo alerted David that his car was here.

When David got inside, he instructed Zheng Bai to take him to the China Palace. Once the car was out of sight, Jianbo grabbed Ping, lifted her, and swung her around by her waist. She wrapped her arms around her husband's neck, grateful for their good fortune.

CHAPTER FOURTEEN

On a cool, brisk evening in early September, Jianbo and Ping waited in front of Shuaifuyuan Alley. At the entrance to the alley stood a decorated archway with the name of a restaurant, Quan Ju De, written in Mandarin. To reach the restaurant, the customer needed to go through the arch and walk down a dimly lit passageway. Jianbo paced back and forth, frequently glancing at his new watch.

"They're late. Are you sure you gave them the right address?"

Ping nodded.

"Don't forget. I want you to tell the American about my plan to open a Chinese restaurant in the United States. If I can get him interested, perhaps he'll help us."

"I don't want him to think that's why we accepted his dinner invitation. Besides, he doesn't even know us. Why would he agree to something like that?"

"When he tastes the food here, I know he'll be interested. This is the best place in Beijing for Peking duck. This could be something we'd offer in our American restaurant."

Ping wondered about her husband and his grandiose schemes based on wishful thinking. She recalled something Auntie Yi Ma had said: *To believe in one's dreams is to spend all of one's life asleep.*

"They're here," Jianbo announced as a black sedan pulled up.

They watched as Zheng Bai got out and opened the rear door on the far side. David exited the vehicle. Zheng Bai sped around to the other side and pulled open the door, bowing to the passenger in the backseat. An elegant hand appeared suspended, awaiting assistance. Zheng Bai offered his arm. The passenger's hand landed lightly, accepting the proffered support. A well-formed leg came into view, joined by another as David's fiancée emerged from the car like an empress ready to greet her minions. Having served his purpose, she dismissed the driver with a flick of her wrist, slipping an arm through David's as she strutted toward the alley. She exuded the confidence of the privileged in a silk wrap-around dress that emphasized her slim waist. In spite of the darkening sky, her South Sea pearl necklace gleamed in the twilight. David, a worthy escort in a gray suit with a light blue shirt opened at the neck, waved.

"They certainly don't look like typical American tourists," Jianbo remarked. "No jeans, no T-shirts."

"Hi," David said. "Sorry we're late. This is Alexis Dunhurst, my fiancée. Alexis, this is Ping and her brother Jianbo."

"David's told me so much about you." Alexis fingered the pearl necklace. "Thanks so much for helping him buy this." Jianbo smiled and nodded.

Alexis glanced around. "Where's the restaurant?"

"It's down this alley," Ping said, indicating the shadowy passageway behind the arch.

Alexis wrinkled her nose and drew David aside. Ping made out some of their conversation. "Even if what's his name, your driver, the boxer..." Alexis began.

"Zheng Bai?"

"Yes, even if he accompanied us down the alley, I wouldn't feel safe. Ask them to take us to another restaurant…one on a well-lit street."

David ran his hand through his hair, an embarrassed look on his face. "Alexis would prefer going someplace else. Do you know of any other restaurant? Perhaps one that's more out in the open and on a main street?"

"What did he say?" Jianbo asked Ping.

"They want to eat somewhere else."

"Tell them this is absolutely the best place in Beijing for Peking duck."

Ping dutifully relayed the message. Alexis crossed her arms and turned to David. "I am not eating here, period."

"Tell your brother I'm sorry, but let's go somewhere else."

On hearing the translation, Jianbo looked disappointed. "Well," he said to Ping. "There's the Dadong Roast Duck on Dongsishitiao."

"Jianbo knows of another restaurant in the Dadong area," Ping said.

Alexis eyed him warily. "Ask him if it's on a main street—not down a dark alley."

In response to Ping's translation, Jianbo nodded.

Pointing to the building beside them, Alexis said, "This building looks a thousand years old. Is this other restaurant more modern?"

Again, Ping translated. "Tell her the restaurant was recently renovated. It is very modern," Jianbo said.

"That sounds like a much nicer place," Alexis replied.

Since Zheng Bai had long since left, Ping asked Jianbo to get a cab.

"Regardless of what this restaurant is like," David said to Alexis in a low voice. "Let's have dinner there. No more changes."

Alexis frowned. "Well, if I don't like it, I'll just order a cup of tea and have room service when we get back to the hotel."

David's lips tightened; he glowered as he escorted Alexis to the waiting cab.

⇥ ⇤

After Alexis rejected the first two tables offered, the two couples finally found themselves sitting on beige banquettes in front of a shiny black table. Alexis nudged David. "Now isn't this better? The restaurant is on a main street. It's very modern-looking and clean. Look, the servers even wear those white sanitary masks when they slice the duck at the table."

"I'm just glad you like it."

"Ping," Jianbo said, "ask them if they want the duck. If they do, I'll order for them."

In response to an apprehensive look from Alexis, David said, "Jianbo works in the kitchen at the China Palace. I'm sure he's capable of ordering for us."

"Just tell him I like my duck *very* crispy."

When the main course arrived, everyone at the table held their breath as Alexis took a bite of the duck. She had just sent back an appetizer for being too cold and the wine for being too bitter.

"This is quite good," she declared. "And I like the presentation, the chef slicing the duck at the table and the waitress showing us three ways to eat it with the different condiments." After taking another bite, she smiled at Jianbo. "Very nice choice."

"What did she say?" Jianbo asked Ping.

"She likes the duck."

Jianbo beamed. "Tell Mr. Bennington about my restaurant. We'll serve duck there, too."

"Couldn't we wait until we've at least finished the meal?"

"No. This is the perfect time. The American lady likes the duck."

Ping stopped eating and placed her chopsticks on the side of the plate. "Jianbo hopes one day to open a restaurant."

"In Beijing?" David asked.

"No. In the United States."

"Where?"

Ping turned to Jianbo. "Mr. Bennington wants to know where in the United States you want to open a restaurant."

"Where does he live?"

"New York City, I think."

"Tell him New York City."

"New York City."

"That's all we need," Alexis smirked. "Another Chinese restaurant in New York. There must be thousands of them."

Just then a waitress passed carrying a tray holding a large chocolate ball about a foot in circumference topped with a sparkler. She placed the dish on the table next to them and slapped the ball hard with a spoon. A second waiter popped a balloon at the same time to simulate an explosion. The chocolate ball burst apart revealing a hollow interior.

Alexis turned to Ping. "Let's order that for dessert. What fun. Maybe Jianbo can serve this in his restaurant."

"What did she say?" Jianbo asked Ping.

"She'd like to order a chocolate bomb for dessert. She also thinks it would be a good item for your restaurant."

"What else did she say about the restaurant? Did she and Mr. Bennington like the idea?"

Not wanting to disappoint her husband by telling him Alexis's initial reaction, she responded, "That was all they said."

Jianbo smiled. "Well at least they're thinking of what we can serve in the restaurant. That's a good thing."

CHAPTER FIFTEEN

After work, Ping bounded down the metal stairs of the service entrance. As she approached the bicycle rack, she noticed her husband talking to a man wearing a light summer suit. She wondered if the businessman was a guest at the hotel. But when she got closer, she recognized the round face and broad grin anchored by two gold teeth: Li Feng.

"*Nie hao*, Feng. What brings you to Beijing?"

"Business," he replied as he ogled Ping. "Beijing agrees with you. You are even more beautiful than the last time I saw you."

Ping blushed and lowered her eyes.

"Feng will only be in Beijing this evening," Jianbo said. "Tomorrow he returns to Chongqing. I'm going to stay with him for a while. He has something he'd like to discuss with me. You can take the bus home, and I'll ride the bike back later."

Ping felt a twinge of annoyance at being so summarily dismissed. Jianbo reached into his picket for some coins. "Here's money for the bus. We'll wait with you until it arrives."

"*Zai jian*," Ping said.

Feng returned her good-bye with a smile broad enough to again reveal the gold teeth.

Once on the bus, Ping glanced out the window to see her husband and Feng already engaged in conversation. In spite of his affable manner, there was something that bothered her about Feng, something she didn't quite trust. She was glad that he lived so far away.

The slight evening breeze did little to dissipate the heat and humidity that had engulfed the city during the day. Feng removed his jacket revealing two dark semicircles of moisture on his light blue shirt below his armpits. Pulling a handkerchief from his pocket, he wiped his brow. The air was oppressive. He coughed, adding his spittle to that already found on the sidewalk. As the two friends trudged along the tree-lined thoroughfare of Dajie, the heavy traffic and loud street noises appeared to heighten Feng's discomfort.

"There's a café. It looks air-conditioned," Feng said. "Let's have a beer."

They took a table well inside the restaurant close to a vent pumping cool air into the room. Feng took a final swipe at the beads of perspiration on his forehead and stuffed the handkerchief into his pants pocket.

"So, how're the newlyweds?" he asked once the server had taken their order.

"No complaints so far."

The waiter returned with two bottles of beer. Feng pulled out a package of cigarettes and offered one to Jianbo.

"Your situation seems to have changed," Jianbo said after a long drag on the cigarette. "What gives? Other than my wedding, I don't think I've seen you in a suit. You look like the businessmen who stay at the hotel."

"Things have improved for me. I quit my job at the restaurant. Do you remember the Guo family in Chongqing?"

"Sure. I hear Mr. Guo is doing very well with his cement business."

"He certainly is. The preparation for the Olympics has quadrupled his business. His plants are running overtime producing cement. He now has a fleet of trucks transporting it up here for new roads and buildings."

"So what does Mr. Guo have to do with you?"

"I'm working for him now, negotiating contracts with construction companies and government contractors. He had to really increase his staff to handle all the new business. My uncle knows him and suggested he hire me. That's why I'm wearing a business suit instead of a cook's apron." Feng adjusted his shirt collar for emphasis.

Jianbo forced a smile. "Well done, my friend. Soon I'll be coming to you for a loan for my American restaurant. I'm glad to see life is treating you so well."

"Maybe too well," Feng replied.

"What's the matter?"

"Mr. Guo has an unmarried daughter. He thinks I would make a good husband for her."

"I don't see the problem. You'll be the son-in-law of one of the wealthiest men in Chongqing."

"True, but I'll also be the husband of one of the homeliest women in the city."

"Oh, so that's it."

"I'm not sure what to do."

"If it were me, I'd marry her. Beauty doesn't last forever. Besides, if you're traveling as much as I think you are, you'll have plenty of opportunity to get involved with beautiful women. And your wife will be none the wiser."

Jianbo leaned back and sipped his drink. He felt fortunate to have a wife as beautiful and smart as Ping, a woman to whom it was easy to be loyal.

"What about children? I could have an ugly son," Feng said.

"So? He'll be very wealthy. It doesn't matter. He'll have his choice of wives."

Feng picked up his cigarette from the ashtray and took a long drag. He closed his eyes, apparently mulling over his friend's words. "You're probably right. I could do worse," he said, releasing a cloud of smoke. "You will be in my wedding party, won't you?"

"Of course. It would be an honor."

Feng signaled the server for two more beers.

"And how about you?"

"Nothing much has changed," Jianbo said. "Ping is doing well in the business center. The guests like her. She's even gotten a small raise. Now she makes more than I do."

"That's great. And how about the future chef?"

"Same situation. Although there's a rumor that one of the sous-chefs might be fired. Apparently, he's been taking some of the stored meat in the freezer home with him. I'd really like to have his job."

"And the restaurant in America?"

"That's in the future. Right now I've got to find some way to make more money."

"What's the hurry? With you and Ping both working you should be OK. Unless you're looking to trade in your bicycle for a car."

Jianbo shook his head. "It's my father. He told me that the steel plant where he works is in trouble. He might get laid off."

"That doesn't surprise me. There've been rumors for a long time about the corruption that goes on in that factory while the government just looks the other way."

"Typical for state-run companies." Jianbo paused to sip his beer. "But if my father does get fired it will be up to me to take care of my parents."

"Couldn't your father find another job?"

"I doubt it. He's too ill. Thanks to all those years of breathing in the fumes from the coke ovens, he has emphysema."

"I'm sorry."

Jianbo stared at the empty bottle of beer. "For forty years he's been a loyal employee of that factory. What does he have to show for it? Months of being paid late or not at all, medical bills that were never reimbursed. And now that he's old and sickly, they'll probably lay him off."

"It's a sad state of affairs," Feng said, "when the government turns its back on loyal employees." After another drag on his cigarette, he continued. "Will you be able to take care of your parents?"

"Yes, but it will be hard to do here on what Ping and I are making. That's why going to America is so important."

Feng gave an understanding nod. "That will be difficult to do."

"Maybe not. We've gotten to know an American. In fact, he and his fiancée took Ping and me to dinner last night. He's very rich. We helped him buy some pearls a few weeks ago. He spent about ninety thousand renminbis for one necklace. He also bought a necklace for Ping and this watch for me for helping him."

Jianbo removed the watch and gave it to Feng for closer inspection.

"Very nice," he said, turning the watch over. "Do you think he'll finance your restaurant?"

"I don't know. I brought up the idea at dinner last night, but nothing came of it."

"Will you see him again?"

"Ping is giving up her day off to take the American woman sightseeing tomorrow. She didn't want to, but I insisted. If we do things for the American couple, they might help us get to the United States."

They talked and drank well into the night. It was almost 2:00 a.m. when Jianbo crawled into bed next to his sleeping wife. *Feng is fortunate,* he decided. How much easier his life would be if Ping had come from a wealthy family.

CHAPTER SIXTEEN

Ping waited in front of Silk Alley. Throngs of tourists packed the narrow lane lined with stalls selling Chinese handicrafts and knockoffs of American and European goods. Vendors hawked their wares; tourists shoved and pushed. If a customer displayed interest in a piece of merchandise, the vender scooted around the counter, sidled up next to the tourist, and punched in a price on a handheld calculator. A hesitation or a shake of the head and the vender would hold out the calculator to the customer to make a counteroffer. The calculator would be handed back and forth until a price was agreed upon. Customers left carrying their merchandise, smug self-satisfied expressions on their faces. Behind them, the vendors grinned and winked at one another.

Ping scanned the crowd hoping to spot Alexis. She had been waiting almost half an hour. Just as she decided that Alexis had probably forgotten about their meeting, a taxi maneuvered toward the curb squeezing between a cyclist and a pedicab. It stopped; Alexis got out. She was wearing white linen slacks topped with a royal blue cashmere sweater set. The sidewalk was wall-to-wall pedestrians, yet the statuesque foreigner stood out.

"Good day, Miss Dunhurst," Ping said.

"Hi, Ping. I thought we agreed the other night that you would call me Alexis. Have you been waiting long?"

"Yes. But it's OK. It gave me time to think about what we could see."

"What do you suggest?"

"I thought we might visit the silk market first since we're here." Ping pointed to the alley behind Alexis. "There are all sorts of merchandise, with many 'knockoffs'—I think that's what you call them—of US and European items. Afterward, we could go to the Forbidden City. Then, if we have time, Tiananmen Square and Memorial Hall. Memorial Hall is very special. Chairman Mao is there. You can actually see him since his body has been—how do you say it?—embalmed."

Alexis wrinkled her nose at Ping's mention of the embalmed body. "It's really too hot to go traipsing around the city," she said, removing her long-sleeved sweater as if to make her point. "Besides, those places will probably be mobbed with tourists. I'd rather just shop."

"I don't think I understood. You don't want to see the Forbidden City?"

"No," Alexis said, examining her fingernails. "Just shop."

"Well, we could start here in Silk Alley," Ping said, somewhat confused. Why would someone travel so far just to shop?

Alexis cast a glance at the market crammed with tourists and aggressive vendors. Once again she wrinkled her nose disdainfully. "What I'd really like to do is go to the Pearl Market, the place where you took David for my necklace."

"We'll need to take a taxi," Ping said. "Sharon's Store is quite far."

She hailed a cab. "Hongqiao Market," Ping instructed the driver in Mandarin.

"It's very sweet of you to escort me around Beijing on your day off."

"It's my pleasure, Miss—I mean, Alexis. Are you sure you don't want to see any sights?"

"No. I don't like being shuttled through monuments with a bunch of other tourists. I prefer buying items that I can't find in the United States or that cost considerably less here."

She looked at her nails again. "You don't happen to have a nail file, do you? I chipped a nail this morning."

"Nail file? I don't know this word."

Alexis held up her well-manicured left hand and made a filing motion with the other hand.

"No, I'm sorry, I don't."

Ping looked at the large diamond ring on Alexis's finger. "That's a beautiful ring."

"It is, isn't it?" She spread her fingers, giving Ping a better view. "This is my engagement ring from David. I've already picked out our wedding rings."

Ping looked confused. "Engagement rings, wedding rings, don't you have these things in China?" Alexis asked.

Ping shook her head.

"In the United States, when a man proposes marriage, he gives his fiancée a ring like the one I'm wearing. Well, probably not as grand. Then, as part of the wedding ceremony, the bride receives another ring. That way, everyone knows she's married."

"We don't do that in China. Jewelry is very expensive, too expensive for young people getting married."

"How do you know if someone is married, then?"

"I don't know." Ping shrugged her shoulders. "Probably how they act when they're together."

"You mean hugging and kissing?"

"No, we are uncomfortable hugging. Often there are special vibrations you feel between the husband and wife. We have a saying that explains it: *Married couples who love each other tell each other a thousand things without talking.*"

"I prefer the diamond ring," Alexis said, lifting her hand to maximize the effect of the light on the stone.

⟞⧾ ⧾⟝

The women spent most of the afternoon at Sharon's Store. Lisa, the same salesgirl who had helped Ping and David before, patiently explained the differences between the strands of pearls. Unlike David, Alexis seemed to enjoy the process, haggling successfully over the cost and the quality of the merchandise. Rather than make Alexis wait while the purchases were customized, Lisa told her she would personally deliver everything to her hotel room after work.

"Do you know of any other nice places like this to shop?" Alexis asked, after taking a cursory look at the items for sale in some of the stalls on the first three floors of the Pearl Market.

Ping understood that to mean more stores like Sharon's. "We could go to the Friendship Store. I haven't been inside, but I've heard many tourists at the hotel speak highly of the quality and variety of the merchandise there. Plus, it's not too far from the hotel."

"What's a Friendship Store?"

"It's a government-run shop. They are all over the country. One American I helped at the business center told me it was similar to a department store in the United States."

"Like a US department store? That sounds like a place I'd like to visit."

Ping took a more active role at the Friendship Store than at Sharon's, as few of the salespeople spoke English. Alexis purchased several ornamental jade pieces, cashmere scarves, jewelry, and a large handmade silk Chinese rug. Ping arranged for the shipping of the rug to the United States. By the time the necessary forms were filled out and payment made, it was late afternoon.

73

"Well, I've had enough sightseeing for one day," Alexis said outside the Friendship Store. "I think I'll see if I can get a massage at the hotel before David and I go out tonight. We're having dinner with some of the executives from the company he's doing business with here."

"I'll say good-bye to you then," Ping said, attempting to hand Alexis the shopping bags she had been carrying. "The hotel is only a few blocks away."

Alexis raised an eyebrow and gave Ping a glassy stare. "I can't carry these packages that far. Besides, it's just too hot to walk more than a few feet. Let's take a cab, go back to the hotel, and have something to drink at Starbucks."

Ping obediently flagged down a taxi and accompanied Alexis to the hotel, helping her carry her purchases from the taxi to the Starbucks next to the mall entrance of the China Palace. They placed the shopping bags on a table in front of the window and stood in line to order behind a young mother with two small children. One of the two, a little girl with large dark eyes and hair in pigtails, pulled on her mother's skirt and pointed to cookies in the dessert case made to look like frogs. Her brother watched from his stroller, an impish grin on his face. Alexis smiled at the little girl, who, tilting her head to the side, stared at the tall blond woman.

"Ping," Alexis said. "Ask the mother of these two adorable children if I can buy them each a cookie."

Ping asked the woman in Mandarin.

"You can," Ping translated. "She is grateful for your kindness."

The young mother grinned broadly, bowing her head in thanks. When it was her turn, Alexis ordered two teas for herself and Ping and two large cookies for the children. The little girl clapped her hands in delight when Alexis presented her with the sweet. Her brother held out his hands in anticipation. Crumbs fell from tiny fingers and clung to rosebud lips as the two devoured their prize.

Seated with their beverages at the table, Ping studied Alexis. She had not seen this softer side. As if reading her thoughts, Alexis said, "I just adore little children. David and I plan on starting a family right away." She took a sip of her tea. "I may not be that interested in monuments and tourist sites, but I am glad I got to meet you and your brother. I think it's more important to get to know the people of a country than spend time exploring deteriorating buildings."

Ping gave Alexis a sideways glance. Perhaps she had misjudged her. Did she really want to get to know her and Jianbo? A chill ran through her body. She felt even more uncomfortable pretending to be Jianbo's sister.

CHAPTER SEVENTEEN

David entered the suite, tossed his jacket on the richly uphol-stered couch in the sitting room, and strode over to the win-dow. He threw open the curtain and pretended to gaze at the view, arms crossed, a scowl on his face.

"Really, David," Alexis said, slamming the door to the suite be-hind her. "Give me a break. Not everyone is as adept as you at using chopsticks. I don't think I insulted any of your Chinese friends by requesting a knife and fork."

David turned to Alexis, lips pressed together, eyes narrowed. "Think. That's not what I was talking about. Don't tell me you have no idea of what you did that might have offended our dinner companions?"

Alexis's pout informed David that not only did she not have any idea but that she didn't much care.

"Look," David said, "As my wife, you'll be entertaining foreign businessmen. I can't worry that you're going to insult them."

"What did I do that was so offensive?"

"Do you remember this?" David waved his hand back and forth in front of his face.

"I'm not going to get lung cancer just to please your Chinese businessmen. If they wanted to smoke, they should have gone outside."

"This is not the United States. There's no ban on smoking in restaurants here."

"Well, there should be."

David sighed, exasperated.

"Is that it, or is there more?" Alexis asked.

"The serving spoon request."

"I thought the waiter forgot to put the serving spoons on the table. It was unsanitary. Everyone kept putting their chopsticks into the serving dishes on the lazy Susan and then putting the food directly into their mouths. My God, David, who knows how many germs were in those dishes?"

"And last but not least, the scream."

"The scream was totally out of my control. When I put my fork into my food, I didn't expect to pull out a chicken foot. I know the Chinese eat anything and everything, but chicken feet?"

David rubbed his forehead. "This conversation is going nowhere. I'm going to go downstairs to the lobby for a few minutes to buy something to read. I'll be back in a little while."

"OK, darling." Alexis walked over to David and put her arms around his neck. "I'll try harder to be more tolerant of secondhand smoke and chicken feet."

Hoping Alexis would be asleep by the time he returned to the room, David bought a *Wall Street Journal* at the newsstand and sat at a table in the bar area.

"Just a glass of beer," he said to the waitress.

Nursing the drink, David listened to the cacophony of conversations around him. The pianist and the costumed greeter at the elevator had long since gone for the day, but the lobby was a hubbub of activity. David watched a steady parade of guests, bellhops, and waiters pass before his table. However, when a well-dressed Asian woman on a barstool gazed seductively in his direction, he shifted his eyes back to the newspaper.

Bothered by his fiancée's behavior, David was unable to concentrate on the words in front of him. Was he making a mistake marrying Alexis? Although he had known her for several years, they had only dated seriously for about three months before their engagement.

"Isn't this a bit sudden?" his mother had asked after he jetted off to Paris with Alexis for a weekend and proposed. But why wait? He enjoyed being with her. They had similar interests, friends in common, and up until now, he had found her charming. But so far, this trip to China had been a disaster. Thank goodness the deal was already signed. His Chinese hosts said nothing, but he could sense their displeasure with Alexis's antics.

If word of this evening got back to his boss, he could forget about heading up the Shanghai office. His main competitor for the position was a South Korean–born American national. David had met the man's wife at a company party. Her demure, reserved manner made her fade into the woodwork. But better that than an insensitive spouse whose only interest in going abroad was to shop.

CHAPTER EIGHTEEN

Ping had just turned on the lights in the cubicles in the business center when she heard the double doors open. It wasn't even 8:00 a.m.; who could need help at this hour? She smoothed her skirt before making her way to the counter.

"Mr. Bennington," Ping said, surprised. "Welcome to the business center. How may I help you?"

"You can relax. For once, I don't need anything. I'm heading back to the United States in a few hours and just wanted to give you this for helping Alexis shop yesterday."

He handed Ping an unsealed hotel envelope. She peered inside and saw several hundred-yuan notes. "Oh no, Mr. Bennington. I can't accept this. I was glad to be of help to you and your fiancée." Ping slid the envelope across the counter back to David.

"I'd like to do something for you. We've taken up so much of your free time."

"Really, it was my pleasure."

"Can't I get you anything? Some small token of thanks? Please, it would make me feel better."

"Well, I enjoy reading English novels. Perhaps a book?"

"That should be no problem. Any particular one?"

"No. I'll enjoy whatever you choose."

"Thanks for everything, Ping."

Without another word, David reached over the counter, kissed Ping gently on her cheek, said good-bye, and left. Ping stood motionless, glad that no one had been in the room to witness the impulsive act, glad that no one was there to see her lift her hand to touch her face where David's lips had been.

Later that day, her manager came over with a bouquet of flowers and a book, *Pride and Prejudice*. Attached to the flowers was a note.

Thanks for making my time in China so special.

Xie Xie, David

That evening, Ping and Jianbo sat on the sofa in front of the bed sipping tea.

"Mr. Bennington and his fiancée returned to America today," Ping said.

"How do you know?"

"He stopped by the business center to give me a book and flowers as a thank you for having spent the day with Alexis."

"Too bad he didn't give you money instead."

Ping lowered her gaze, remembering the envelope filled with yuan. She didn't feel right accepting money. In any case, Jianbo would have insisted she turn it over to him. She could have taken it and not have told him, but lies and secrets do not belong in a marriage.

Jianbo frowned. "Are they coming back?"

"I don't know. He didn't say."

"I guess that's the end of my restaurant unless we meet another rich American."

Jianbo sipped his tea, shoulders hunched forward, eyes down-turned. Ping put her cup on the table, sad to see her husband so dejected.

"Why is opening a restaurant in America so important?"

"It's an opportunity to make a lot of money. The uncle of one of my friends started with one restaurant there and now has three. He's very wealthy."

"Did an American sponsor him?"

"No, he married a Chinese woman who had become a US citizen. Now he's a citizen, too."

Ping bit her lip. She felt she had somehow let her husband down. She remembered Alexis's remark about the many Chinese restaurants in New York City. "The city probably has many Chinese places to eat."

"Yes, but not many chefs have had the experience I have, working in the kitchen of a large luxury hotel. I see what tourists order. I know what the best-selling items are."

Maybe Jianbo's idea isn't so crazy, Ping thought. *What he says seems to make sense.* "What would I do in New York?"

"You'd help me in the restaurant—maybe wait on tables or be the cashier. You know English and can talk to the customers."

"How long would I have to do that?"

"I don't know. Until we make enough money to hire someone else."

Ping smiled, but her heart sank. It sounded like it would be years until she could continue her education. Although she and Jianbo shared the same bed, they dreamed different dreams.

CHAPTER NINETEEN

Late September 2004

Jianbo shifted on the hard seat, careful not to awaken Ping, who was asleep, her head against his shoulder. He wished he had splurged and purchased a sleeper berth. They could have taken turns stretching out during the twenty-five-hour train ride from Chongqing to Beijing. The railroad car in which they traveled consisted of two rows of hard benches separated by a center aisle. The benches were arranged in couplets facing each other. Each bench had room for two travelers.

The steady rocking of the car caused Jianbo to nod off. He dozed intermittently, awakening when the train stopped briefly in Baofeng and then again three hours later in Zhengzhou. Ping stretched and sat up bleary-eyed as the train pulled out of the Zhengzhou station. The sun, piercing through the mist, announced the day.

"I'll be right back," Jianbo said. He walked down the central aisle of the car and returned a few minutes later with a bottle of soda and small cakes with a lotus-seed paste filling. He unwrapped the sweets, letting the wrappers slide to the floor, adding to the pile of debris dropped by passengers since the start of the journey. Jianbo offered a cake to Ping. She took it along with several sips of soda. "It's a long trip," Jianbo said. "But I'm glad I was there to see Feng get married."

"It was very nice, and the reception—I've never seen so much food."

"Feng is fortunate. He's married the daughter of one of the wealthiest men in Chongqing—one who could afford a lavish wedding."

"You sound jealous."

"Not at all. His wife seems nice, but she is not very attractive. Feng will earn his money."

"I don't know. Feng is no prize. He's always burping and spitting."

"So, what's wrong with that? That's what men do."

"Perhaps. But I don't find your friend particularly attractive."

Ping turned her face toward the window, watching as the train passed by an occasional flat-roofed dwelling. The early morning sun illuminated the gently rolling countryside, still a lush green from the late summer rains. A white-breasted osprey swooped down into a shallow, reed-filled lake and emerged with a silver carp in its beak.

Attempting to find a more comfortable position, Ping shifted from one spot to another on the bench. It had been unbearably hot in Chongqing for the wedding—a typical searing late summer day. In spite of the heat, she had enjoyed the visit. She was able to see Baba and Auntie Yi Ma. Ping told her aunt about her husband's plan to open a restaurant in the United States and confessed she did not want to go. If they stayed in Beijing, she might be able to continue her studies. There were many universities to choose from. Maybe she could go part time. Auntie Yi Ma told her not to worry. How could Jianbo possibly afford to go to America and open a restaurant? It would never happen.

"How much longer before we get to Beijing?" Ping asked.

"About seven hours. We still need to stop at Handan and Shijazhuang."

"I'll be back in a few minutes." Ping stood up and joined the long line for the toilet. Jianbo followed, standing behind her massaging her shoulders while the two waited their turn. When Ping went back to the wooden bench, she pulled out a book from her backpack.

"Is that the book the American gave you?" Jianbo asked as he sat down next to her.

"Yes. It's called *Pride and Prejudice.* It's in English."

"What's it about?"

"A young woman is in love with a wealthy man, an aristocrat. He loves her, too, but he's concerned because she's not from the same class; she's of lower birth."

"What happens?"

"I don't know. I haven't finished the book yet."

"It's not a good idea for people of different classes to marry," Jianbo said. "I'm happy that we're from similar backgrounds."

"Me, too," Ping replied, sliding closer to him.

They conversed little during the next hour as Ping read and Jianbo tried unsuccessfully to sleep. "Feng's lucky," he finally said. "Mr. Guo bought him a car and a house adjacent to his. He'll make good money, but he'll have to earn it; his father-in-law will expect him to get to work early and stay late."

"That's nice," Ping said, absorbed in her book.

"If you're going to read and ignore me, let me sit by the window. At least that will give me something to do."

The two switched seats. The unvarying *clickity-clack* of the train, as it sped northward, was echoed in the monotone ambers and greens of endless stretches of wheat fields and terraced hillsides. Jianbo glanced out the train window. A road and farmhouse appeared and disappeared at the side of the track. A peasant flashed by in loose black pants and white shirt pulling a two-wheeled cart overflowing with wheat. A circular wide-brimmed straw hat protected him from the harshness of the sun.

When his eyelids started to flutter, Jianbo took a sweater from his backpack and put it between his head and the back of the wooden bench. He had not been truthful with Ping. He was envious of Feng's good fortune. It was he, Jianbo, who had always been the more successful of the two. Didn't he have the beautiful wife? Wasn't he the one working in Beijing? However, his position at the China Palace was going nowhere. The sous-chef job had gone to a nephew of the manager not half as capable as he was. Every night, he would think about what he had learned that day in the kitchen that would be useful in his American restaurant. It was only that dream that made work at the China Palace bearable.

The train slowed as it approached the town of Handan. The platform quickly filled with passengers shoving and pushing, impatiently waiting to board. Ping gently shook Jianbo. "Wake up, the train is going to be very crowded. We need to put our backpacks by our side so we can keep an eye on them."

Jianbo awoke to the influx of passengers scrambling for a spot on the hard benches. Within seconds, every seat was taken. A few minutes after the train pulled out of the station, a short, thin man in black slacks, gray T-shirt, and flip-flops appeared pushing a beverage and snack cart through the crowded car. Jianbo purchased a bottle of water and another cake to share with Ping.

A family of three now occupied the once empty bench facing them. The parents were not much older than Ping and Jianbo. Sitting between them was a child of three or four, a bowl-shaped haircut framed his cherubic face. Ping smiled at the child offering to share some of her cake. The boy took the sweet and shoved it into his mouth; a residue of crumbs fell on his clothes.

"*Xie xie*," said his mother, looking adoringly at her child. She pulled a hanky from her purse and brushed the crumbs to the floor. The boy's father smiled at Ping, asking where she and Jianbo were from. He and his family were returning to their home in Shijiazhuang after spending the weekend with relatives in Handan. Talking to the parents and playing with the child made this part of the voyage pass more quickly. Before long, Ping caught sight of the smokestacks of Shijiazhuang in the distance. When the train pulled out of the station after a brief stop, an elderly couple had replaced the family.

"The little boy was adorable, wasn't he?" Ping said to Jianbo. Without waiting for a reply, she continued wistfully, "It would be nice to have a child."

Jianbo's jaw dropped. This was the first time Ping had mentioned starting a family. "We can't have a child now."

"Why not?"

"How could we afford it? You'd either have to stop working to stay with the baby, or we'd have to hire someone. Either way, it would be expensive."

"I could go back to Chongqing with the child and find a job there. Between Auntie Yi Ma and your mother the baby would be well taken care of."

"You really want to live in Chongqing and have me stay in Beijing?"

"No, I'd miss you too much."

Jianbo squeezed her hand. He was tempted to tell her that even though they were saving much of their salaries each week, it would be difficult to support both themselves and his parents. But that burden was his alone. It was his duty to provide for his family. To do otherwise would be to lose face.

Jianbo found the final four hours between Shijiazhuang and Beijing difficult. While Ping alternately slept and read, he paced up and down the aisle longing for a cigarette, ready to defy the "no smoking" signs plastered throughout the car. The cakes had done little to satisfy his hunger. He reached into his pocket. Just enough to pay the bus fare from the train station to the apartment. The trip to Chongqing had been expensive. In addition to a gift for Feng and his bride, he and Ping had bought presents for their families. He wanted to show his parents, father-in-law, and Auntie Yi Ma that they were doing well, that he was a good provider. He wished now that they had selected less expensive gifts.

When the train finally pulled into the station in Beijing, Jianbo woke Ping. "We're home."

Ping opened her eyes, smiled at him, stretched, and collected her belongings. She put the novel into her bag.

"I finished the book," she said.

"How did it end?"

"The two married. The aristocrat loved the woman too much to give her up."

"I understand how he feels," Jianbo replied as he helped Ping down from the train.

CHAPTER TWENTY

Autumn arrived without fanfare in Beijing. The hot, steamy summer slowly transitioned into the temperate weather that would last into November when the freezing winds from Siberia enveloped the city. Ping and Jianbo wore light jackets over their uniforms as they biked to work. As usual, Ping rode sidesaddle on the back rack of the bike, her arms around Jianbo's waist, her face lifted upward, refreshed by the cool morning breeze.

However, once they joined the flow of vehicles that filled the wide boulevards, the ride became less pleasurable. Ping released one arm from around her husband's waist to cover her nose and mouth from the fumes and dirt wafting through the air, compliments of the coal burned in the homes and businesses lining the street. By the time they reached the hotel, their jackets were covered with a thin layer of soot.

Ping waited by the service entrance while Jianbo chained and locked the bike. They walked up the stairs, greeted the guard at the door, and entered the building. Before going into the business center, Ping visited the ladies' room to remove the grime from her clothes and hair. She undid her chignon, bent over and shook her head. Satisfied that any residue from the bike ride had fallen from her dark tresses, she carefully redid her hair. After brushing off her clothes, she made her way into the business center through the employees' entrance.

Her manager was removing the older periodicals and newspapers from the tables and shelves and replacing them with more updated editions. "*Nie hao,* Ping," he said. "There was a telephone call for you a few minutes ago."

"For me?" Ping responded, concern in her voice.

"I don't think it was an emergency. The gentleman said he'd call back."

Ping sighed in relief. If something had happened to her father or Auntie Yi Ma, whoever telephoned would have left a message or at least a phone number so she could return the call. It was probably a guest or former guest of the hotel needing help with a translation. She had become quite proficient in English since she spoke it most of the day. Her manager now referred the majority of translation requests to her.

The phone rang. The manager told Ping to answer it.

"Good morning. This is the business center. May I be of help?"

"Ping?" a familiar voice asked.

"Yes?"

"It's David Bennington."

"Oh, good morning, Mr. Bennington," Ping said. She was grateful that her manager was busy arranging the magazines and did not notice her face redden and her hand shake.

"Are you busy now, or can we talk?"

"There's no one in the office at present, sir."

"Good. Alexis and I were discussing how helpful you and your brother had been during our trip to Beijing. We really appreciated it. We decided to do something for you. How would you and Jianbo like to come to the United States for a week as our guests?"

Ping stood open-mouthed. Had she understood correctly? Sometimes she had trouble comprehending English over the phone.

"Are you still there?"

"Yes, Mr. Bennington. I'm sorry for not answering, but I'm not sure I understood you correctly."

"Alexis and I would like you and Jianbo to come to the United States as our guests for a week. I'll pay for the trip. You can stay at my mother's home. She has plenty of room. It's our way of thanking you for all your help."

"I...I don't know. I'll have to talk with Jianbo."

"Please do that. I'll call you tomorrow about the same time for your answer. Is that all right?"

"Yes, and thank you very much for the invitation. You are very kind."

Ping placed the receiver in its cradle. Her heart raced; beads of perspiration formed on her forehead. She needed to sit down.

"Is everything OK?" her manager asked. "You didn't receive bad news, did you?"

"No, just a very unexpected invitation."

CHAPTER TWENTY-ONE

After work, Ping waited by the bicycle for Jianbo, unsure of what to do. She felt that nothing good could come of this invitation. Her husband would see it as the opportunity he had been waiting for. He would want to talk to Mr. Bennington and to whoever else would listen about his restaurant. What if someone did sponsor him? What if the money became available? Mr. Bennington certainly seemed wealthy enough.

If I don't tell Jianbo, no harm will be done, she thought. I'll tell Mr. Bennington that we just can't go—that the hotel won't give us the time off. But then she wondered what Jianbo would do if he ever found out about the invitation. He would certainly feel deceived. He would think she was disloyal and unworthy of him.

"Hi, Ping, sorry I'm late," Jianbo said. "There was a group seated right before the dining room closed."

Ping jumped, startled by her husband's sudden arrival. After he unlocked the bicycle, she positioned herself on the rear rack for the ride home. The bike flitted in and out of traffic. Even though it was night, she could see the ominous outline of black clouds in the dark evening sky.

"You're awfully quiet," Jianbo said as they sat drinking jasmine tea later that evening on the couch opposite the bed.

Feeling she could no longer postpone the inevitable, Ping revealed her conversation with Mr. Bennington. In his excitement, Jianbo almost spilled his cup of tea. "What luck," he said. "Of course you accepted."

"No, I told Mr. Bennington I would check with you first. He's calling again tomorrow morning for our answer."

"Tell him yes, yes, of course, yes."

"But what about our jobs?" Ping asked. "We might not be able to get the time off."

Jianbo took Ping's hands in his and looked directly into her eyes. "Don't you understand? This could be our big chance. Even if it means losing our jobs, we have to go."

Ping's hand shook; her chin trembled.

"I know you're afraid, but trust me. Everything will be all right. I'd never let anything bad happen to you."

His words did little to sooth Ping's concerns. "America is so far away," she said. "Mr. Bennington and his fiancée seem nice, but we don't really know them. So much could go wrong. What if they find out that we're not brother and sister?"

"We'll only be going for a week. And unless you say something, how will they know?"

"But it's wrong to deceive Mr. Bennington, especially if we accept his hospitality."

"It's really no different from what we did when he and his fiancée were in Beijing. It didn't seem to bother you then."

"It did. I was uncomfortable pretending to be your sister. But since it was only for a few days, I didn't think it would be too terrible. Now we'll be staying at Mr. Bennington's mother's home. We will be deceiving more people. If we're found out, it would be shameful."

"We'll just have to be careful no one finds out; that's all," Jianbo said. "This invitation is an opportunity. We must accept. Just think: we'll be visiting America. This is my dream."

"We'll be punished for our dishonesty."

"Don't be so negative. Look at the trip as an opportunity. You'll get to practice your English. You'll be even more fluent when we come back."

"What if no one understands me?"

"Why do you think they won't? It's you your boss asks for whenever a guest needs something translated. You'll manage perfectly in the United States. I'm not worried about my English, and all I can say is 'How do you want your eggs?'"

Ping smiled in spite of herself. "You could go without me. Fall is the busiest season at the hotel. If you get in trouble for leaving the kitchen shorthanded and lose your job, at least I'll still have mine."

"The reason that I'm not worried about my English is because you'll be with me to translate. How could I possibly get along by myself?"

"Just like you do at the omelet station."

"When we were out with Mr. Bennington and his fiancée, I had no clue what you were talking about."

Ping said nothing.

"Look how excited you were when we visited the Forbidden City. Think of all the places to see in New York. There's the statue of that woman with the torch."

"The Statue of Liberty?"

"Yes. Plus, all the skyscrapers. And if you do ever teach English, you can tell your students you've visited one of the greatest cities in America."

"Let me think about it tonight, and I'll tell you tomorrow morning."

Jianbo's eyes narrowed; his face became taut. "No. I've tried to reason with you. This trip will be good for both of us. There will be no more discussion. Tell Mr. Bennington we accept his invitation."

"Alexis will be very glad to hear you're coming," David said when Ping told him she and Jianbo would travel to the United States. "Is the last week in October good for you?"

"That would be fine."

"How about if you come Friday, the twenty-sixth, and return the following week on November second? With the time change, you'll arrive in New York around midday on Friday."

Ping knew her boss would not be happy if she was gone during that week, one of the busiest for the hotel. But Jianbo had insisted she accept whatever dates Mr. Bennington proposed.

"That will be fine," she answered, a tremor in her voice.

"Good. I'll have my travel agent FedEx the tickets to you. Where should I send them?"

"The hotel business center would probably be best."

"The tickets should arrive no later than the day after tomorrow. If they don't, please call me." David gave Ping his work and home phone numbers.

Ping thanked David again for his kindness. She could feel beads of perspiration rolling down her back. Before replacing the phone in its cradle, she took a tissue from under the counter to wipe off the residue of her sweaty palms from the receiver.

The following day a large white envelope arrived for Ping at the business center. Her heart pounded; her head ached as she held it in her hands. Dutifully, she delivered it to Jianbo, who was waiting for her at the bicycle rack after work. He took the envelope from her and opened it. "Our tickets to a better life," he said, before sliding the package inside his jacket.

CHAPTER TWENTY-TWO

October 24, 2004

A banging on the door woke Jianbo as he lay next to Ping. He bolted out of bed and glanced at his watch. Six thirty in the morning. Who could it be at this hour? He opened the door a crack and peered out. It was his neighbor, the only resident in the courtyard complex with a telephone.

"Yes?" Jianbo asked, heart pounding.

"It's your father. He's very ill. He was taken to the hospital a few hours ago by ambulance. Your mother called. She wants you to come home immediately."

"What's the matter?" Ping asked, sitting up in bed and rubbing her eyes.

Jianbo had already pulled his backpack from the armoire and was stuffing it with clothes. "My father's been taken to the hospital. I'm going to Chongqing."

Ping located her bag and began filling it.

"What are you doing?" Jianbo asked.

"Packing."

He put his hand on her backpack. "You're not coming with me," he said, lips pressed together, chin firm. "We're supposed to go to America in two days. If I'm not back, you will go. Once my father is better, I'll join you."

Ping stared at Jianbo, her lower lip quivering. "You want me to go by myself?"

"Yes."

"Couldn't we tell Mr. Bennington we can't come now? He could change the date, wait until after your father recovers."

"No. Everything is set. Who knows what will happen with my father?"

Jianbo opened a small drawer in the armoire and pulled out Ping's plane ticket, passport, and money. "Take your ticket and passport, and don't lose them." He counted out five twenty-dollar bills. "Here's one hundred American dollars."

"Where did you get this?" Ping asked.

"Feng loaned me the money. This should be enough for a week in America."

Ping handed the ticket, passport, and money back to Jianbo. "I'm not going by myself. We'll wait until your father is well, and we can both go together. In the meantime, I'm going with you to Chongqing. What will your family think if I don't show up?"

Jianbo grabbed Ping's arm as she reached for some clothes to put in her backpack.

"You're hurting me," she said, struggling to free herself.

"You're not coming with me. You will go to America as planned the day after tomorrow."

"No. I'm not going."

Face flushed, eyes like burning coals, Jianbo spun Ping around and slapped her hard on the face. The force of the strike sent her reeling backward onto the bed. She stared up at him, mouth agape, eyes wide, fingers touching the welt on her cheek. Appearing almost as shocked by his action as Ping, Jianbo placed his hands on the sides of his head and paced back and forth. Finally, when he had expunged whatever demon had possessed him, he sat down beside Ping. Trembling, she moved away from him, shielding her face with her arms.

Jianbo reached out. "Please, Ping, don't…don't move away." He folded his hands in his lap. He hung his head. Lowering her arms, Ping eyed him warily.

"I'm sorry if I hurt you. But you must go to America. If I could, I would send you to Chongqing, and I would go. But you know I can't do that."

Ping stared at Jianbo through red-rimmed eyes.

"Please, Ping. This is our chance, an opportunity to improve our lives. I'll explain to my family what a sacrifice you're making by going to the United States and not accompanying me to Chongqing. Don't let me down."

In a low tremulous voice, Ping finally spoke. "I know something horrible will happen if I go. We have lied to Mr. Bennington and his fiancée."

"What we did was not so terrible. What difference does it make if the Americans think I'm your brother or your husband?"

"Something inside me says we'll pay dearly for this deception. You know what they say: it is only a clear conscience that does not fear midnight knocking. See, your father has already been stricken."

"He's in the hospital because he has been ill for a long time. There is absolutely no connection between this event and our trip to America. And look how fortunate we were. With help from Feng's father-in-law, we were able to get passports and visas in less than a month. That's a sign we should go."

Jianbo got up and finished packing. He walked over to Ping, who had not moved from the bed. She raised her head and looked forlornly at him. He sat beside her. "Our situation is not good," he began, his voice softer. "If my father does not fully recover and cannot go back to work, we will have to take care of my parents. That will be very difficult on what we're making at the hotel."

"Don't they have savings?"

"Very little. It will be up to us to provide for them."

Ping covered her face with her hands. She thought of the photo of Baba and his sister, her auntie Yangmei. She remembered her father's words— "those with money never go hungry."

"Please look at me. This is important," Jianbo said.

Obediently, Ping raised her head.

"You must go to America and talk to Mr. Bennington about the restaurant. Remind him I'm an experienced cook, that I know the type of Chinese food that pleases foreigners. And that before the China Palace I worked in a restaurant in Chongqing."

"But you were a waiter there, not a cook."

"Don't tell him that. Tell him I worked in the kitchen."

"But that will be another lie."

"Damn it, Ping. Don't be so frustrating."

She cowered before him.

Jianbo ran his hand through his hair; he tapped his foot on the floor. "I need an answer, Ping. Will you go to America with or without me? Remember, our well-being and the well-being of my parents depends on your answer."

Ping trembled and gingerly touched her burning cheek. She now knew the consequences of refusing her husband's requests. "I'll go," she said in a barely audible whisper.

"Good. Remember, talk to Mr. Bennington about the restaurant."

Grabbing his backpack, Jianbo opened the door and left. Ping lay back on the bed, arm over her face, a nauseous feeling in her stomach. She touched her swollen cheek and mourned her relationship with Jianbo—a relationship now irrevocably changed.

CHAPTER TWENTY-THREE

Imitating the travelers in front of her, Ping showed her documents to the official at passport control. "Where is the receipt for the departure tax?"

"Departure tax?" Ping replied, a note of panic in her voice.

"Yes, you must pay the ninety-yuan departure tax before you can proceed to the boarding area." The official indicated the direction of the cashier's window where payment should be made.

"Can I pay in American dollars? I don't have enough yuan."

"Yes, I'm sure you can," the official replied.

Ping left the line and did as instructed. She was starting the trip with one hundred American dollars. When she returned to passport control with the departure tax receipt, she had less than ninety. Although the foreign money represented a month's salary for her, she was concerned that this would not be enough for her stay in America.

Sleep had eluded Ping the night before. Images had raced through her mind—missing the flight, not having the correct documents to exit China, arriving in New York with no one to meet her. What if Mr. Bennington forgot she was coming? He was a busy man. She checked her backpack for the fourth time to make sure she had the phone numbers he had given her.

She envied the other passengers as they crisscrossed through the terminal, striding purposefully toward ticket counters and gates. Her stomach churned. She had no idea what she was doing.

Once through passport control, she followed those in front of her to luggage inspection. Ping had not checked any suitcases. The backpack she carried contained a few articles of clothing and gifts for her American hosts.

In the departure lounge she checked in. "Everything is in order," the woman behind the counter informed her. "This is your boarding pass. We'll start boarding in approximately thirty minutes. Just take a seat until then."

Ping unzipped a small compartment in her backpack and put the boarding pass inside. Then she sat down next to an elderly Chinese couple, two of only a few Asians in the departure area. Through the window she could see the jet waiting to transport her to a land she knew only through books. In spite of the jacket she wore, she shivered, wishing desperately that Jianbo was there with her.

She wondered whether the other passengers could tell this was her first plane trip. No one else seemed nervous. Everyone was either reading, chatting on a cell phone, or talking to a companion. Ping pulled out a book Auntie Yi Ma had sent her, a guide to New York City. She opened it and pretended to read.

"We are now boarding rows thirty-five to forty," the woman announced from behind the counter.

Ping turned to the Chinese couple. "I didn't understand the announcement. What are we supposed to do?"

"They're boarding the plane by row number. Your number is printed on your ticket. You must wait until it is called."

Removing the boarding pass from her backpack, Ping found her assigned row. She sat patiently as the waiting area emptied. Only one or two passengers remained.

"Anyone holding a ticket on Flight 128 to New York should now be on board."

Grabbing her backpack, Ping raced to the entry door.

"I'm sorry," she said. "I never heard my row number called."

"Didn't you hear me say business class? Passengers in first and business class board first."

Red-faced, Ping ran quickly down the gateway. On board, the flight attendant indicated that her seat was toward the front of the plane. Ping glanced to her right. The narrow aisles were filled with passengers stuffing bags in overhead compartments. Turning left, she entered business class. There were fewer seats, and it was less crowded in this section. With the help of a flight attendant, she found her place next to a window. Before sitting down, she put her backpack in the overhead bin as she had seen the other passengers doing.

No sooner had she buckled her seat belt than the elderly gentleman in the seat next to her bombarded her with questions in English. Where was she from? Was this her first trip to America? Ping welcomed the distraction. Before the plane taxied down the runway she found out that the old man ("Call me Jim," he had insisted), was returning from three weeks in China. He was enthusiastic about her country. She listened while he described his boat trip down the Yangtze River and an excursion to Xian to see the Terracotta soldiers.

"But, of course, you've seen all these sights," Jim said.

"No, I haven't. And I even grew up in Chongqing, where most of the Yangtze River tours begin."

"I guess it's like me. I've lived in Queens all my life, and I've never been to the top of the Empire State Building." Ping made a mental note to look up the Empire State Building in her guidebook.

She got the impression that Jim was lonely. She learned that he was eighty-four years old, that his children didn't want him to take this trip to China by himself, that his wife of sixty years had died of cancer, and that he missed her terribly.

After an elaborate lunch, including wine, which Ping ginger-ly sipped, Jim reclined his chair to take a nap. Before doing so, however, he showed Ping how to raise the footrest, operate the individual viewing screen, and select a video. Ping switched back and forth between film offerings until she found one that seemed interesting.

Shortly after the film ended, a snack was served. Jim woke up, and the two conversed over fruit and cheese. She was grateful to the old man. He seemed to have no trouble understanding her English. In fact, he complimented her several times on how well she spoke. After the trays had been removed, Ping noticed a small black bag in the compartment in front of her.

"What is this?" she asked Jim.

"It's filled with toiletries. It's yours to keep."

"Really?" Ping said, surprised to be receiving a gift from the airline.

She unzipped the bag and examined its contents. She'd give the razor to Jianbo but would keep the tiny toothbrush, tooth-paste, and slipper socks. Ping leaned back in her seat and sipped her tea. She liked riding in planes.

CHAPTER TWENTY-FOUR

After clearing immigration and customs, Ping walked through the opaque sliding-glass doors into the terminal area of Kennedy Airport. A wide, chained-off passageway separated arriving passengers from a noisy crowd shouting to familiar faces or holding placards with names of individuals to be picked up. Ping paused, muscles tense, heart racing, unsure of what to do.

"Ping, over here."

She turned around and saw Alexis waving to her from behind the barrier. With a sigh of relief, she walked around the chains to join her.

"Where's your brother?"

"His father is ill. He had to go to Chongqing to be with him."

"His father?" Alexis asked.

Ping bit her lip. This is what comes from deception. She would have to be careful with every word uttered. "I mean 'our' father," Ping said, her face flushed. "Sometimes my English isn't very good."

"Didn't you want to be with your father, too?"

"I did, but Jianbo insisted I come." Ping felt her answer was inadequate, but she couldn't think of anything better to say.

Alexis looked puzzled but smiled at Ping, "Well, I'm very sorry about your father. I hope he recovers quickly."

"Thank you."

"Where's the rest of your luggage?" Alexis asked, glancing at Ping's backpack.

"This is all I have."

"Really. I must have had three suitcases for my six days in Beijing. I can't believe you travel so light."

"Is Mr. Bennington here, too?"

"No, we'll see him later. He's at work. I'm going to drive you to his mother's house and get you settled."

"Where are the big buildings? The skyscrapers?" Ping asked. "I didn't see any when the plane was landing."

"The airport's quite a ways out of the city. We'll see them when we get closer to Manhattan."

At this point, Ping found more similarities between China and the United States than differences. Except for the signs in English, Kennedy Airport was indistinguishable from Capital Airport in Beijing. They were both crowded with frenzied travelers coping with similar procedures. The small homes she had seen as the plane approached the airport reminded her of those in her country. The weather was identical. The chilly October air that greeted her outside the terminal building felt the same as what she had just left behind in Beijing.

"I'm in short-term parking. I was lucky and got a parking space pretty close to the terminal," Alexis said.

Ping nodded even though she understood nothing of what Alexis had just said. When they reached the parking lot, Alexis guided them toward a dark green sedan. She used a special device to unlock the doors. Ping heard them click open as they approached. Another press of the device and the trunk popped up. Alexis took Ping's backpack and put it inside.

This automobile was the first big difference Ping noticed between the two countries. In China, the nicest vehicle Ping had ridden in was the black sedan hired by Jianbo's parents for their wedding. She had felt so luxurious in the backseat in her red *cheongsam*. But this one was far more elegant—the tan leather seats, the wooden dashboard, the slot where Alexis slid in a disc. She had never seen such a beautiful car.

During the forty-five-minute drive to David's mother's home in Alpine, New Jersey, Alexis entertained Ping with the minutiae of her wedding preparations. Half listening, Ping turned a curious eye to the scenery outside. She tingled with excitement scarcely believing she was in America. But nothing she saw impressed her, especially the crowded highway they were traveling on, lined with abandoned tires and trash.

"This is the Cross Bronx Expressway," Alexis said as if reading Ping's thoughts. "It's one of the ugliest highways in the area, if not in the United States. It looks like something you'd find in a third-world country, not in America." Alexis winced. "Oops, sorry. China is really an emerging-market country, not third world. At least that's what David says."

Grateful that Alexis had been at the airport when she arrived, Ping chose to ignore the "third world" comment—although she hadn't seen anything yet more impressive than her homeland. She preferred the wide streets of Beijing with their hodgepodge of vehicles and bicycles to those she had seen so far in America. In China, it was not unusual to see a bicycle-wagon contraption hauling a goat down a major thoroughfare. On this highway, the only variety was in the size of the vehicles, big, bigger, and biggest—cars, vans (which Alexis called SUVs), and large trucks.

Suddenly, the road changed into an eight-lane bridge spanning a river.

"This is the Hudson River," Alexis said. "We're on the George Washington Bridge, named after the first president of the United States." Ping nodded remembering the name from one of her English classes at school. "If you look to the left, you can see the skyscrapers."

Ping's heart beat faster. This was the New York she expected to see—the famous skyline that appeared in newspapers and on TV. She was captivated by the row of increasingly taller buildings lining the east side of the Hudson River. With the morning sun reflected in the windows and on the water, the concrete and steel panorama was more beautiful than she had ever imagined.

Midway across the bridge, a sign announced that they had passed into New Jersey. They turned onto a parkway that was more like the roadways Ping had expected: wide, few cars, no trucks, and a landscaped island separating north- and southbound lanes. Ping craned her neck at each break in the trees that permitted a view of the New York side of the Hudson River. Alexis exited the parkway and followed a road that meandered by sizable estates with meticulous lawns and gardens. She pulled the car into a circular driveway in front of a large brick residence.

"Is this a hotel?" Ping asked.

"No. This is my future mother-in-law's house."

Ping stared in awe; she had never seen such a large private home.

CHAPTER TWENTY-FIVE

P ing followed Alexis as she climbed the two wide, curved stone steps leading to the double-door entrance of the Bennington estate. Before Alexis had an opportunity to ring the doorbell, the door opened and a heavyset middle-aged woman appeared. "Hello, Miss Dunhurst," the woman said, greeting Alexis in a heavily accented voice.

"Hi, Greta. This is David's and my friend from China, Wang Ping."

"Nice to meet you, Miss Ping," Greta said.

"It is a pleasure to meet you, also."

"Mrs. Bennington is waiting for you on the veranda." Greta took Ping's backpack. "I'll put this up in your room. Where are your other suitcases?"

Alexis rolled her eyes. "This is all she has."

Greta gave Ping a reassuring smile as she stepped aside to let her enter. Inside, the house was flooded with light pouring in from a multitude of sources: the French doors at the end of the hall, the enormous windows in the living and dining rooms, and the huge skylight two stories above. The light contrasted with the dark, hardwood floors; reflected off mirrors and glass tabletops; and shimmered on satin drapes and rich, textured fabrics. Sweet scents of lilies, gardenias, and peonies wafted through the air from a large floral arrangement on a console table in the entryway. *So, this is how foreigners live,* Ping thought, comparing this home to the small, cramped, dwelling in which she had grown up with its rank odors of cigarette smoke and age.

"Come," Alexis said. "I'll introduce you to David's mother."

Ping followed Alexis down the wide center hall, feeling swallowed up by the vastness of the house. Katherine Bennington was sitting at a wrought-iron table on the veranda. A large green striped umbrella protected her from the sun as she read a newspaper and sipped her coffee. The stone patio stretched the width of the house. In front of the veranda was a kidney-shaped swimming pool and spa. Next to the pool was a cottage. A series of carefully cultivated gardens ended in front of a row of high hedges.

"Good morning," Alexis said as she embraced David's mother.

Tall and slender, Katherine Bennington was dressed casually in off-white slacks and a dark blue sweater, her gray hair pulled back into a low ponytail. Her eyes captivated Ping, soft and green like a lily pad.

"Welcome to America," Mrs. Bennington said warmly, extending her hand. "You must be Ping. David and Alexis have told me a great deal about you and your brother. Is your brother still outside?"

"Their father is ill," Alexis said. "Her brother is with him."

"And you didn't want to be with your father, too?" Mrs. Bennington asked turning to Ping.

After her blunder with Alexis, Ping realized she needed a good reason for why she came alone. She had prepared one during her ride from the airport.

"Jianbo felt that one of us should come. It would be rude to do otherwise given your kind invitation."

"What's wrong with your father?"

"It's a sickness of the lungs," Ping said. "I forget the English name."

"Emphysema?" Mrs. Bennington suggested.

"Yes, that's it. He's doing much better now. The doctors think he'll be able to go home from the hospital very soon. When that happens, Jianbo will join me here."

Apparently satisfied by Ping's explanation, Mrs. Bennington suggested that she might want to shower and change her clothes after the long plane ride before they lunched.

"I'll show her to her room," Alexis said.

Ping followed Alexis up the large staircase in the foyer to the second floor. They passed several bedrooms before Alexis ushered her into what was to be her room. The first thing Ping noticed was how out of place her worn backpack seemed on the crisp, chintz quilt of the king-size bed, like a weed in a garden of lilies.

Inside the room, Ping turned around slowly, her mouth agape. The bedroom was enormous, almost as large as her entire apartment in Beijing. Marble-topped mahogany nightstands were positioned on either side of the bed. On the opposite side of the room stood a matching dresser with a large tripod mirror. A stately armoire rested against an adjoining wall. The chintz pattern of the quilt was repeated on two armchairs in front of a large window overlooking the rear of the house. Ping glanced out the window into the garden. From her vantage point she could see the small house by the pool. She also discovered that behind the row of high hedges she had seen from the veranda was a tennis court.

"Does anyone live in the little cottage?" Ping asked.

"You mean the guesthouse? Greta and her husband, Ulrich, live there. They take care of the house and grounds. Greta cleans and cooks; her husband tends to the landscaping, pool, and tennis court. He also drives Mrs. Bennington wherever she needs to go. They've worked for Katherine for many years."

"Greta has an accent. Where is she from?"

Alexis waved her hand dismissively. "I don't really know. Croatia, Latvia, one of those countries." She grabbed some hangers from the closet and handed them to Ping.

"You might want to unpack, so your clothes don't get wrinkled."

Ping pulled out a pair of black slacks, a few tops, a dark skirt, and a change of underwear from the backpack. She hung the slacks and skirt in the closet along with the jacket she had just taken off.

"Put your sweater and other things in the dresser," Alexis said.

After doing as instructed, Ping stood awkwardly in front of the bed uncertain what to do next.

"You can finish unpacking; we have time."

"That's all I brought."

"For the week?"

Ping nodded, feeling she had somehow displeased Alexis. "I do have some gifts," she said, fumbling around in the backpack. She produced two cashmere scarves. "These are for you and Mr. Bennington."

"Oh, his and hers matching wool scarves—rather nice for imitation Burberry. That's very sweet of you."

"I brought this paperweight for Mrs. Bennington," Ping said, taking a box from the backpack. "Do you think she'll like it?" Ping carefully removed a glass paperweight with two blue porpoises jumping over a transparent globe. The gift had cost her a week's salary.

"I'm sure she will," Alexis said, wrinkling her nose. "If you want, I'll give it to her when I go downstairs."

"Thank you," Ping said, handing the paperweight to Alexis.

"Well, I guess you'll want to take a shower after that long plane ride." She opened the door next to the closet. "This is your bathroom."

Ping peered into the largest bathroom she had ever seen—even bigger than those at the China Palace. The floor was set with 18-inch gray-and-white stone tiles arranged on the diagonal. A contrasting pattern covered most of the walls and the glassed-in shower stall. The vanity and the Jacuzzi tub were in white marble.

"Will Mrs. Bennington be using this bathroom, too?"

Alexis scoffed. "No, she has one about three times this size. Plus, there are two other bathrooms besides this one and Katherine's as well as a powder room."

Ping thought about the outhouse she and Jianbo shared with the other residents of the courtyard. There were twelve people using the one facility, and in America here was one woman with four bathrooms and a powder room. This country was indeed different from China.

⇌ ⇌

Alexis left Ping and went downstairs. She found Katherine still reading on the patio. "This is for you from your houseguest," she said, handing her the paperweight. "I was going to do you a favor and drop it on the stairs."

Katherine frowned and stared at Alexis. "Why would you want to do that?"

"It would save you the trouble of hiding it in the basement."

Katherine slid her hand over the glass globe and porpoises. "This is a lovely gift and something I don't have. It will be perfect on my desk."

Alexis moved a chair next to Katherine wondering when her future mother-in-law had lost her sense of taste. "We do have a problem," she said.

"What is it?"

"Ping has nothing appropriate to wear to the club this evening."

Katherine lowered her glasses and stared at Alexis, green eyes no longer soft. "Everything Ping brought was in that backpack. Most of it was filled with gifts, not clothes." She pulled out the scarves Ping had given her. "She brought these for David and me."

Katherine fingered the wool scarves. "They're nice, very soft. Burberry, aren't they?"

Alexis sneered. "Imitation Burberry. The Chinese have knock-offs of just about everything."

"It's still a lovely gesture on Ping's part. For her, these were most likely expensive purchases."

"You're probably right. I did thank her for them."

"How sweet of you," Katherine said, unable to hide a touch of sarcasm. After a pause, she continued. "I think I'll have Ulrich take Ping to Saint John's after lunch. Debra, the saleslady I work with there, should be able to outfit her for this evening."

Alexis's mouth dropped open. "Saint John's? Isn't that a bit excessive? Macy's would work just as well."

Katherine smiled and got up from the table. "No. I think Ping deserves something special. You'll have to excuse me. I need to call and make sure Debra is at the store and can help." She picked up the paperweight. "I also want to put this in a prominent place on my desk."

Alone on the patio, Alexis gazed at the carefully landscaped yard with its pool and tennis court. One day this would probably be David's and hers. She sensed a coldness from Katherine when discussing Ping's gifts. Perhaps she had better appear humbler; she didn't want to alienate her future mother-in-law.

CHAPTER TWENTY-SIX

Ping sat uncomfortably on the padded chair in the large, mirrored dressing room, clad in only her panties and bra. After bringing her a cup of tea, Debra, an attractive saleswoman in her forties, had left Ping alone to search for appropriate clothes for her client. She returned with various items draped over her arms.

"Let's try some of these on for size. With your slender build, I pulled some zeros and twos. I think they'll fit."

Ping now understood why Alexis didn't want to spend time at Silk Alley and the stalls in the Pearl Market. This is how rich Americans shopped, relaxing in large dressing rooms, drinking tea while saleswomen ran all over the store looking for clothes for them to try on.

"How do you know Mrs. Bennington?" Debra asked.

"My brother and I helped her son in Beijing. He and his fiancée invited us here for the week."

"Lucky you. Is this your first trip to the United States?"

Ping nodded as Debra handed her a two-piece ecru suit with gold metal trim around the collar and cuffs. Four elegant gold filigree buttons adorned the jacket. The drop-pleated skirt fell to just above Ping's knees.

"Stunning," Debra said as Ping positioned herself at the three-sided full-length mirror. "It fits perfectly."

Ping tried on several outfits, but Debra felt the ecru suit was the most spectacular. In addition to the suit, Debra charged a pair of elegant gold sling-back shoes and matching clutch to Mrs. Bennington's account.

"You have beautiful hair," Debra told Ping, "but instead of wearing it down, let's try pulling it back. It will show off your face."

She combed Ping's hair into a high ponytail and then asked her to step outside the dressing room and take a look at herself in a larger mirror. Customers and sales personnel paused to gaze at the stunning Asian woman. One whispered something to Debra. "They think you're a model," she said to Ping when they returned to the dressing room. "You'll be the belle of the ball this evening."

"I'm sorry. I don't understand that expression."

"You will," Debra said.

That evening, Ping tried the Jacuzzi tub in the guest bathroom for the first time. Greta had placed a number of bath products on the tile ledge above the tub for Ping to use. To the sound of classical music coming from the radio on the nightstand, she laid her head against a waterproof pillow suctioned onto the tub, luxuriating in the hot, sudsy water, fragrant bubbles up to her neck.

She stared at the decorative tile border encircling the tub, a vacant look in her eyes. She envisioned Jianbo at his father's bedside. Hopefully her father-in-law would improve and Jianbo could join her. Ping wished he were here now to accompany her to the country club. This must be a very special place, or why had she been whisked into New York for appropriate clothes? Were Mrs. Bennington and Alexis concerned she might embarrass them?

Ping would have preferred staying in for the evening reading one of the books from her host's library.

Reluctantly, she shut off the Jacuzzi, lifted the stopper, and climbed out of the tub. She wrapped herself in the largest, softest towel she had ever seen. A bath sheet, Greta had called it when she handed it to her earlier along with several plastic bottles of skin lotion. Opening the caps, she sniffed each one, finally selecting the jasmine scented.

Ping slipped on her underwear, the only items she would be wearing that weren't from Saint John's. Seated on the chair in front of the marble-topped vanity, she brushed her hair until it shone then pulled it back into a high ponytail as the saleslady had suggested.

Greta had taken the purchases and hung them in the closet on the valet bar—another new expression she had learned. Gingerly, she took the ecru suit off the hanger and put it on. In the mirror, she tried on the necklaces her father and David had given her. David's, with the three pearls, was the more elegant and looked perfect with the outfit. She held the *mother-daughter* necklace in her hand and then placed it in the new gold clutch. Ping needed her mother to be with her this evening.

CHAPTER TWENTY-SEVEN

P ing descended the stairs from the second floor to the entryway of Mrs. Bennington's home, the pleated skirt swaying gracefully as she moved. A whistle escaped Ulrich's lips; Mrs. Bennington's lily pad eyes showed their approval.

"You look lovely," she said as Ping reached the bottom of the staircase.

"Thank you for these clothes. I've never worn anything so beautiful."

"It was my pleasure. I must remember to call Debra and let her know how delighted I am with her selection. Of course, with your build and height, most anything would look good on you."

Ping lowered her eyes, a blush creeping up the sides of her face.

"Well, we don't want to be late." Mrs. Bennington walked toward the front door as Ulrich rushed to open it.

Once in the car, Mrs. Bennington told Ping that another couple, good friends of Alexis and David, would also be joining them for dinner. The husband, Roger, was an attorney. He and David had been friends since grammar school. Roger was to be best man at her son's wedding. "I think you'll like his wife, Marjorie," she said. "She is not one to mince words."

"Mince words? I don't understand this."

"Oh, I'm so sorry, my dear. Your English is so good that I forget it's your second language. 'To not mince words' means to tell it like it is, be direct, be truthful."

"Now I understand."

"By the way, thank you for the lovely paperweight. It's perfect on my desk in the study."

"I'm so happy you like it," Ping said, beaming.

Mrs. Bennington patted Ping's hand. "I hope you feel at home here."

"I do. You have been so kind." Ping looked away, concerned that Mrs. Bennington would see the tears forming in her eyes. She had never met anyone as generous and caring as Mrs. Bennington. For the first time since she had arrived, she felt relaxed and, in a strange way, protected.

"Here we are," Mrs. Bennington announced as Ulrich stopped the car under a large porte cochere. Before Ping could place her hand on the door handle, two men, one on each side of the car, opened the rear doors and extended their arms to help the women out. Ping waited for Mrs. Bennington to circle the front of the automobile. The two men charged ahead of them to open the doors to the clubhouse.

"Enjoy your evening," they chimed in unison.

"Ah, Mrs. Bennington, good evening," said a man dressed in a black tux and bowtie. "The rest of your party has already been seated."

The maître d' led the women to their table. As Ping made her way across the seemingly endless dining room, she was aware of voices suddenly hushed and eyes that followed her. Why were they staring? Was she doing something wrong?

A woman at a table they passed motioned to Katherine. "Just a minute," she said to the maître d'. "Come, Ping, I'll introduce you to some friends of mine." As they approached, the two men at the table stood up.

"These are my good friends Anne and Bennett Hunt and Lillian and Andrew Buchman. This is Wang Ping, my guest from China."

"Good evening," Ping replied, bowing her head.

"Well, Katherine," Lillian said. "You told me she was lovely, but your guest is absolutely stunning."

Ping could feel her face flush.

"Every man in here is drooling," Anne said with a wink. "Even my husband. Sit down, Bennett."

After some small talk, Katherine and Ping left and followed the maître d'. Ping asked Katherine, "I didn't understand. What does drooling mean?"

"It's an expression. Anne meant every man in the place would like to be with you."

"Does that mean I look all right?"

Katherine put her arm around Ping's waist. "My dear, you look like a princess."

Ping held her head higher as they approached the table where David Bennington sat. His admiring gaze and welcoming smile increased her feeling of well-being.

The maître d' placed Ping between David and Mrs. Bennington. Introductions were made and greetings exchanged as the two women took their seats.

"Well, Ping, you certainly attracted attention in that exquisite outfit. I think every eye in the room was on you when you walked in," Marjorie said.

"It is a lovely outfit," Alexis remarked. "But I don't think that was why people were staring at Ping. Anytime someone different comes to the club, it creates a stir. Remember that African-American woman who was a guest of the Perrys and all the attention she received?"

Mrs. Bennington stared in disbelief at Alexis; Marjorie rolled her eyes. In an attempt to rescue the group from an uncomfortable situation, Roger lifted his glass. "A toast to beautiful women, the four most beautiful of which happen to be at this table."

"Here, here," said David, eyes focused on Ping.

The waiter distributed large leatherbound menus. "If you need any help in understanding how these dishes are prepared," David whispered to Ping, "just ask me."

"Thank you, Mr. Bennington."

He winced. "Please call me David. We're not at the China Palace. You don't have to be so formal."

"Thank you, David," she repeated.

Sitting to the right of David, Alexis leaned forward and glared at Ping, who shifted uncomfortably in her seat. Had she done something wrong? Something that angered Alexis? But, sandwiched as she was between Mrs. Bennington and David, Ping felt safe.

When everyone was settled and appetizers served, Roger turned to Ping. "My parents are going to China next month. What sights do you recommend they see?"

"There are many things to see in my country, but I have not traveled much outside of Chongqing and Beijing, so I can't tell you firsthand. Most tourists want to see the Terracotta warriors at Xian."

"That's a place I'd like to visit," David said. "The army of warriors is one of the most significant archaeological discoveries of the century."

"What are they?" Marjorie asked.

"About thirty years ago, peasants digging a well unearthed some pottery dating from the second century BC. Archaeologists uncovered more than seven thousand artifacts, including a whole army of life-size horses, soldiers, and chariots. They were made from terracotta and buried along with the emperor. What's truly amazing is that most of the figures are intact. Plus each soldier's face is unique—modeled after a different person."

"I can't believe you didn't go when you were in China," Roger said. "It sounds like an archaeologist's dream."

"I'll get there. My company plans on sending me to China frequently."

Alexis moaned. "I hope not. I don't think I can take many more trips to a third-world country."

David's jaw dropped. Mrs. Bennington shook her head and turned to Alexis. "My dear, have you forgotten we have a guest?"

"Excuse me. I meant a developing country," Alexis said, cocking her head and taking another sip of her wine.

Roger gave her a curious look before continuing. "What do you recommend my parents see in Beijing? They'll only be there a couple of days."

"Jianbo and I visited the Forbidden City last month. It is very beautiful."

"And if you want," Alexis said. "You can even see Mao Tse-tung—in the flesh, so to speak. Isn't that right, Ping?"

Ping stared at Alexis, unsure of her intentions. As the others appeared to be waiting for a response, she answered. "Yes that's true. His body is embalmed. It is on display in Memorial Hall."

"Your parents would like to see that, wouldn't they, Roger?" Alexis asked snidely.

Ignoring the remark, Roger headed into what was usually safer territory—restaurants. "What are some restaurants you would recommend in Beijing, Ping?"

"Guests at the hotel where I work have said Tiandi Yijia is very good. It is near the Forbidden City."

"Isn't that the one where your Chinese business friends took us, David?"

"I don't think so."

"Well, if it is, Roger, I don't think your parents would enjoy it—unless, of course, they like chicken feet."

"Chicken feet?"

"Yes, they eat chicken feet over there."

"What's wrong with you?" David whispered to Alexis, anger in his voice.

Alexis glared at him, lifting her wineglass to her lips. All eyes turned toward Ping.

Ping lowered her head and breathed deeply to control the anger roiling within her. How could Alexis make such unkind remarks about her country? She could remain silent no longer. "Let me tell you something about China," she began sweetly, flushed cheeks the only hint of her ire. "It is true that we eat chicken feet and other things that you may not find to your liking. But there is a reason. About fifty years ago there was a great famine in my country. No one knows exactly, but it is believed between thirty to forty million people died from hunger."

No one spoke at the table. Alexis shifted uncomfortably in her seat.

Emboldened by the silence around her, Ping continued. "Because we have so little in my country, we value things that others may not. One New Year's holiday, when I was maybe eight or nine, my father gave me a gift that was very special—an orange. I remember peeling it carefully so as not to lose any of the nectar. I spent much time separating each segment, sucking out the juice, chewing the pulp. I can still taste the sweetness of the orange in my mouth."

Ping glanced around the table. All eyes were upon her. "I saved the pits and planted them in the ground in the spring hoping to recreate this beautiful fruit. I put the orange rinds in a special place in a drawer. The aroma lingered for several days before the peelings finally dried up. I thought I was indeed fortunate to have this wonderful present. This was my very first gift."

Except for Alexis, who kept her eyes focused on her lap, everyone at the table looked at Ping with a mixture of sympathy and admiration. David leaned back in his chair, a smile of approval on his lips.

Ping sat taller, chin lifted. She was glad she had not minced words.

CHAPTER TWENTY-EIGHT

"Good morning, Mr. Bennington," Greta said as she opened the front door. "I thought Ulrich was to drive Miss Ping into the city this morning."

"I decided I would. I need to talk to my mother about something. Where is she?"

"In the morning room finishing breakfast. Would you like something to eat?"

David paused. "How about your blueberry pancakes. I can't get anything like them in the city."

"I just happen to have some frozen blueberries in the freezer. It'll just be a few minutes," Greta said and headed toward the kitchen.

David found his mother at the breakfast table engrossed in the morning paper.

"Well, this is a pleasant surprise," Katherine said, reaching up to kiss her son. "I didn't expect to see you this morning."

"I need to talk to you."

Katherine put down her paper, her face solemn, her eyes somber.

David pulled up a chair next to his mother's. "I'm having second thoughts about marrying Alexis."

Sighing deeply, Katherine patted her son's hand. "I'm so sorry."

"I don't know what to do. With our friends and my American business associates, she's fine. But out of her element, she's a disaster. In Beijing, she insulted our Chinese hosts at dinner. And then her racial and ethnic comments last night." David shook his head. "In my position with the company, I can't risk having a wife that might embarrass me."

"Have you told Alexis how you feel?"

"I tried to in Beijing, but she just acted like I was being unreasonable."

David stood and began pacing. "And what was with her last night?"

"She might have been jealous of Ping. It's not often that Alexis is upstaged."

"Do you think that was the issue?"

Katherine shrugged her shoulders. "Most likely."

"I suppose you're right. But my heart went out to Ping. Although she did a great job of defending herself."

"I was impressed."

"But even if Alexis's behavior was caused by jealousy, there's still a problem. It doesn't sound like she wants to return to China."

"Is that important?"

"Yes. I'm in the running to head the Shanghai office that will be opening in a year or so. That'll mean at least two years abroad."

"Does Alexis know?"

"I've mentioned it, but it doesn't seem to have registered."

Conversation stopped as Greta arrived with the pancakes, which David dug into with relish. "Just as delicious as I remembered."

"It's nice to cook for someone so appreciative," Greta replied as she poured coffee for both David and Mrs. Bennington.

As soon as Greta left the room, David stopped eating and looked beseechingly at his mother. "What should I do?"

"Do you love Alexis?"

"I don't know anymore. I thought I did. But now every time she opens her mouth, I cringe. I'm afraid of what might come out."

Katherine moved closer and put her arm around her son. "I'll listen to you, I'll share your grief and your joy, but I can't tell you what to do. That has to be your decision."

"After what I saw last night and in China, I don't see how I can marry her."

"You don't have to decide today. Think it over a few days. Wait at least until after your guest leaves."

Katherine sat back in her seat; David picked up his fork and began eating the pancakes. After several bites, he turned again toward his mother. "Speaking of my guest, what do you think of Ping?"

"She's a lovely girl and speaks English extremely well. And, of course, she is very beautiful. Is that why you invited her?"

"Of course not. It wasn't even my idea to have her here."

"It couldn't have been Alexis's with her feelings about China."

"Actually it was. She read a story somewhere—I think it was the *New York Times,* about parents hiring Chinese nannies so that their kids could learn Mandarin. According to Alexis, Mandarin is a must if you want your child to get into the best schools. Her idea is to hire Ping as a nanny."

"Is Alexis pregnant?"

"No. She just wants to make sure she has bragging rights when our yet-to-be-conceived child enters preschool."

"So Mandarin is the language du jour. When you were young, it was French."

"I don't remember learning French."

"You didn't. I thought the whole foreign language craze to get your toddler accepted by a top preschool was ridiculous."

David stopped eating and stared, an admiring look in his eyes. "I'm glad my mother is so wise."

CHAPTER TWENTY-NINE

Ping exited the theater, eyes rimmed in red, blowing her nose in the handkerchief David had handed her. "Did you enjoy the play?" Alexis asked.

"It was beautiful," Ping replied, dabbing at her eyes. "I'm sorry I was so emotional."

"Don't worry," Alexis said. "This is the third time I've seen *Phantom of the Opera,* and I still get choked up."

She glanced at her watch. "You'll have to have dinner at the club without me this evening. I'm meeting my mother for another fitting for my wedding gown." She kissed David on his cheek. "Please call me later, darling, when you get home."

David watched as Alexis pulled away in a taxi. When the cab was no longer visible, he turned to Ping. "Let's have dinner in the city, tonight. You've already eaten at the club once. I'll take you somewhere new."

As Ping didn't object to the change in plans, David took out his cell. "I'm sure my mother will understand if we don't join her tonight." He called his mother on the phone and left word on her answering machine not to expect them for dinner.

"It's such a nice evening," David said. "I thought you might enjoy Tavern on the Green. It's in Central Park and has some beautiful views."

"It sounds nice. I would like to go to this tavern."

After retrieving his car from a nearby parking garage, they drove into Central Park. "We're a little early for dinner," David said as he handed the car keys to the valet. "Let's sit outside and have a drink." He led Ping to an outdoor bar overlooking the park.

"This reminds me of China," Ping said pointing to the colorful string-light lanterns overhead.

When the waiter asked Ping what she would like to drink, she looked helplessly at David. "Two kirs," he said. "I think you'll like this. It's made with cassis and white wine."

A quizzical look from Ping caused David to further define the drink. "Cassis is a type of berry, a black currant."

"This is very good," Ping said after the waiter had served the drinks. "I don't know if we have this drink in China."

"So, what do you think about America?"

"Everyone has been so kind and helpful. You have made me feel very welcome."

"And New York?"

"I'm comfortable in this city. I see many nationalities, many Asians like me. I listened to conversations when we walked to the theater. I heard people speaking Mandarin and Cantonese."

"I had the opposite experience on my first trip to Beijing. One afternoon I went to Tiananmen Square. I think I was the only Caucasian there. I felt very isolated because I heard no English. I couldn't communicate with anyone."

"Were you afraid?"

"No. The faces were kind. The people I passed smiled at me."

"Did you like my country?"

"Very much. One day I'll go back for an extended stay. There is so much I want to see."

David signaled for the waiter to bring the bill. "Should we go inside now?"

Ping nodded. As they walked into the restaurant, she thought how fortunate she was to have met Mr. Bennington. He was so kind and thoughtful. Unlike Alexis, he appreciated her country. He could see beyond chicken feet.

"We'd like a table where it's quiet," David said, discreetly slipping the maître d' some money. He led the couple through a series of banquet rooms, each more elegant than the last. Finally, David and Ping were ushered into a glass pavilion opening onto a garden, lit by Waterford crystal chandeliers. In the center of each linen-covered table was a purple and blue flower arrangement. The maître d' sat them at a table overlooking the garden.

Since Ping was unfamiliar with most of the items on the menu, David suggested he order for the two of them. They started the meal with oysters on the half shell, accompanied by a French Vouvray. David watched Ping delicately detach the oyster from its shell. As she raised the fork to her lips, he noticed her necklace. "Is that Mandarin on your necklace?"

Ping nodded, unable to speak as she chewed. "It says 'mother and daughter,'" she finally said.

"Was it a gift from your mother?"

Normally Ping would not discuss subjects close to her heart with someone she barely knew. Perhaps it was the intimate setting. Perhaps it was the wine, but she answered David's question. "No, from my father. He had bought it for my mother, but she died giving birth to me."

"I'm sorry," David said. "I didn't know."

Eyes lowered, Ping focused on another oyster. As he ate, David glanced at Ping, seemingly saddened by her revelation.

For the entrée, David selected filet mignon. After the waiter had placed their steaks in front of them, he uncorked a bottle of Cabernet Sauvignon. David sampled the wine and nodded his approval. "So, your father raised you?" he asked.

"Along with my Auntie Yi Ma, my mother's older sister. She has been with me since I was born."

"Are you close with your father?"

Ping tilted her head and gave David a curious smile. This was a strange question. She hesitated before responding. "We are very close. Moving from Chongqing, where I was raised, to Beijing was difficult. I miss Baba—my father—and Auntie Yi Ma."

"Then why did you move?"

"Jianbo wanted to."

"Do you always listen to your brother?"

Panic flashed in Ping's eyes. She reached for her wineglass. By the time she placed the goblet on the table, her composure had returned. "It was time to leave Chongqing."

"You're fortunate to have a father that you care for so deeply. I wish I had the same feelings toward mine."

Ping stared at David, wondering why he was telling her something so personal. Apparently interpreting her gaze as an indication of interest, he continued. "My parents divorced when I was in high school. Right after the divorce my father married a woman only slightly older than me."

"So this woman is your...your..."

"Stepmother."

"Yes. Stepmother. Do you like her?"

David's lips tightened; his eyes narrowed. "The short answer is no, but it's not really her fault—although she probably only married my father for his money. I'm really angry with him, and I think it just spills over."

"You're angry because of the divorce?"

David played with the dessert fork on the table before answering. "The divorce was painful, but there were other things he did."

Ping's eyes, dark, luminous, and compassionate, invited him to continue. "My father wanted me to go into business and work in his office. But I didn't want to. I graduated college with a major in anthropology and applied to Michigan University's graduate program—one of the best in the country. When I received the acceptance letter, I went to share the good news with my father."

David paused and swilled the red wine in his goblet. The reflected light from the chandeliers added sparkle to the liquid. "I should never have gone to see him."

"Why?"

"He refused to read the acceptance letter, dismissing archaeology as a hobby. In addition, he compared me to my friend Roger— the fellow you met last night. At the time he was going to Yale Law School. I'll never forget my father's words." He paused as if still pained by the memory. "He said, talking about Roger, 'Now there's a son a father can be proud of.'"

"What an unkind thing to say," Ping remarked.

She reached out as if to touch David's hand but pulled back. They sat in silence; their eyes communicating what their lips could not say.

For dessert they shared a chocolate soufflé. Her face flushed from the wine, Ping confessed to David her desire to complete her English studies at the university. For his part, David revealed that he had entered Harvard's MBA program instead of going to Michigan. "I guess, deep down, I needed my father's approval."

"In my country we are taught to respect our father's wishes," Ping said.

"Perhaps that's wise."

CHAPTER THIRTY

Outside Tavern on the Green, just as David was about to hand his ticket to the valet, a hansom cab pulled up to the door, depositing its passengers.

"Do you want to take a ride?" David asked, pointing to the horse-drawn carriage.

Ping nodded, the afterglow of the drinks removing any reservations she might have had.

The driver helped Ping into the carriage and handed the couple a light blanket to protect them from the chill of the night air. The two rode in an easy silence, enjoying their proximity to each other. The noises from the street provided a background to the steady refrain of the horse's hooves and the taffeta sounds of the breeze dancing through the branches of the tulip trees.

David's hand found Ping's beneath the blanket. Surprised, she did not pull away. The warmth of his touch radiated up her arm and throughout her body. Her heart beat wildly. What was happening? She was Jianbo's wife. How could she feel this weak and helpless at David's touch?

Fearful that if she looked at him, her face would disclose too much, she turned her head away, watching as the moon played hide and seek among the trees. Somewhere a police siren sounded, somewhere a dog howled, but inside the carriage it was secure and warm.

All too soon, the hansom cab pulled back up to the restaurant. The driver reined in the horse. A series of syncopated clops from the horse's hooves brought the cab to a halt. David pushed aside the blanket and climbed out of the carriage. He held out his hands to help Ping down. His arms around her waist, he slowly lowered her to the ground.

They stood inches apart by the side of the carriage. David reached down and lifted her face to his. Ping felt weak; her head spun as he pressed his lips against hers. For a fleeting moment, she resisted and started to pull away. But in the end she remained in his arms, accepting his embrace with an eagerness that matched his own.

The whinny of the horse and the voices of a group coming out of the restaurant reminded them they were not alone. Slowly, reluctantly they pulled apart. David put his hands on Ping's shoulders. "I guess we'd better get going," he said softly.

As in the carriage, the two were silent during the drive back to David's mother's house. Only this time the silence was uncomfortable. David was concerned by his precipitous action. Had he taken advantage of Ping's slightly inebriated state? Did she think less of him for having kissed her? After all, he was engaged to be married. But with his arms around her, he felt powerless. His attraction to Ping was strong—stronger than it was toward any woman, including Alexis.

David broke the silence. "I'm sorry for what happened. I don't know what came over me. Perhaps I had too much to drink."

"Perhaps we both did," Ping said.

He gave a sideways glance to her face. Did he misinterpret her expression, the tone of her voice? There was no hint of anger—her eyes sparkled; her words flowed sweetly. Relieved, he allowed himself once again to take pleasure in her nearness.

As the car pulled into the circular drive at his mother's home, David was surprised to see the house ablaze in light. It was close to eleven o'clock. His mother liked to retire early. But before he even stopped the car, she appeared at the front door.

"What's the matter?" David asked.

When Ping walked into the foyer, Mrs. Bennington drew her into her arms. "I'm so sorry. You received a call from China. Your father passed away."

Ping's eyes widened in disbelief. Her body shook. Cascading tears accompanied deep sobs of despair.

"I must go back to China immediately. Jianbo needs me," Ping finally said when she was able to speak.

Mrs. Bennington led her into the living room and turned to her son, who trailed behind. "I'll get Ping a glass of water. Please call the airline and get her on the next flight home."

David left the room, his heart as heavy as Ping's but for a very different reason.

CHAPTER THIRTY-ONE

November 2004

After his father's funeral and their return to Beijing, Ping and Jianbo tried to settle back into their familiar routine, but some things had changed. Jianbo was preoccupied with settling his father's affairs and making arrangements for his mother. The changes were subtler for Ping: a loss of concentration, a far-off look as she worked with the guests at the hotel, guilt and remorse as she lay next to Jianbo in their bed at night.

She thought often of David. When she was not busy at work, she replayed the carriage ride and kiss in her mind like a streaming video. Although the memory brought her pleasure, it also filled her with shame. She was married; she should not be thinking about another man.

Preoccupied with funeral arrangements, Jianbo did not question Ping much about the trip. He only asked if she had discussed the restaurant with Mr. Bennington. He was not happy when she told him she hadn't but accepted her excuse that there had been no time during the interrupted visit to do so.

However, as soon as he settled his father's affairs, he wanted to know all about the trip. Ping told Jianbo about the flight over, the helpful elderly American in the seat next to her, the small TV screen that each person in her section of the plane had available to them. She described in detail Mrs. Bennington's home, the number of rooms, the swimming pool, the gardens, and the tennis court. She reported on her day in Manhattan with David and Alexis, the sights she saw, the wonderful play she enjoyed, the food she ate.

"America must be very different from here," Jianbo said to Ping as they sat on the couch drinking tea.

"Less than I would have thought. Although I have never seen a home as large and as elegant as Mrs. Bennington's, there were smaller dwellings like here. There were no wide avenues in New York City like we have in Beijing, and I saw only two people riding bicycles. There were mainly buses and yellow taxicabs on the streets."

"Did you see any Chinese?"

"Not at Mrs. Bennington's country club, where we ate my first night. But I saw many on the streets of New York. And Alexis told me there was a whole section of the city with mainly Chinese. It's called Chinatown. If I hadn't come back early, she would have taken me there."

"How about Chinese restaurants, did you see any?"

"There were many. In one section we went through, there was one on almost every street corner."

Jianbo's look darkened. Ping took their empty cups to the kitchen to pour more tea.

"Were they nice to you?" Jianbo asked when Ping returned.

"They tried to be, but I felt very uncomfortable when I first arrived." Ping paused to sip her tea. "I got the feeling that they were afraid I'd embarrass them."

"What do you mean?"

"Well, Americans wear something different every day. Evidently, when they travel they take many suitcases. They all asked about my luggage. They didn't understand how I could fit everything into my backpack. I guess they didn't like my clothes. The first place they took me was to a store to buy an outfit."

"Let me see it."

"I left it there."

Fortunately, Jianbo didn't ask her why. Although Mrs. Bennington told her to take her new clothes, she left them in the guest-room closet. They would only remind her of her trip to the United States, a trip on which she had been disloyal to her husband.

At night Ping tossed and turned, her heart filled with remorse. How could she and David have embraced? He was engaged; she was married. Pangs of regret accompanied her everywhere.

Three weeks after her return she lay on her side next to Jianbo exhausted but unable to fall asleep. The light from the full moon seeped in through the single window in the room, enabling Ping to make out her husband's features as he slept. She studied his face, the thick black hair falling on his forehead, the minute lifting of his chest in response to the steady intake of air, the low sonorous emissions. Ping placed her arm across her husband's upturned body. The movement caused Jianbo to open his eyes.

"What's the matter?" he asked.

"I need to tell you something."

"What is it?" Jianbo turned to face her.

"Something happened in New York," Ping began.

And with that introduction, she confessed to her husband the carriage ride with David Bennington that culminated in an embrace. Jianbo said nothing.

"Please say something. I'm so ashamed."

"Why didn't you pull away from him?"

"I don't know. We had so much wine with dinner, I wasn't thinking straight."

"What happened after the kiss?"

"Nothing. We barely spoke to each other on the car ride home. We both realized what we had done was wrong. I'm sure he was thinking about Alexis."

"Interesting," Jianbo said. "The American probably thought you were innocent, that you did nothing wrong since he didn't know you were married. Or had you told him?"

"No, I never did."

"Why not?"

"Because," Ping said, irritation in her voice, "you told me not to. He still thinks we're brother and sister."

"So he does."

For several days, Jianbo said little. Ping's guilt was replaced by feelings of shame. But she was glad she had confessed. There should be no secrets between a wife and her husband. And besides, Jianbo was not without some culpability. If he had not insisted that they present themselves to David and Alexis as siblings, the incident would never have occurred.

One evening a few days later during their nightly tea ritual, Jianbo told Ping he forgave her indiscretion. Grateful, Ping kissed him. How fortunate she was to have such an understanding husband.

CHAPTER THIRTY-TWO

David stood at the counter waiting for two fruit and yogurt shakes, strands of ash blond hair plastered against his wet forehead. After paying, he carried the drinks to a table where Roger sat. The men had identical diamond-shaped areas of sweat on the backs of their white tennis shirts. Several women in revealing spandex outfits strutted by the health bar and waved to them. Bathed in the bright fluorescent lighting of the sports club, members could forget the cold, bleak New York day visible only through the skylight overhead.

"Thanks," Roger said, gulping down the drink. He set the half-empty plastic cup on a small table. "I'd better enjoy this. It's not often I win and you have to buy the drinks."

Wiping his brow with a well-used towel, David forced a smile. "I couldn't focus on the game."

"What's the matter?"

"I can't marry Alexis."

Roger's mouth dropped open. "Are you serious?"

"I'm going to tell her tonight."

"She'll go ballistic."

"I know."

Elbows on the table, David ran his fingers through his hair. He lifted his head to return the greeting of a perky brunette hustling by.

"What happened? Did you have a fight?"

"No. Nothing like that." David took a sip of his drink before continuing. "My boss called me this morning. I'm no longer in the running to head up the Shanghai office."

"What happened?"

"One of the partners was over in Beijing checking on the joint venture I had set up. Apparently our Chinese colleagues found Alexis's behavior offensive and would prefer that I'm no longer involved."

"Is that enough of a reason to call off the wedding? Why don't you sit on it a few days? You just got the news. Maybe you'll see things differently tomorrow."

"I doubt it. This assignment was important if I was to make partner early."

"Why the rush?"

"It's a bad reason, I know, but I just wanted to see my father's face when I told him I made partner. I'd be at least ten years young-er than he was when he made it at his firm."

"So Alexis becomes the victim of this modern-day Greek trag-edy, this competition between father and son?"

"No, it's more than that. I can't spend the rest of my life with someone so self-centered and bigoted."

"Don't tell me this is the first time you realized this?"

"It's bothered me all along. But it really hit home that evening when we were at the club—that evening when Alexis insulted Ping. I find myself disliking her more and more every time we're together."

"If that's how you feel before the wedding, you'd better break it off. It doesn't get any easier after you're married."

"I just keep wishing Alexis was more like Ping."

"I'm sure if you were engaged to Ping you would be picked to head up the Shanghai office. Once your boss took a look at her there'd be no question about the promotion."

David leaned back in his chair deep in thought.

"Wait a minute," Roger said. "I'm not suggesting you get engaged to Ping. I was just making a joke."

"I know. But you just gave me some food for thought." David looked at his watch. "We'd better go. I don't want to be late getting back to the office."

The two men picked up their tennis bags and rackets. Roger took the empty glasses and threw them in the trash. "Just tell me when and where you're going to tell Alexis tonight," he said as they walked toward the locker room. "I want to be as far away as possible from the explosion."

CHAPTER THIRTY-THREE

Beijing, December 2004

It had been almost a month since Ping's trip to the United States. The idyllic days of autumn were gone; the cold winds from Siberia had invaded the city. On mornings when winter jackets offered little relief from subfreezing temperatures, Ping and Jianbo would abandon the bicycle for the relative warmth of the bus.

In spite of the bitter cold, Ping was happy. She and Jianbo had managed to spend a few days in Chongqing. Although the majority of the time was spent with her mother-in-law, she was able to slip away to see Auntie Yi Ma and her father. America and David Bennington seemed far away, her visit there a fading memory.

The only interruption in her tranquil routine was the occasional visit from Li Feng. After seeing his friend, Jianbo would become dejected and irritable. When Ping questioned him after Feng's last visit, he confessed to being jealous. Thanks to his father-in-law, Feng led a prosperous life. The fact he was married did not prevent him from enjoying the company of other women on his many out-of-town business trips.

"Is that what you would like to do?" Ping asked Jianbo.

"No, I'm very happy with my wife. I don't need anyone else. But I always did better than Feng, and now he has moved ahead of me."

"You tell me you're happy," Ping said.

"That's true most of the time. But what do I have to show for my three years of hard work? We live in a rented one-room apartment where we must wear our coats in the winter to stay warm. And I'm concerned we don't have enough money to take care of my mother, too."

"If we put some money aside every month, maybe we'll be able to buy a small apartment."

"No," Jianbo said. "Even with both of us working, that won't happen. Beijing is too expensive. The only chance we have to live like Feng is to go to America. There, everyone has a house and a car."

Ping didn't know if this was true, but based on the number of cars she saw on the road during her trip to the United States, she thought Jianbo might be right. She did know that she didn't need a house and a car to be happy.

⤝⬩⬩⤞

Late one afternoon at the business center, Ping's boss told her that Jianbo was at the back door and wanted to speak to her.

"Guess who's here?" Jianbo asked Ping.

"I don't know. Li Feng?"

"No, Mr. Bennington."

Ping felt her knees go weak and her heart beat wildly. "What does he want?"

"He has something important he wants to talk to me about. I'm to meet him after work."

"I don't want to see him."

"He didn't ask for you. He's coming with an interpreter."

"Please don't go," Ping pleaded, convinced nothing good could come of this meeting. "I have a bad feeling about this."

"Don't worry, nothing will happen. Trust me." Jianbo handed her some money. "Here's fare for the bus. I'll bike home after my meeting with the American."

CHAPTER THIRTY-FOUR

It was almost one o'clock in the morning when Jianbo arrived home. Ping had fallen asleep on the couch reading *Sense and Sensibility*, an English book her Auntie Yi Ma had sent her,. She awoke when she heard the door open. Jianbo entered the house, red-faced from peddling home in the wintry night. He removed his gloves and wool cap, unzipped his jacket, and sat next to Ping.

"Your hands are so cold." Ping massaged Jianbo's frozen fingers.

"Why don't you make us some tea? We need to talk," he said.

Ping put a kettle of water on the hot plate. While it heated, she opened a bag of tea leaves and placed some in a pot. Waiting for the tea to steep, she tried to guess what the American talked about with Jianbo. Did he decide to invite them again to the United States? Did they discuss Jianbo's restaurant? Or did David feel a need, like she had had, to confess their inappropriate actions that night in Central Park?

By the time Ping placed the cups of tea on the coffee table, Jianbo had settled in on the couch. "What did the American want?" Ping asked.

"He wants to marry you."

Ping dropped to the couch as if she had been shot. "That's not possible. I'm married."

The grim twist of Jianbo's mouth and his serious expression indicated he thought otherwise. Ping's pulse raced as she took a sip of tea. The teacup rattled precariously as she placed it on the table.

"Anyway, David can't. He's engaged."

"He's broken off his engagement."

Ping could not stop her hands from shaking. "You told him we were married, didn't you?"

Jianbo did not answer.

Ping's chin trembled. "You did tell him we were married, didn't you?"

Jianbo looked away.

"Please, please tell me you told him we were married."

"I didn't."

Ping closed her eyes. A feeling of nausea crept through her body. When she reopened them she asked, "Why did he ask you? Why not me?"

"He said he would have asked our father, but since he was deceased, he thought it appropriate to ask me. He didn't want me to think he was just swooping down and whisking you away."

"Let me tell you what's not appropriate," Ping said, eyes narrowed, voice rising. "Asking me, your wife, to wed another. You must tell him we are married."

"Now isn't a good time."

"If you won't tell him, I will. This deception has gone on far too long."

"Don't," Jianbo said, grabbing Ping's wrist. "I want to tell you my plan. Do not speak until I have finished."

As Ping listened in disbelief, Jianbo explained that this was a once-in-a-lifetime opportunity, the opportunity that would allow them to escape this downtrodden life and live like wealthy Americans.

"The plan is very simple. We will divorce, and you will marry the American." Jianbo put two fingers on his wife's lips to stop her from interrupting him.

"Don't say anything until I'm finished."

Resigned, Ping sat back.

"You marry David Bennington and become an American citizen. Then you divorce him and remarry me. The spouse of an American automatically becomes a citizen, too."

Ping sat in shocked silence, her stomach in turmoil.

"How could David want to marry me? He doesn't even know me."

"He told me he was attracted to you the first time he saw you in the business center. Plus, if he marries you, he's sure his company will send him to Shanghai to open an office there. I'm trying to remember exactly what he said. Oh yes, you'll be an asset, a big help in his career."

"But he doesn't even know me," Ping repeated as if in a trance.

"He thinks he does. He said what he likes most about you is your honesty and your innocence."

"My honesty?" Ping shook her head. "I've deceived him from the first moment we met."

"He doesn't know that. And I didn't tell him otherwise. Plus—and this is another benefit of the plan—I told him how we had to support our relatives and how little money we had. He said if you married him, he would give me $15,000."

"What? Am I a piece of merchandise to be bought and sold?"

Pushing Jianbo aside, hands clasped over her mouth, Ping rushed to the kitchen sink and vomited. Holding on to the side of the sink as she heaved, her body rid itself of everything inside her. Finally, pale and sweating, she slid to the floor, defeated.

"Don't touch me," Ping said to Jianbo as he approached her. "Get away from me. Just leave me alone." Turning abruptly, Jianbo zipped up his jacket, took his scarf and gloves, and left. She heard the whir of the bike tires on the courtyard stones as he rode off. Such was her anger and despair, she didn't care that he was gone or even where he was going. All she knew was she would never forgive him for what he had asked her to do.

CHAPTER THIRTY-FIVE

When Ping awoke the next morning, she thought she had dreamed the nightmarish events of the prior evening. But Jianbo's side of the bed was empty, and the stench of vomit from the kitchen permeated the apartment. It was almost noon; she was late for work. But even if she had wanted to go to the China Palace, it would have been impossible. She had no money for the bus.

Ping cleaned up and discarded the mess in the kitchen sink. Ravenous, she looked around for something to eat. There was nothing. Since she and Jianbo usually ate their meals at the hotel, the only thing she found was tea. Weighed down by sadness and unable to satisfy her hunger, Ping crawled back under the covers.

Toward dusk she was awakened by a pounding on the door. "Damn it, Ping, the door's locked. Let me in."

Slipping into her shoes, she padded over to the door. Once the door was open, Jianbo pushed himself through. Face livid, he glared at Ping. "Why the hell did you lock the door? This is my house. How dare you keep me out."

Ping stepped back, lips trembling, keeping the open door between them. Jianbo slammed the bag he was carrying on the kitchen counter. "I told everyone you were sick. The cook made this for you. Not that you deserve it."

Treading softly, Ping made her way into the kitchen and pulled out a container of broth with noodles from the bag. It was cold. She turned on the hot plate to heat it up.

Jianbo stomped toward the door. "I'm going to pee. When I get back, we will talk."

Shivering, Ping pulled a blanket from the bed and wrapped it around her. Her long hair was matted and tangled. Her lips were dry; her mouth tasted foul. When the soup was hot, Ping poured it into a bowl and shuffled over to the couch. She quickly consumed the broth and noodles. But the food did little to bring back her energy.

Slamming the door behind him, Jianbo strode back into the apartment. Ping cringed as he approached. She placed the empty bowl on the end table and folded the blanket around her. Jianbo sat on the couch, one arm across the top of the couch, the other on the armrest. He tapped his foot impatiently.

"The American is getting a fiancée visa for you."

"Wha—what do you mean?"

"You are going to the United States to marry him."

"No," Ping cried out, vehemently shaking her head from side to side.

Jianbo pressed his lips together; his face tightened. "You have no say in this. We're divorcing, and you're marrying the American as we planned."

Ping pulled her arms from beneath the blanket and lunged toward Jianbo striking him on the chest with her fists. "No. I won't do it. You can't make me."

Jianbo grabbed her wrists. His nails cut into her skin. Ping's eyes opened wide in terror as he lifted his hand. With a guttural roar, he brought his palm down hard against her face. Ping tried to protect herself. But he struck her again and again. Finally when she was no longer able to resist, when she lay down and curled up her knees into her chest, when all she could do was whimper, he stopped.

She felt him get up from the couch and heard him clomp into the kitchen and open the refrigerator. He returned. Ping covered her head with her arms. "Here, take this. Put it against your face."

Slowly she looked up. In his hand he held a towel filled with ice cubes. She took it and placed it on her cheek. The coldness on her face made her flinch. Her skin felt raw. Tears filled her eyes.

The wind whipped against the window, rattling the panes of glass. The antiquated heating system was no match against the subzero weather. "It's freezing in here," Jianbo said. "I'll make some tea."

In the kitchen, he put water in a pot and stood waiting for it to boil, his back toward Ping. Covered by the blanket, she trembled, less from the cold than from fear. Returning from the kitchen, Jianbo placed a cup of tea on the side table nearest her. She grasped the porcelain cup in both hands allowing the heat to warm them before putting the beverage to her lips.

"Sharing you with another man is not what I want," Jianbo said, sitting down next to Ping. "But I see no other way to move beyond where we are now. The good jobs at the restaurant go to the friends and relatives of the head chef. If we don't do something, five years from now I'll still be asking guests how they want their eggs."

He paused, apparently waiting for Ping to respond. She said nothing.

"This will be a sacrifice for both of us. Do you think I want another man touching you, sleeping with you?"

Ping looked away.

"The arrangement will only be for a short time, just until you become an American citizen. Then you will send for me, and we'll be back together again. We probably don't even need to divorce."

Ping's eyes widened, her indignation stronger than her fear. "I cannot be married to two men at the same time. I would sooner be dead."

Hands clasped between his knees, head bowed, Jianbo appeared contrite. "I'm sorry I hit you, but," he said, turning toward Ping, "you just wouldn't listen to reason." He shifted uncomfortably as he stared at her red and swollen face. "We'll divorce before your marriage to the American if that's what you want."

"That's what I want."

"You know, if we live in America, we can have as many children as we want. We'll live in a well-heated house. We won't have to sit wrapped in blankets to keep warm."

"There'll be a sacrifice initially," he continued. "We'll be apart for a few months, but afterward we'll live well for the rest of our lives. We'll be able to give our children things we never had. We'll also be able to give many gifts to your Baba and Auntie Yi Ma."

Ping muttered under her breath. "We will bring shame on our families."

"No." Jianbo shook his head. "I've figured it all out. We'll tell our families that you've been sent to America by the China Palace to make your English even better. They will be proud that you were selected for this honor."

"And my boss?"

"We will tell him that you must go to Chongqing to take care of your father. We'll say he's ill."

Ping shut her eyes. What could she do? She felt like a trapped animal. If she obeyed her husband, she would be dishonored and vilified, forced to share another man's bed. But if she disobeyed him? She touched her swollen face.

"How long will it take for me to become an American citizen?"

"I don't know exactly, but I've been told you're a citizen the day of your wedding."

"So I could divorce Mr. Bennington the day after the ceremony?"

"I think so," Jianbo said, with a look that told Ping he had no idea if this were true.

"And no one need ever know what we did?"

"Not unless you tell them."

Ping fingered the *mother-daughter* necklace she wore. She prayed for the strength to defy her husband. But instead of power, Ping felt limp; instead of vigor, she trembled beneath her blanket; instead of an inner force, she felt empty and hollow.

"Tell Mr. Bennington I will marry him."

PART TWO

"A clay figure fears rain, a lie fears truth."

—Chinese proverb

CHAPTER THIRTY-SIX

Chongqing, January 2005

Jianbo stared at the pale yellow liquid, focusing on the gaseous bubbles colliding their way to the surface of the glass. Across the table, Feng exhaled ringlets of smoke. They sat huddled in a booth in the back of a café as far from the entrance as possible, but there was little they could do to protect themselves against the penetrating chill. Most of the patrons sat wrapped in winter coats and jackets; some did not even remove their gloves.

Feng raised his glass of beer. "Here's to your divorce."

"How quickly things change," Jianbo said, making no move to lift his glass. "It was not that long ago that we were toasting my wedding."

"Well, if things go according to plan, the next time I toast you, it will again be for your wedding."

"Who knows when that will be," Jianbo replied, his mouth downturned, his eyes wistful.

"Then let's toast your trip to the United States. That's closer. That's next week."

"I wish I weren't going."

"I thought this was your dream. What happened?"

Jianbo shook his head, wrapped his scarf more tightly around his neck, and leaned back against the wooden booth.

"Anything else?" the waiter asked, removing the two empty beer bottles.

"Two more beers," Feng replied.

Jianbo waited until the waiter had left before he answered Feng's question. "I have to give Ping away."

"Give Ping away? What does that mean?"

"In American weddings, someone has to give the bride away. Usually it's the father that hands the bride over to the new husband."

"Tell Ping to have her father do it."

"That's what I did. She reminded me he was dead."

"Zhao Jiang died?" Feng asked.

"Of course not. But when Ping and I were pretending to be brother and sister and my father died, the Benningtons naturally assumed it was her father as well. Now they think she's an orphan—no mother, no father, just her brother."

The waiter returned and placed two bottles of beer on the table. Jianbo poured some into his glass and took a sip. "But even if the Benningtons didn't think Ping's father was dead, it wouldn't work. Zhao Jiang knows nothing of what we're doing. Her family thinks we're still married and that the China Palace sent her to the United States for special English training."

"Are you sure you and Ping want to go through with this?"

"I'm not so sure anymore; I really miss her."

"There's still time if you want to change your mind. The ceremony isn't until next week."

"We've come this far. The divorce is official. The wedding is set. It's too late to back out. I just have to keep my mind on the payoff—fifteen thousand dollars and American citizenship. That will make it bearable."

The door to the café opened as a couple entered, bringing with them gusts of bone-chilling wind and rain. It was only four thirty in the afternoon, but darkness had descended.

"Is the weather nice in New York this time of year?" Feng asked.

"According to Ping, it's pretty much the same as here."

"I'm surprised the American didn't wait until the spring or summer. Who wants to get married in weather like this?"

"He didn't want to wait. Besides, from the time Ping arrives, they have ninety days to get married or else she has to apply for a fiancée visa all over again."

"When does Ping become a US citizen?"

"As soon as she marries the American."

"So she can divorce him in February and remarry you in March?"

"Something like that. I'll have Ping check."

"What?" Feng stared at Jianbo in disbelief. "Don't tell me you didn't find this out before you divorced?"

"Everyone I talked to told me if you marry an American, you automatically become a US citizen."

"But what if everyone is wrong?"

"If they are and it'll take too long, Ping will come home immediately."

"What if she doesn't want to?"

Jianbo's eyes narrowed. "What do you mean?"

"The American is wealthy. She might not want to give up a rich life in the United States."

"She will do what I say." Jianbo picked up his glass and slammed it down with such force that it cracked. Beer seeped across the table and dribbled to the floor. The waiter rushed over with a cloth. Jianbo jumped up but not before the liquid had dripped onto his clothes and slithered down his jeans. He stood, his body tense, fists clenched by his side. "She will do what I say."

CHAPTER THIRTY-SEVEN

David handed his keys to the valet and hustled to the other side of the car, where Ping waited. As they walked toward the entrance of the country club, gusts of wind whipped freshly fallen snowflakes into small eddies of white. Close to the building, isolated branches of evergreen emerged from beneath a white cover to peer through steamy windowpanes.

In the foyer, David removed his and Ping's wraps and handed them to the coat-check girl. The festive atmosphere inside the club contrasted with the cold, white, ethereal landscape outside. Waiters holding large trays sashayed among the tables. The clang of metal as warmers were removed and stacked accompanied the ring of silverware against china.

They followed the maître d' to where Marjorie and Roger sat waiting. Burning logs in a large stone fireplace crackled behind their table. Occasionally, an ember shone briefly only to extinguish itself against the mesh screen.

Before taking a seat, David circled the table. He patted Roger's shoulder and then stooped to kiss Marjorie on the check. Rising,

Roger gave Ping a hug; Marjorie forced a smile. "Sorry we're late," David said. "My mother had a plumbing emergency."

"It's a good thing you weren't any later, or Marjorie and I would have been three sheets to the wind."

Ping looked curiously at Roger, who grinned. "You don't understand the expression, do you?"

She shook her head.

"'Three sheets to the wind' means you've had too much alcohol to drink."

"I see," Ping said, noting the empty martini glasses.

"What kind of plumbing problem did your mother have?" Roger asked.

"Pretty serious. Something's leaking in her bathroom. When I arrived to pick up Ping, water was seeping through the ceiling onto the first floor. A plumber did some work on the pipes a few weeks ago. My mother couldn't get hold of him, so I called in Paul Bronski, the guy who's doing the renovations at my place."

"Did he fix the problem?" Roger asked.

"We left before he finished, but he did manage to stop the leak."

"Sorry to interrupt this fascinating conversation," Marjorie said, "but I'm starved. Plus I've had a bit too much to drink. I need to eat something, or who knows what I'll do."

"By all means, let's order," David replied, opening his menu, a twinkle in his eye. "Can't have Marjorie dancing on the table."

Ping perused the menu but couldn't help noticing Marjorie staring at her, eyes cold, mouth pinched. Her stomach churned. She would have given anything to be back in Mrs. Bennington's kitchen. *Better a dinner of herbs than a stalled ox where hate is.*

After the waiter took their orders and returned with salads and wine, Roger tapped his knife against his glass and raised his goblet in a toast. "Here's to your and Ping's wedding next week."

David and Ping lifted their glasses of wine in response. But instead of joining the others in a toast, Marjorie searched through her purse for a tissue and blew her nose. "Excuse me. I think I have a cold coming on."

Roger glared at his wife, then took a sip from his glass. Finished with her purse, Marjorie hung it on the back of her chair, seemingly oblivious to the uncomfortable silence at the table. "Is there anyone coming from China besides your brother?" she asked Ping.

"No."

"No aunts, uncles, cousins?"

"Come on, Marjorie, give Ping a break, and let her at least finish her salad before putting her through the third degree," Roger said.

Marjorie glowered at her husband.

"That's all right," Ping replied. "I don't mind the questions. It's difficult for my family to come to the United States. It is very expensive, although David said he would pay for anyone I wished to invite." She smiled at him. "But my relatives don't speak English. It would be very awkward for them."

Apparently satisfied, Marjorie continued eating her salad. After a few more bites, she put down her fork and turned to David. "I have to tell you, David, I think what you did to Alexis was despicable."

"Marj—"

"No, let me finish, Roger. You know me; I have to say what's on my mind. After all, I was the one who introduced Alexis to David."

"How is Alexis?" David asked.

"Devastated. How did you think she'd be?"

"She seemed OK when we talked about calling off the wedding."

Marjorie shook her head. "She's a class act. She wasn't going to fall apart in front of you."

"I told her to keep the engagement ring, the pearls, and the other gifts I'd given her."

"How generous of you, Mr. Bennington," Marjorie said. Ping shifted uncomfortably in her seat.

"I'm cutting you off." Roger reached for Marjorie's wineglass. She quickly moved it away from him.

David shook his head. "Look, Marjorie, I would give anything to go back in time and not have proposed to Alexis." He sat back as the waiter removed his salad plate. "In any case, I'm covering all the costs her family incurred in planning the wedding."

"Why do men always feel if no one loses money, everything's OK?"

"What would you want David to do, Marjorie? Marry someone he doesn't love?" Roger asked.

"You drop Alexis six months before your wedding date. Then you marry Ping less than two months after you break the engagement. You could have waited a reasonable period."

A tear slipped out of the corner of Ping's eye and slid down her cheek. The teardrop did what Roger had been unable to do—silence Marjorie. He turned to Ping. "Please forgive my wife. She and alcohol don't mix well together."

Marjorie stared angrily at her husband and sat back, arms folded across her chest. No one spoke as the waiter removed the salad plates and served the dinner. Ping looked at David. Why didn't he defend himself against Marjorie's accusations?

"I'm very sorry that Alexis is hurt," David said as if reading Ping's thoughts. He reached over and took her hand. "But I love Ping. I want to spend the rest of my life with her."

David's words almost atoned for Marjorie's behavior. Ping beamed, grateful for his declaration. Yet, she wondered how many of his friends and family members felt like Marjorie.

"Where are you going on your honeymoon?" Roger asked.

"Hawaii," David answered.

"Isn't that where you and Alex—?" Marjorie began.

"Maui, not the big island," David said before she could finish.

"Will you live in your Tribeca loft when you return?"

"I've hired a decorator to redo the place," David replied. "It looks too much like a bachelor's pad now."

Marjorie turned to Ping. "Have you seen it yet?"

"Yes."

"Is it larger than what you had in Beijing?"

"Oh, yes. The apartment I had in China was very small."

"You're lucky to be marrying David. Not only is he good-looking, but he can afford to buy you very nice things," Marjorie said.

Roger kicked his wife under the table. Seemingly unfazed, Marjorie took a mouthful of sea bass. Ping put down her fork, no longer hungry.

—⟨⊢ ⊣⟩—

Later that evening, alone in what used to be David's room at Mrs. Bennington's, Ping sat at an ornate desk and wrote a letter to Jianbo on stationery she had found in the drawer.

Dear Jianbo, she began in Mandarin, *I cannot go through with this marriage. I am all alone here. There is no one I can talk to who will give me the strength and courage I need to continue this farce. David's friends do not like me. They seem suspicious of my intentions. Mrs. Bennington is very kind, but sometimes I catch her staring at me as if she, too, does not trust me. In spite of a good heating system and a comfortable bed, I cannot sleep at night. I have nightmares that I will be found out and thrown out of the house...*

A sharp blast of wintry wind shook the windowpanes. Ping paused, walked over to the window, and peered out. A full moon illuminated the fresh snow. In the dark unlit recesses of the yard, naked tree limbs fought to survive against the wind.

Sighing, she moved toward the bed with its inviting mattress and comforter. She stopped briefly at the desk, ripped up the unfinished letter, and discarded the pieces in a wastepaper basket. It was a futile effort. Even if she posted the letter early in the morning, Jianbo would not receive it before he left for the United States. She would wait until he arrived to tell him she could not go through with the wedding.

CHAPTER THIRTY-EIGHT

"Ping's not back from her fitting in the city," Katherine said to David as he joined her in the library.

"That's a problem. We need to leave soon if we're going to meet Dad on time."

He sat down in a rich chocolate leather chair opposite his mother. Feathered orange flames in the fireplace and a brightly colored area rug contrasted with the dark wood flooring and the mahogany furniture. The comfortable setting made the library a pleasant retreat on this wintry day.

"So how's the plumbing problem? Did my guy fix everything?"

"Yes," Mrs. Bennington replied. "But I'm very upset with my plumber. He refuses to compensate me for what I had to lay out because he didn't do the job right in the first place."

"Do you want me to get the lawyers involved?"

"Not yet. Let's wait and see what happens."

David stared at the red flames leaping in the fireplace and tapped his fingers on the arm of his chair. He turned toward the doorway as Greta entered the room. "I'm sorry to interrupt, but

Ulrich just called. The fitting is taking longer than expected. He and Miss Ping will be late."

"Please call him back," David said, glancing at his watch. "Ask Ulrich to take Ping to the Carlton Hotel on Madison and East 29th. We're meeting my father there for lunch at noon."

"That's going to be a problem. I need Ulrich to drive me to the club by eleven thirty," Mrs. Bennington said.

"Don't worry. I'll drop you off on my way into the city. Ulrich will be back in time to pick you up."

"I hate to take you out of your way, but I can't be late. My garden club is having its annual luncheon. We'll be selecting officers for the coming year."

"Will Alexis's mother be there?" David asked.

"Probably."

"I'm sorry if I've made things uncomfortable for you at the club."

"Well, except for a comment about Asian grandchildren, she's been remarkably civil."

"How do you feel about it?"

"About what?"

"Asian grandchildren?"

"I really don't care what they look like; I just want grandchildren."

David smiled at his mother. "I wish Dad was more like you. I'm worried about how he'll react when he meets Ping."

"You told him she was Chinese, didn't you?"

"No."

"For heaven's sake, why not?"

"I didn't want to deal with his reaction." David pursed his lips. He clasped his hands together. "But that might have been unfair to Ping. Hopefully, he'll behave at lunch."

CHAPTER THIRTY-NINE

"You're late," Mr. Bennington Sr. said as the maître d' ushered David to the table.

"Hello, Dad. Good to see you, too." He nodded to the well-endowed blonde sitting next to his father. "Hi, Christy. Sorry, but I was at Mom's, and the traffic into the city was brutal."

"Well, where is the bride-to-be? Or have you decided to ditch this young lady like you did Alexis?"

"No, she should be here soon," David replied, ignoring his father's remark.

"I'm anxious to meet my future daughter-in-law. You haven't told me anything at all about her."

"What do you want to know?"

"Is she from a respectable family?

"Yes."

"What does her father do?"

"He passed away a couple of months ago."

"Sorry to hear that. Was he a member of your mother's club?"

David shifted in his chair. He cleared his throat before speaking. "Her family wouldn't be able to get into the club."

His father's eyes widened. "She's not black, is she?"

"No, she's not."

"Thank God for that."

Mr. Bennington tapped his fingers on the table. Christy pulled out her compact to check her lipstick. David leaned back in his chair, arms crossed, wondering how his mother could have married such a bigot. His head ached. How would his father react to Ping?

Seated facing the entrance, Mr. Bennington Sr. stared in the direction of the revolving glass door. "Now, there's a beautiful young lady."

Christy and David turned to see an elegantly dressed woman removing a fur-lined black coat and handing it to the coat-check girl. She wore a stylish red and black wool suit with black leather high-heeled boots and a matching handbag.

"The lady in red happens to be my fiancée," David said as the maître d' showed Ping to the table. "Let me introduce you. Ping, this is my father and his wife, Christy."

"I'm pleased to meet you," Ping said extending her hand.

"It continues to amaze me that David can attract such beautiful women." Mr. Bennington Sr. took her hand in his and brought it to his lips.

Ping blushed and lowered her eyes. David sighed, relieved. Apparently beauty trumped ethnicity.

"Are you from Japan?" Christy asked after Ping sat down.

"No, China."

"Your father promised me we'd go on a cruise to the Orient," Christy said turning toward David. "But," she added pouting, "all he ever does is work."

Ignoring his wife, David's father turned to Ping. "How did you meet my son?"

"We met at the business center of the China Palace Hotel in Beijing. I was working there assisting guests."

"Ping helped me copy documents I needed for a meeting. I told you about it, Dad, remember? I was trying to get the management of that Chinese company to do a joint venture with my client."

"That was rather recent, wasn't it?"

"Last summer."

"Then you haven't known each other very long," Mr. Bennington Sr. said, his brow furrowed.

"Can't we continue this conversation after we order?" Christy asked. "I'm famished."

The waiter scraped the crumbs from the tablecloth in preparation for dessert and coffee. David and his father sat alone. Ping and Christy had just excused themselves to go to the ladies' room.

"Well, what do you think of Ping?"

"She's exquisite. Seems intelligent. Speaks English well."

"I hear a 'but' in there somewhere."

"You're right, David. But what do you really know about her? What's her family like?"

"Her mother died at birth, and, as I said before, her father passed away a few months ago. All she has left is an older brother."

"What's the family name?"

"Wang. It's rather common in China."

"How do you spell it?"

"W-a-n-g."

Mr. Bennington Sr. took a pen and small pad from his pocket and wrote down the name.

"Is she from Beijing?"

"No. Her family comes from Chongqing. She'd only been in the capital about two months when I met her."

"What's the name of the city again? How do you spell it?"

"Wait a minute. Why all the questions?"

"I'm going to do what *you* should have done before you brought that girl to the United States—a background check."

"If you do anything like that, I don't want you at the wedding."

"Are you afraid I'll find out something?"

"Not at all. But doing a background check is an insult. If she ever found out, she would think I don't trust her. And I do."

"Then you're a greater fool than I thought."

"What's the matter, Dad? Is my arm candy sweeter than yours?"

"Don't be ridiculous. I trust you had her sign a prenup?"

"No, I didn't."

"Look, the girls are coming back. Here's my attorney's card." Mr. Bennington pulled a business card from his wallet and gave it to David. "Please call him. He prepared my prenup with Christy." David took the card from his father and put it in his pocket.

When Ping and Christy returned, they glanced at the dessert menu and decided to forgo any sweets. Over coffee and tea, the four chatted about the approaching wedding. When they parted outside the restaurant, David took the card his father had given him from his pocket, ripped it up, and threw it in the trash.

CHAPTER FORTY

Ping put on her *mother-daughter* necklace. Today, she needed her mother's strength. Today, she would tell Jianbo she could not go through with the wedding.

Checking her image in the full-length mirror, she smoothed down the cashmere sweater Mrs. Bennington had bought her. Glancing at the clock on the nightstand, she grabbed her coat and ran down the stairs. Greta greeted her in the front hall and handed her a letter. "This came for you this morning."

"Thank you," Ping said as she made her way outside to where Ulrich waited to take her to the airport. He held the rear door open. Ping would have preferred sitting up front, but David frowned on this. "Ulrich is our chauffeur," he explained. "Please sit in the back and let him do his job."

Ensconced in the rear seat, Ping opened the envelope. Her heart was heavy as she unfolded the letter and recognized Auntie Yi Ma's carefully formed Mandarin characters.

Dear Ping,

Your father is so proud of you. He tells all his friends that a big hotel in Beijing has sent you to America to study English. We have not heard from you since you left. What is life like in the United States? Are the Americans friendly? Do you live with other students? We looked on a map and found Alpine. We are confused. It is in a place called New Jersey, not New York where you go to school. Public transportation must be good in America.

Jianbo came by last weekend when he visited his mother. He said you are happy in America. He told us that the hotel is sending him to see you for a few days. We are glad he is going. You must be lonely without him.

I am thankful you have this opportunity, but I hope you will come home soon. Baba and I miss you.

Please write and send pictures of America.

Auntie Yi Ma

Ping reread the letter several times before folding it and placing it in her purse. "What have I done?" she muttered to herself, her chin quivering. "How could I have let things go this far?"

"Is something the matter?" Ulrich asked, peering at her through the rearview mirror.

"No, everything's fine," Ping said, forcing a smile.

"I checked with the airline. Your brother's plane is on time."

Ping struggled to maintain her balance as the crowd pushed and shoved with each opening of the frosted sliding doors. A steady flow of international passengers emerged onto the chained-off passageway struggling with luggage of various shapes and sizes. Standing on tiptoe, Ping peered over the people in front of her for some glimpse of Jianbo. As a new group of arrivals came forward, she recognized his cocky swagger, his confident grin. Her stomach churned. Pasting a smile on her face, she called his name. Jianbo waved, quickened his pace, and circled around the noisy crowd to greet her.

"How was your trip?" she asked in Mandarin, taking his arm and guiding him to the terminal exit.

"Good."

As the two walked out to where Ulrich was waiting with the car, Jianbo studied Ping. "You look different," he said. "Those clothes, the way you're wearing your hair…"

"David's mother has been very kind. She makes sure I dress properly."

Ulrich helped Jianbo put his backpack into the trunk of the town car. Once settled, Ping listened as her former husband waxed lyrical on being in America.

After several minutes of feigning interest, she interrupted him. "I want to tell you something important," she said in Mandarin. "I cannot go through with this marriage. I want to go back to China."

Jianbo's mouth dropped open. "What?"

"I want to go back to China."

"Absolutely not."

"But what we're doing is wrong. David and his mother are good people. They don't deserve to be deceived."

Jianbo's eyes became hard; his lips tightened. Glancing at the rearview mirror, Ping could see Ulrich eyeing them.

"Ulrich is watching us," Ping said.

"So what. He can't understand what we're saying." Nonetheless, Jianbo forced a grin and spoke in a softer tone. "Why are you backing out now—after all we've gone through to get this far?"

"David believes our stories, but I don't think his friends do. Eventually something will happen—I'll forget and talk about my father, or one of David's business contacts in China might know our families—and he will learn the truth. And then what will happen? I am alone here. I have nowhere to go if he kicks me out of the house."

"You're being silly. If our plan is uncovered, you contact me. I'll find a way to get you home. If necessary, Feng will lend us the money for the airfare."

"I received a letter from Auntie Yi Ma today. She wanted to know how my English studies were coming along, and what I thought of America. We're not only lying to the Benningtons but to our families as well."

"I spoke to your father and aunt before I left. They are very proud of you. All their friends and relatives have heard the story of your studying in America. I told them that you were considered such a valuable employee that the hotel was sending me to the United States for a few days to be with you. If you tell them the truth now, your father and Auntie Yi Ma will be humiliated. Why make them lose face in front of their friends?"

Ping turned and looked out the window. It had seemed so simple. She would just tell Jianbo she could not marry David. She had forgotten how clever and cunning those born under the sign of the Monkey could be. Now, according to Jianbo, the honor of her family was at stake if she did not go through with the marriage. As the car neared Mrs. Bennington's home she turned again to Jianbo. "I will say no more now because we are almost there. But I am not finished. I want to go back to China."

"We'll see about that," he said as the car pulled into the circular drive.

CHAPTER FORTY-ONE

In spite of Ping's description of the estate, Jianbo appeared un-prepared for the luxuriousness of the house. Standing in the foyer, mouth agape, his eyes wandered from the elegant furnish-ings to the central staircase to the large skylight above his head.

"*Nie hao*," Mrs. Bennington said, rushing in from the study to greet her guest.

"*Nie hao*," Jianbo responded.

He reached into his backpack and pulled out a colorfully wrapped gift. "For you," he said, bowing. Ping had suggested he buy his hostess some silk scarves.

Mrs. Bennington unwrapped the package. "How beautiful. *Xie, xie.*"

"You speak Mandarin," Jianbo said.

"Ping's been teaching me a few words. I think I've used up most of my vocabulary."

Unable to understand her, Jianbo looked questioningly at Ping.

"Should I take Jianbo to his room?" she asked, ignoring his silent request.

"Of course. When he's unpacked, come back down. Greta's baked her special chocolate cake to celebrate his arrival."

Jianbo followed Ping up the wide staircase to the second floor. Once inside the guest room where Ping had stayed the first time she had come, he closed the door, grabbed her by the waist, and spun her around.

"Put me down. Put me down. Someone will hear us."

"This house is amazing. Maybe one day, we'll have something like this."

"I don't think so. Most Americans don't live this well." But caught up in his enthusiasm, she added, "Wait until you see the rest of the place."

Trailing behind Ping, Jianbo peered out the large window. Although less impressive in winter, the rear of the estate with its tennis court, swimming pool, now covered until spring, and guesthouse appeared to dazzle him. Next, Ping showed him the bathroom.

"Look at this," Ping said, opening the shower door. "When you take a shower, water comes out from all these nozzles. It feels like a massage."

"A Jacuzzi, right?" Jianbo asked, pointing to the large tub. "Just like the China Palace. I didn't think people could have these in their homes. I guess anything is possible in America."

A knock on the bedroom door interrupted the tour. It was Greta.

"I just wanted to make sure there were enough towels."

"Everything's fine. Thank you," Ping said. "Greta, this is Jianbo."

"Glad to meet you. I've heard a lot about you from your sister."

Jianbo smiled engagingly at Greta, although Ping knew he had not understood a word she had said.

Once Greta left the room, Ping sat in the armchair by the window to watch Jianbo unpack. "You cannot make me marry David."

He paused, turned, and glared at Ping.

Chin firm, voice strong, Ping announced, "I'm going to tell David the truth. He'll never marry me then."

"And what will you do when he tells you to leave?"

"I'll go back to China with you."

"That will be difficult. I have a return ticket. You do not."

Ping turned ashen; beads of sweat appeared on her upper lip. "You wouldn't leave me behind."

"Why wouldn't I if you tried to destroy everything we've worked for?"

"David or Mrs. Bennington would buy me a ticket home."

Jianbo sneered. "Why would they want to help someone who betrayed them?"

Ping slumped forward in the chair, her head spinning. She opened her mouth as if to protest, but no words came out.

───

In the three days leading up to the wedding, Ping and Jianbo spent little time together. Angry at his reaction to her request to return to China, she avoided him whenever possible. Each morning at breakfast, Mrs. Bennington and Jianbo would discuss what sights he should visit using Ping as an interpreter. David would give him the money for entry fees, meals, and transportation. Ulrich would drive him to the ferry terminal in the morning and pick him up in time for dinner.

In spite of the cold weather, Jianbo usually rode on the uncovered upper deck of the ferry. He told Mrs. Bennington through Ping that he enjoyed the press of the wintry air against his face. From his vantage point, he could watch as the ferry zigzagged between the large chunks of ice floating in the Hudson River. He claimed to never tire of seeing the magnificent skyline as the boat approached the Manhattan ferry terminal.

At dinner, occasionally at the country club, but more often in Mrs. Bennington's elegant dining room, Ping would translate

Jianbo's daily adventures. David's mother seemed to enjoy these tales told from her visitor's perspective—trips to the top of the Empire State Building, boat tours around Manhattan, visits to the United Nations. Seeing the city in which she had grown up through another's admiring eyes seemed to make it all the more special.

Jianbo's enthusiasm appealed to Ping, but it could not dissipate her resentment of him for putting her in this untenable position. True, his desire to come to the United States to improve his position in life was admirable as was his objective to provide well for her and his mother. But this should not come at the price of her self-respect.

CHAPTER FORTY-TWO

On the eve of her marriage, Ping placed the tray holding a pot of tea, two cups, and a plate of cookies on the carpet outside the guest room. She would make a final appeal to Jianbo to call off the wedding. She lifted her hand to knock but then lowered it. She fingered her necklace and said a silent prayer to her mother for courage and strength. Taking a deep breath and pushing back her shoulders, she knocked.

"Who is it?" Jianbo asked in Mandarin.

"It's me."

Dressed in sweat pants and a T-shirt, Jianbo opened the door. Ping padded into the room holding the tray.

"I asked Greta to prepare jasmine tea for us."

"So you finally decided to spend some time alone with me," Jianbo said, helping Ping set the tray on the table in front of the window flanked by two wingback chairs. "You've been avoiding me all week."

"I've been busy getting ready for the wedding."

Ping poured the tea into the cups and handed one to Jianbo. She took hers and sat down in one of the chairs.

"I don't think I can give you away tomorrow," Jianbo said, taking a seat opposite her.

Ping's face brightened. "Does this mean I can go back home with you?"

Jianbo pushed back the hair from his forehead; he bit his lower lip.

"We can still call it off," Ping said, eyes hopeful. "I'll just say I can't live in America. I want to go back to China."

"But go back to what? To a life where we barely have enough money to live?"

"I was happy with you in Beijing. I liked our little apartment. I liked riding behind you on the bicycle to work, drinking jasmine tea, and chatting before going to bed."

Jianbo said nothing. He got up, pulled Ping from her chair, and tried to embrace her. She placed her hands against his chest and pushed him away. "Please don't, not if I'm marrying David tomorrow."

"You're punishing me, aren't you? Don't you realize how much this hurts me?"

"Probably less than the hurt I felt when you asked me to share another man's bed."

"You're angry."

"Yes."

"I just want us to have a good life. Marrying the American will help us do that."

"You just want to have a better life than Feng's."

"That's not true. I don't want to end up like my parents. My father worked hard all his life and had little to show for it when he died. My mother has nothing. She is totally dependent on us."

Jianbo slumped back into his chair and buried his face in his hands. Ping thought she would enjoy seeing him suffer for what he had done to her, but instead his remorsefulness saddened her. She sat on the carpet next to him, letting her head rest against his knees. She felt his despair in the touch of his fingers on her face. Tears slid down her cheeks and disappeared into the plush fibers of the carpet. In the stillness that surrounded them, they could hear the slight tremor of the windowpanes beaten by the wind, the throbbing of their heartbeats, and the aggravating tick of the clock on the nightstand, reminding them that they'd soon be separated.

"Why is the American spending the night here in his mother's house?" Jianbo asked.

"The American's name is David."

"To me he's just the American who will help us get citizenship."

"The church is nearby," Ping said. "It would take David a long time to get here from Manhattan."

"Will he be sleeping with you tonight?"

"Of course not. Why do you ask me something like that?"

"I'm sorry." Jianbo placed his empty cup on the tray and leaned back, eyes closed.

Ping glanced at the alarm clock. "It's late. I'd better go."

Jianbo jumped up. "Don't leave me alone tonight."

"I cannot sleep with you on the eve of my marriage to another."

"We don't have to sleep like husband and wife. We can even stay dressed."

Sleep like husband and wife? Didn't Jianbo realize he was no longer her husband? He could no longer ask her to share his bed—even if they did nothing.

"Please. I promise I won't even kiss you. I just want to hold you close, feel you in my arms. That will sustain me until we're together again."

"I cannot sleep with two men."

Jianbo grabbed her arm. "You will stay with me tonight."

"No," Ping said firmly, struggling to free herself.

He tightened his grip and pulled her toward him. Ping's lips pressed together; her jaw was set. "Stop, or I'll scream."

She opened her mouth. A look of panic crossed Jianbo's face. He released her. Without a word, Ping turned and walked toward the door and left.

CHAPTER FORTY-THREE

"Let me help you with that," Greta said, lifting the ivory gown over Ping's head. Staring at her image in the full-length mirror, Ping adjusted the off-the-shoulder neckline and ran her hands over the form-fitting bodice. Greta bent down and fluffed up the cascading skirt made from petals of crisp silk taffeta. Seated on a chair, Mrs. Bennington watched the scintillating swoosh of the gown as Ping glided toward her, eyes eager for approval.

"I don't believe I've ever seen a more beautiful bride," she said. Greta nodded in agreement. Ping beamed.

Fumbling in her bag, Mrs. Bennington produced a small rectangular jewelry box. "Are you familiar with the American wedding poem?"

Ping shook her head.

"It goes like this. 'Something old, something new, something borrowed, and something blue.'"

"What does this poem mean?" Ping asked.

"The 'something old' suggests a continuation with the past. 'Something new' is the hope for good fortune."

Memories of the good luck lady combing her hair caused Ping to flinch. The traditions she had followed for her first wedding did not bring happiness. Perhaps Western customs would be different.

Mrs. Bennington opened the jewelry box and pulled out a ring. "I am lending you this for the wedding," she said and handed it to Ping.

Ping held the ring up to the light entranced by the glittering multifaceted blue stone. Greta came over to look. "It's a sapphire," Mrs. Bennington said. "My father gave it to my mother on their wedding day."

"It is so beautiful. Thank you. I will be very careful with it." Ping placed it on her finger.

"Let me see." Mrs. Bennington examined her outstretched hand. "It fits perfectly. Now you have something old, something borrowed, and something blue all in this one ring."

"What do 'borrowed' and 'blue' represent?"

"'Borrowed' means that our friends and family will always be with you. We hope to share in, that is *borrow*, some of your happiness. 'Blue' symbolizes your faithfulness, purity, and fidelity to David."

Ping lowered her eyes. Her joy at receiving the ring diminished. The blue stone did not represent her; she was anything but pure.

"Is something the matter?"

"No." Ping shook her head. "I'm grateful for your kindness."

Mrs. Bennington's lily pad eyes shone. She reached again into her purse. "David wanted me to give you the 'something new.'" She held up a strand of pearls.

Ping gasped. It looked like the one David had bought Alexis. She glanced at the name on the box: Sharon's Store. Mrs. Bennington waved her hand to Greta, who took the strand and fastened it around Ping's neck.

Jianbo strode into the church rectory, stopping short when he spied Ping by the minister's side resplendent in her wedding dress. He frowned, seemingly disappointed that her gloomy demeanor of the prior evening had been replaced by a radiant glow. She stood tall, face flushed, her dark tresses piled high on her head behind a beaded tiara holding a short veil.

"You look more beautiful today than you did on our wedding day."

Ping put a finger to her lips and cast a glance at the minister standing nearby.

"I'm sure he doesn't understand Mandarin," Jianbo said, grinning at the clergyman.

The minister smiled back. "Good day to you, too. Your sister is truly a vision of loveliness this morning."

"Would you mind if I speak to my brother alone?" Ping asked.

"Of course not. You have a few minutes before the ceremony begins. My assistant will come for you." The minister left and closed the rectory door behind him.

Ping approached Jianbo and reached for the boutonnière hanging precariously from the lapel of his tuxedo. "Let me fix this for you," she said, repositioning the flower.

As she stepped back to review her work, Jianbo's eyes were drawn to her neck.

"Isn't that the pearl necklace the American bought for his fiancée?"

"It's similar. It's a wedding gift."

"How much did it cost?"

Ping's eyes narrowed. "It was a gift. How would I know how much it cost?"

Jianbo came closer to examine the pearls. "These are as fine as the ones he bought in Beijing. We'll be able to sell the necklace for a lot of money."

Ping's fingers reached for the necklace. She had no intention of keeping it if she divorced David. Everything she had been given—the clothing, the luggage, the jewelry—would remain behind.

"We're alone," Jianbo said, glancing around the rectory. He put his hands on Ping's shoulders. Pulling her closer, he tried to kiss her.

Ping turned her face to the side and pushed him away. Jianbo frowned. "This will be the last time we are together for a while. How can you refuse me one kiss?"

"Why are you doing this? I told you last night, I cannot be embraced by you now and another this evening. I am not a...I am not a whore." She struggled to hold back tears.

"Don't cry. People will become suspicious." Jianbo wiped away a tear inching down her cheek. "I am filled with sadness, too. I didn't think our separation would be this painful."

They stood without speaking, Jianbo's sorrow palpable. But Ping felt no pity for this man who had treated her like chattel. Finally, she broke the silence. "Is it today that I become an American citizen?"

Jianbo bit his lip. "I think so."

"What do you mean, 'you think so'?"

"That's what I was told. But ask David to be sure."

Ping felt a sudden tightness in her chest. If she became a citizen upon her marriage and her divorce was indeed imminent, she had decided not to sleep with David like a husband and a wife. Performing acts of love with two men was abhorrent. But what if gaining citizenship took longer? She could not dishonor her marriage vows indefinitely.

The minister's assistant, a middle-aged woman with wire-rimmed glasses, poked her head inside the room. "They're ready for you."

Ping took a deep breath, adjusted her gown, and walked to the door. The assistant lowered the veil to cover Ping's face. Not too long ago, Auntie Yi Ma had done the same, only this time the veil was white, not red.

The assistant guided Ping toward the door and handed her the wedding bouquet, a mixture of cascading pearl and pale yellow roses. "Follow me," she said as she positioned Ping and Jianbo at the entrance to the sanctuary and placed his hand on her elbow.

As the first strains of Mendelssohn's "Wedding March" filled the church, those attending rose to their feet. Ping and Jianbo began their walk down the aisle. He tightened his grip on her arm. She cast a sideward glance toward him. He wore the look of someone marching toward the gallows.

As they continued their walk, all eyes were on Ping. Through the chords of the music, she heard whispers of "beautiful," "stunning," "striking." She lifted her head higher; she walked taller. But as Ping neared the altar, she trembled. The exuberant lilt of the wedding march had ended. For the second time in less than a year, she would leave behind everything familiar. Even though she was angry with Jianbo, her heart was heavy with loss. She glanced at him. His face was sullen, his eyes downcast. "Smile," Ping said in Mandarin.

"I can't."

"You must, or people will suspect something."

Jianbo responded with a halfhearted grin.

Waiting at the altar, David exuded joy. Reluctantly, Jianbo released Ping's arm and handed her over to him. As she stood before the minister reciting her vows, she felt faint. David steadied her shaking hand. He slipped the wedding ring on her finger. At the end of the ceremony, he drew her close. She did not push him away as she had Jianbo earlier. His kiss evoked the same exhilaration as the first time he had embraced her in Central Park. Once again, her knees weakened; she could hardly breathe.

As Beethoven's "Ode to Joy" sounded from the organ, Ping, with David at her side, turned to begin their march up the aisle as husband and wife. In contrast to the smiling faces that greeted them, Jianbo stood on the side in his black tuxedo, lips pinched together, eyes menacing—a dark presence lurking in the background.

CHAPTER FORTY-FOUR

Maui

"Look, a trail of bougainvillea." Leaving David and the bellboy in the front hall of their hotel suite, Ping followed the violet petals through the sitting room with its colorful wicker furniture and into the bedroom. The trail forked off in one direction, stopping at a bedside table on which there was a bottle of champagne in an ice bucket and two long-stemmed flutes. A second trail of blossoms led into the bathroom. It ended at the side of a large Jacuzzi tub. Above it was a shelf stacked with aromatherapy oils and candles.

As the bellboy showed David how to regulate the air-conditioning and informed him of the various hotel restaurants, Ping wandered back into the bedroom and onto the balcony that ran the width of the suite. The ocean's spray captured fragments of the early morning sun. A series of terraced gardens filled with exotic flowers sloped down to the white sandy beach and the cobalt sea. Although familiar with some of the plants, Ping had never seen so many varieties. Multiple hues of hibiscus were interspersed with neon-colored ginger blooms. Wild vines embellished with orange blossoms mingled with purple cattleya. Orchids in all colors, shapes, and sizes peeked from behind palm leaves. The salty ocean air competed with the fragrant scents of yellow acacia and white hibiscus.

Transfixed by the beauty of the setting, Ping inhaled deeply, filling her lungs with the perfumed air that surrounded her. Closing her eyes, she felt the soft breeze from the ocean caress her face. She had indeed found paradise. Standing next to the railing, mesmerized by the symphony of colors before her, Ping remained on the balcony long after she heard the bellboy leave.

"Are you going to stay out there forever?"

Reluctantly, Ping turned and made her way into the bedroom. "Oh, David, you should see the beauti—"

Ping brought her hand to her mouth; her eyes widened. Waiting on the bed, David lay naked. Ping stared, horrified. His erect penis seemed like a sword waiting to thrust itself hard and deep into its intended victim.

Apparently confused and embarrassed by Ping's reaction, David jumped out of bed. He reached into the closet for his monogrammed white terrycloth robe—a gift from the hotel—and quickly wrapped it around him.

Ping stood trembling by the balcony door.

"I'm sorry," David said as he moved beside her. "I didn't mean to frighten you."

"Please forgive me." Tears rolled down her cheeks.

"Don't worry." David put an arm around her slumped shoulders. "I guess I went too fast. You tell me when you're ready."

Comforted by his words, the tension slowly dissipated from Ping's body. "Why don't we put our clothes away and then decide what we want to do?" David said.

Ping carefully hung her dresses and slacks on hangers and placed T-shirts, shirts, underwear, and bathing suits in drawers. She left the negligees Mrs. Bennington had helped her select inside the locked suitcase crammed behind her shoes in the closet. A long T-shirt would do for sleeping. A feeling of nausea and shame overcame her when she thought of going to bed that evening with David. She was in a state of limbo—divorced but still committed to Jianbo, married but only until she obtained US citizenship. How could she have let Jianbo put her in this situation?

When she rejoined David in the sitting room, he was studying the pamphlet left by the bellboy, detailing the activities included in the honeymoon package. "What would you like to do today?" David asked, passing the pamphlet to Ping.

"Whatever you would like."

"I want you to choose."

Ping turned her head toward David, a smile inched across her face. With Jianbo what she wanted to do wouldn't have mattered. "Really, you want me to choose?"

"Yes. I know I'll enjoy doing whatever you select."

"There's a tai chi class on the beach that starts in twenty minutes. Could we do that?"

"I've never done tai chi, but I'd like to learn. And after the class?"

"Maybe the boat trip to Molokini?"

"Sounds good," David said. But a look of disappointment on his face made Ping think he probably would have preferred the more intimate massage for two at the spa or the private picnic prepared by the hotel and served on an isolated stretch of beach.

Although athletic, David had trouble executing the tai chi moves. Ping, on the other hand, danced through the series of positions effortlessly, balancing on her right leg while extending the left hip high out to the side, bending deeply on one knee with her other leg stretched along the sand, buttocks almost touching the ground.

"You've done this before," David said after the class.

"Yes. This is something we do in my country in large groups early in the morning."

"I felt very awkward."

"That's because this is your first time.

David looked at his watch. "We'd better change if we want to take that excursion to Molokini."

A few minutes later, dressed in bathing suits and cover-ups, they got on the hotel bus that took them and other passengers to the docks where they boarded a boat. From the upper deck David and Ping watched as the craft approached the crescent-shaped crater of Molokini.

"Are you ready?" David asked as the boat slowed to a stop.

"For what?"

"Snorkeling."

Ping paused, her brow furrowed. Those nearby donned face masks, snorkels, and fins. "I don't understand."

"That's the purpose of the trip."

She watched wide-eyed as passengers jumped into the crystalline waters off the back of the boat.

"I didn't know what this snorkeling was," Ping said. "I've never done this thing. I thought we were just taking a boat ride."

"C'mon, I'll be right by your side. Nothing will happen."

Ping reluctantly took David's hand as he led her to the equipment. After slipping on the fins she waddled to the edge of the boat. She stared at the water, muscles tense. "I can only swim a little."

David handed Ping a boogie board. "Here, this will hold you up. You won't sink." Then he jumped into the water.

Ping donned her face mask, knelt on the deck, and gingerly put her hand into the sea to test the temperature.

"Jump," David said, preparing to grab her once she hit the water. "There're people waiting behind you."

Turning her head, Ping saw a line had formed. Embarrassed, she stood up, adjusted her goggles, grabbed the boogie board, closed her eyes, and leaped off the edge of the boat. The moment she hit the water, she felt David's arms around her waist. After adjusting her mask, she hung onto the boogie board, kicked her feet, and put her face in the water.

"Well, what do you think?" David asked when Ping lifted her head for air.

"The water is beautiful. Look, I can see all the way down to the bottom through these goggles. It's so clear."

Clinging to the boogie board, she followed David as he swam away from the boat. Rainbow-colored fish circled within inches of her feet. Resting her chest on the board, she peered into the depths of the sea. Through the goggles she noticed a slightly larger fish skimming along the ocean floor.

"David, look at the big fish on the bottom. What is it?"

"A baby shark."

Ping made a U-turn, kicking franticly in the direction of the boat. David caught up with her. "Whoa, no need to panic. It's not going to bother us."

"Are you sure?"

"Absolutely. If he tries to eat you, I'll distract him, and you can escape to the boat."

Ping frowned at David but then broke into a smile. They remained in the water until a whistle blew indicating it was time to return to the boat. As the vessel pulled into the harbor, Ping turned to David, who stood next to her at the railing, her eyes radiant. "Thank you. I've had such a wonderful day."

Ping did not resist when David kissed her tenderly. They walked down the short gangplank hand in hand. Sitting on the bus on the way back to the hotel, his arm around Ping, David seemed eager to get back to their room.

CHAPTER FORTY-FIVE

Although Ping did not resist when David kissed her in the privacy of their suite, she flinched when his hand touched her breast. *Still too soon I guess,* David thought. In the hope that an evening meal by the sea would encourage Ping to consummate their marriage, he had reserved a table on the outdoor terrace of the hotel for what the honeymoon brochure described as "the ultimate romantic dinner."

"What an elegant couple," an elderly matron whispered to her male companion as Ping and David passed their table. Overhearing the remark, Ping, stunning in a lilac spaghetti-strap chiffon dress, smiled self-consciously. The maître d' led them to a table overlooking the ocean.

The setting sun emblazoned the sky with bold strokes of rose, orange, and sapphire, colors reflected in the azure waters of the Pacific. Gentle waves broke on the now empty beach. Rows of pink lokelani and white kukui blossoms separated the candle-lit tables on the terrace from the sand. The murmuring surf accompanied the cries of egrets and herons as they searched the shore for food.

While the waiter took their order and the sommelier placed a bottle of sauvignon blanc in the silver wine bucket beside the table, Ping sat entranced watching the sun slowly disappear on the horizon. "I wish we could stay here forever," she said turning to David.

"I think Maui is perfect for a week, but to live here all the time would be boring."

"I don't think so. Every sunset would be different. It would take forever to learn the names of all the flowers, to identify the songs of all the birds."

"But what happens if you're not into flowers and birds?"

Ping laughed. David reached across the table and took her hands in his.

"I was thinking today about what makes a good marriage," he said.

"And did you come up with an answer?"

"Yes. Are you familiar with the term *synergy*?"

Ping shook her head.

"It's a business term used when the whole is greater than the sum of its parts. It's like saying two plus two equals five."

"I don't quite understand how this relates to us."

"You and I together are better than you and I apart."

Ping tilted her head to the side and pursed her lips. David continued. "Before today, I never did tai chi, and you never snorkeled. Together we've done more than we would have done apart." Ping smiled. She liked this definition of marriage.

The waiter arrived and placed salads of shrimp and smoked duck in front of the couple. The sommelier uncorked the bottle of wine and poured some for David to taste.

"Very nice," David said. The sommelier filled their glasses.

They selected two different entrées to share: sautéed fresh Hawaiian red snapper and pan-fried Hawaiian saltwater shrimp served on Macadamia nut rice.

"You know with all the wedding and honeymoon preparations, we never really talked about what you would like to do when we get back to New York," David said to Ping over dessert.

Ping lifted her eyes. She had thought often of what she wanted to do but had been reluctant to say anything. David had allowed her to select the day's activities, but would he let her choose a career? "I could get a job teaching Mandarin."

"You don't have to work. We can live very well on my salary."

"But what would I do all day?"

"My friends' wives like to shop."

"Why? I have all the clothes I need."

"You could do charity work. Help out at hospitals, become a docent at a museum."

"I want to talk again about synergy," Ping said, showing little enthusiasm for David's suggestions.

"OK."

"Our marriage should be a growth experience for both of us. Just by being from different countries we help each other—you teach me American ways, and I help you understand my culture. You say your boss is thinking of sending you to China. I can teach you acceptable and unacceptable behavior in my country. This will help you grow in your job."

"It will."

"I'd like to grow, too."

"How can I help?"

"Do you think it would be possible for me to finish my college degree in New York?"

"Is that what you'd like to do?"

"Yes. I liked going to the university when I was in Chongqing."

"We can look into it when we get back. There are a lot of colleges and universities in Manhattan. What would you study?"

"In China I studied English. I wanted to become an English professor. Here that wouldn't work. I could never speak English as well as a native."

David opened his mouth as if to contradict.

"No," Ping said, shaking her head. "A foreigner teaching English in America is like a duck teaching a fish to swim. But what I could teach is Mandarin and Cantonese. I wouldn't mind studying other Asian languages as well."

"The spring semester probably starts at most colleges in a week or two. But since you'd be a transfer student, we might be able to get you admitted. I know someone in the admissions office at NYU who could help."

Ping took a sip of wine and smiled at David. "Thank you. You have made me very happy."

"We should go to bed early tonight," David said after they returned to their suite following dinner. "Our tour to Haleakala leaves at four thirty tomorrow morning."

Preparing for bed, Ping thought about unlocking the suitcase and wearing one of the negligees. After several glasses of wine combined with the exotic setting and the possibility of continuing her university studies, Jianbo and Beijing seemed light-years away.

"I think there are other elements to a good marriage besides synergy," David said climbing into bed in his pajama bottoms. "Like honesty. A husband and wife should never lie to each other."

Ping's heart skipped a beat.

"I do know everything I should about you, don't I?" David asked.

"Yes," Ping said, feeling a crimson wave sweep over her body. With renewed visions of Jianbo, she pulled a long T-shirt out of the drawer and slipped it on using it first to wipe her moist palms. Shutting off the light on the nightstand, she slipped into bed beside David.

"My father wanted to hire a detective to check your background."

Ping held her breath.

"But I told him no."

The moonlight sneaking through the open door to the balcony was not bright enough to reveal the panic in Ping's eyes. Regaining her composure, she turned toward David. In response, he wrapped his arms around her and drew her close. Aroused, he slipped his hand under her shirt. Ping's body stiffened. With a sigh, David turned onto his back.

Ping reached over and kissed him affectionately on the cheek. "You are so kind and good to me. I wish..."

"What?"

"Nothing," Ping said as she turned away from him and closed her eyes tightly to hold back tears.

CHAPTER FORTY-SIX

At four thirty the following morning David and Ping sat in the van that would take them from sea level up more than ten thousand feet to the summit of the volcano Haleakala. At the top they were joined by other tour members and given one-piece orange jumpsuits to wear over their clothes. The jumpsuits served two purposes: to protect the group against the predawn chill and to be easily spotted by the guides.

Ping stared across the barren, black cone-studded remains of the once active volcano. "This must be what the moon looks like," she said to David.

"And we look like two astronauts in these orange suits."

Ping admired the starkness of the terrain. "I feel like an explorer, setting out on a new adventure."

"You are," he replied, squeezing her hand. "Look," David said. "You can see the top of the sun beginning to rise over the crater."

They watched spellbound, arms around each other's waists as the bright orange sphere slowly ascended over the stark black landscape. The sunrise complete, the surface looked less foreboding.

Streaks of red, yellow, and gray appeared, tracing the course of centuries of lava flows.

The guide instructed the group to go to a small truck from which tour personnel rolled out bicycles. After each member of the tour selected a bike, and seat adjustments were made, the group followed a guide single file down the steep road from the top of the crater. As the cyclists made their way leisurely across the twenty-nine switchbacks, the landscape changed from barren and rocky with only the hardiest plants and shrubs surviving, to vegetable truck farms and botanical gardens. Once on the bottom, the guide led the group to a restaurant, where a champagne brunch was served. After the meal, the van returned to take the newlyweds to their hotel.

In the van, Ping rode silently next to David. If she were to re-marry Jianbo in just a few months, she could not consummate her marriage to David. If she did, she would be no better than a prostitute. But what if Jianbo was wrong, and marriage did not make her a citizen automatically?

"Am I an American citizen now?" she asked David.

"Why would you think that?"

"Because I am your wife."

David drew his brows together. "It's not that easy. Even if you're married to an American, it takes years."

"Years?"

"It doesn't happen on your wedding day. Why would you think that?"

"Jianbo told me it did."

David's eyes narrowed. "Well your brother gave you wrong information. Would you like to become a US citizen?"

Ping nodded.

"When we get back to New York, I'll have my attorney find out exactly what's required."

"Thank you," Ping said.

Years. How could Jianbo be so wrong? She frowned, furious that he had misled her. She could no longer refuse David. He was her husband now and would be for quite a while—perhaps forever.

"Can we take a nap before dinner?" Ping asked as she entered the suite.

"Sure," David said, sitting on a chair to take off his shoes.

In the bathroom, Ping found vanilla-scented candles that she lit and placed on the nightstand. She pulled down the covers of the bed and folded back the top sheet. As David watched hungrily, she unzipped her shorts. They fell to the floor. She lifted her T-shirt over her head revealing a slender waist, tight abdomen, and a sheer pink bra. She unhooked the bra. The straps slid over her shoulders and down her arms to expose soft, rounded breasts. Bending over, she removed her lace panties. She stood naked before David shoulders back, breasts high, nipples erect, her dark tresses falling seductively around inviting eyes. His face flushed and breathing heavily, David quickly removed his clothes and walked to where Ping waited.

Lying on the bed, their bodies entwined, Ping felt David's hardness against her leg. As his hand glided down her back, her heart beat faster. When his fingers slid below her waist, she flinched. Only Jianbo had ever touched her there. But as David gently stroked her buttocks, Ping relaxed. She felt like a peony opening its petals to greet the dawn.

Slowly, methodically, David's hands explored Ping's body. He moved his fingers between her legs and inserted them into her vagina. She moaned with pleasure, inviting wetness oozing onto her thighs. His hands cupped her breasts. She felt his tongue playing with her nipples like a hummingbird gathering nectar from a sweet flower.

David moved his head lower, lips sliding along her abdomen. As he inched further down her body, she spread her thighs apart. She felt his tongue between her legs. The hummingbird sucked the sweetness from the pistil of the peony.

Ping had never been so aroused. Her moans grew louder as David entered her. The pink petals of the peony opened wider, fully exposing its moist, creamy center. The hummingbird flapped its wings louder and louder, faster and faster. Pink petals twirled and spiraled into the air, colliding in an explosive crescendo.

As David rolled over beside her, Ping lay motionless. Warmth radiated throughout her body, tears of joy careened down glistening cheeks. Something wonderful had just happened.

⚬⚬⚬

They did not leave their room for the rest of the day. Dinner did not entice them as their appetites were only for each other. When they were finally sated, David held Ping close as she drifted off to sleep. It was 1:00 a.m., but he was wide awake. His marriage was finally consummated, but his satisfaction was not complete. Ping's resistance had misled him. The way her brother had chaperoned her in Beijing made him think she had never been with a man. David caressed Ping's back; she snuggled closer. He could hardly fault her for not being a virgin, but he wished he had been her first lover.

CHAPTER FORTY-SEVEN

A whirlwind of activity greeted Ping on the couple's return to New York City—parties with David's friends and colleagues, meetings with the interior decorator, thank-you notes for wedding gifts, and luncheons at the club with Mrs. Bennington. On this particular evening two weeks after their return, Ping was thrilled that she and David had no plans. Earlier she had taken a walk to Chinatown, which was not far from their condo, and had purchased food to make dinner. On the way home, she had stopped in a used-book store and bought a copy of F. Scott Fitzgerald's *The Great Gatsby*. Since she was living in the United States, she wanted to become familiar with American authors.

From the refrigerator, Ping took out the fresh broccoli and placed it on the marble countertop. She would make stir-fry beef and broccoli tonight. Just as she opened a cabinet to pull out a pot, the phone rang. It was Jianbo.

"I can't talk long. I came to work early to use the phone," he said in Mandarin.

Ping glanced at the kitchen clock. It was 5:30 p.m. here, which meant 5:30 a.m. in Beijing.

"I have not heard from you for several weeks."

"There was a lot to do after the honeymoon."

"Did you talk to the American about my restaurant?"

"No, but his lawyer is going to let me know how long it takes to become a US citizen."

"So as the American's wife you're not automatically a citizen?"

"David said no."

"Whatever you need to do," Jianbo said after a brief pause. "Do it quickly. I am very lonely here without you."

The following evening after dinner, David produced a folder from his briefcase. "My attorney faxed me the requirements for citizenship."

Ping, who had been cleaning up in the kitchen, felt a chill careen through her body. She wiped her hands on a dishcloth and joined him on the living room couch. "Right now," David began. "You have conditional resident status. A few months before our second anniversary, we'll apply to remove the condition." He looked up from the paper. "According to this, I must sign the request. I guess there's a concern that a foreigner might marry an American just to become a citizen."

Ping looked away and swallowed hard. David shot a glance at her. "Is something the matter?"

"No," Ping said, her face flushed. "I just didn't realize it would take so long."

David's brow furrowed. Ping felt a fluttering in her stomach. "So in two years I can be an American?"

"Not quite. You have to wait another year before you can apply."

Ping winced; her breathing became shaky.

"Are you all right?" Ping nodded. David moved away from her and stared. "Why is this citizenship thing so important?"

"It's not," Ping said, her brow glistening.

"When did you think you'd be a citizen?"

Ping looked down and fiddled with the button on her blouse. "On our wedding day."

"Who told you that?"

"I told you, remember? Jianbo."

Ping's face turned ashen. Did David suspect her motives for marrying him? And what would Jianbo say when she told him it would take years to become a citizen? David shook his head and rubbed his brow. "I'm going to ask you a question. Don't be frightened. I'll believe whatever you say."

Ping lifted her head, hands clasped tightly together.

"Did you marry me just to become an American citizen?"

Through trembling lips, she answered. "No."

CHAPTER FORTY-EIGHT

"Good morning, Mrs. Bennington, may I help you with those packages?"

"Thank you, Xavier," Ping said handing the plastic grocery bags to the doorman as she stepped out of the taxi.

"Do you want me to have a porter take these to your apartment?"

"No, thank you. I'll carry them upstairs."

Ping knew if David were with her, he would insist that the porter carry the bags. But she was uncomfortable having people wait on her. She found it demeaning to ask others to do something she could easily do for herself.

"That's their job," David would explain. "That's why we'll give them a big tip at Christmas."

The doorman set the bags inside the elevator and pressed the ninth-floor button before getting out. During the car's ascent, Ping retrieved the keys from her shoulder bag. Every time she opened the door to her new home and stepped inside she trembled with delight. The dramatic two-story entryway with its suspended semi-circular metal stairway to the second floor led into a large living and dining room area. The sweet scent of fresh orange blossoms on a long narrow table in the foyer greeted her as she stepped inside.

The grocery bags unloaded, Ping put some loose tea in a pot, filled it from a hot water spout by the sink, and set it on the counter to steep. She had left the house early that morning and walked to Chinatown. At 9:00 a.m. she had joined a group in Columbus Park doing tai chi. Afterward she wandered the crowded streets, stopping at markets to buy food for dinner.

It had been several days since she had talked with David about citizenship. They had not made love since, even though she wore the negligees Mrs. Bennington had given her. Did he suspect she had married him only to become an American? Ping wished Auntie Yi Ma were here; she would know what to do.

At the sound of the front door opening, Ping's heart beat faster, glad that her husband was home early. "You have a letter," David said as he entered the apartment, mail in hand. "It looks like it's from—drumroll here, please—NYU."

"Oh, please, let me see," Ping said, grabbing the envelope and tearing it open.

She read the letter.

"Well?"

Beaming, she handed it to David.

"Dear Mrs. Bennington," David read, "The College of Arts and Sciences is pleased to inform you that you have been accepted as a transfer student into the Department of East Asian Studies." David hugged his wife. "Congratulations."

Ping glowed.

The ringing of the phone interrupted their rejoicing. David answered and passed the receiver to Ping. "It's your brother."

Her hand shook as she put the phone to her ear. She had written to Jianbo describing the process for US citizenship. Undoubtedly, the letter prompted his call. "*Nie hao*," she said, watching David climb the stairs to their bedroom.

Jianbo had just received her letter. He was not happy about having to wait three years for Ping to apply for citizenship. "Are you sure you are correct?" he asked in Mandarin. "No one ever mentioned 'conditional permanent residence status' when you marry an American."

"David's attorney gave me the information."

"Then come home immediately. I cannot wait three years."

Ping could feel her stomach roiling. She did not want to return; she wanted to stay in America with David. "Perhaps the attorney is mistaken," she said.

She could almost see Jianbo's face, the creased forehead, the cold, dark eyes, as he mulled over the possibility. "OK. Check with immigration. But if it is three more years, you will come home."

Ping raised an eyebrow and held back a desire to laugh. How could Jianbo feel he had the right to demand she return? They were divorced. She owed him nothing. She would have said as much only she was afraid he might somehow contact David and inform him of her involvement in his plan to become a citizen.

"I hope you're not getting used to the apartment you're living in. So, David told you it was worth several million US dollars. It must be very special."

"It's nice."

"Don't you think it's unfair? You live in a home with three bathrooms and a fireplace while I live in a hovel."

No, I don't, Ping thought. *This was your idea, not mine.*

After a pause, Jianbo continued. "Without your salary, I am having trouble paying the rent. I want you to send me some money."

Ping shook her head in disgust. He had managed the rent payments quite well on what he earned before they were married. "How much do you need?"

"Send me six hundred dollars every month."

"Six hundred a month? That's more than what I was earning at the hotel."

"I know. But the American is wealthy. He will give it to you. You shouldn't be the only one benefiting from your situation."

Between clenched teeth, Ping responded. "I'll see what I can do. I must go now. David is expecting dinner."

"Well, we certainly don't want to keep him waiting. Make sure I get the money within the week."

Ping closed her eyes tightly to keep from crying. How could she have married such a monster?

—◁+▷—

"Is everything all right?" David asked as he entered the room. His eyes focused on Ping's face. "You look troubled."

"No, everything is fine. It's just that Jianbo needs money. The apartment is too expensive without my being there to help pay the rent."

"Tell me how much he needs, and I'll wire it to him."

"No, you have already been too generous. I'll send him some from what you give me."

"But I only give you $250 a week. If you're going to give some to Jianbo, I'll give you more."

Only $250 a week? That was $1,000 a month, a fortune in China. "Please, don't give me any more. I have enough."

"What do you do with it?"

"I put it in the checking account that you helped me open at the bank."

"And?"

"It stays there. I take some money out once in a while to buy a book to read."

"You're amazing. Most women I know would have spent the money and have asked for more."

Ping shrugged her shoulders.

"But that's why I married you: because you aren't like most women." David sat next to Ping on the couch and slipped his hand under her T-shirt. She slid her body under his as he un-hooked her bra.

The last vestiges of sunlight slowly retreated from the room. Early evening sounds from the street below filtered into the apartment joining the moans and sighs from the couple on the couch.

CHAPTER FORTY-NINE

February 2005

"Are you lost?" a voice asked Ping in accented English.

Grateful for assistance, she looked up from the map she was holding to see a slight-built Asian woman dressed in jeans and an NYU hoodie. "I'm trying to find this building," she said pointing to an address on a slip of paper. "I have a class that starts at twelve thirty, and I have no idea where it is."

"I'm taking that course, too. It's not far. Just on the other side of Washington Square Park."

"Are you Chinese?" Ping asked.

The woman nodded. "*Wo xiang zhongquo ren.*"

Ping smiled broadly. As they passed beneath the triumphal stone arch at the entrance to the park, they switched from English to Mandarin. "My name is Haiyan, but everyone calls me by my American name, Helen."

"I'm Ping. I don't have an American name."

"You don't need one. Your name is easy for Americans to pronounce." After a pause, Helen continued. "How long have you been in New York?"

"Just a few months. How about you?"

"About seven years."

"That's a long time. Don't you miss China?"

"Sometimes, when I hear a dove sing, when I see a lily, or when I smell dumplings being cooked in Chinatown."

Ping understood; she felt the same way. How nice to meet another woman from China and to be able to speak Mandarin. For the first time she realized how much she missed her friends Meihui and Zhilan.

Ping and Helen neared the exit. In spite of the winter weather they passed chess players wearing gloves absorbed in games played on checkered squares etched on stone tables. The intricacies of the game made for unusual pairings—an Asian youth sat across from an African American, a teenage boy with a nose ring faced off against a white-haired wrinkled man. Ping and Helen hurried by mothers pushing infants in carriages, senior citizens reading and chatting on peeling green benches. Once through the park, they made their way to a building on an adjacent street.

"Here's where the class is." Ping looked at the gray building before them, a building very similar to those at the university in Chongqing. Helen led Ping up a flight of stairs and into a classroom. "Sit next to me," Helen said, pointing to a chair in the front row.

Ping sat down, settled in, and checked out the room. There were several students already there. They chatted in a variety of languages. Occasionally, Ping identified a Cantonese or Korean word emerging from the cacophony of sounds around her. Ping felt at home; most of the students in the room were Asian and female. Since the course was Asian-American Women in Literature and Film, the composition of the class was not surprising.

An attractive, slender woman in her forties entered carrying a worn attaché case. She strode to the front of the classroom. The steady din of voices subsided. After removing a set of papers from her briefcase, she distributed them to the students. Ping glanced at the syllabus and noticed the list of required texts and readings. This looked like a very interesting course.

Helen leaned over. "I've heard good things about the professor," she said as the teacher began to speak in accented English.

"Good afternoon. I am Dr. Hwang. This semester we will examine the Asian-American woman as seen through writings and film."

As Dr. Hwang read the list of required texts and readings, Helen passed a note to Ping asking if she wanted to have a cup of tea after class. Ping nodded to her new friend.

⟞⟝ ⟞⟝

"We'll go to my apartment," Helen said as the two left the classroom. "It's not far from here."

"Do you live by yourself?" Ping asked.

"No, I'm married. In fact, I have a little boy, Nathan. He's almost eight years old."

"Is he home?"

"No, he's at school. He gets dropped off around four. How about you? Are you married?"

"Yes. I married an American about a month ago."

"Congratulations," Helen said as she slipped on her hoodie. "I'm married to an American, too. We met in Beijing."

"What a coincidence. That's where I met my husband."

"Are you from Beijing?"

"No. Chongqing, and you?"

"Not too far from there. I grew up along the Yangtze, too, in Yichang."

"We have much in common."

Helen stopped before a tan brick building. "Here's my home." She removed a set of keys from her book bag. In the entry hall she walked over to a row of mailboxes and unlocked the one labeled "Glauber." A look of consternation crossed her face as she put her hand in and pulled it out empty.

"My husband must be home. He usually isn't here until dinnertime."

"If you'd like we can do this another day," Ping said, sensing Helen's discomfort.

"No. Come upstairs. If my husband's working, the door to his office will be closed. Since we'll be in the kitchen we won't bother him."

Ping followed Helen up two flights of stairs, pausing on the landing as her friend opened the door. They stepped into a large living room lined with bookcases. Helen cracked open one of the two windows that faced the street. The wintry air dissipated the musty odor that pervaded the room.

"You have so many books," Ping said, her eyes scanning shelves packed with hardbacks, paperbacks, journals, and manuscripts.

"My husband is a finance professor," Helen said matter-of-factly as if this explained the voluminous collection.

She glanced at a closed door halfway down the hallway and ushered Ping into a small kitchen. "Why don't you sit here?" she said pointing to one of the three blue vinyl cushioned chairs surrounding a rectangular Formica table. To optimize the available space in the room, the table had been pushed against a wall. The apartment was much smaller and considerably older than hers and David's. She probably would not invite Helen to her home—it would seem too much like showing off.

After putting some water on to boil, Helen opened a tin and spooned tea leaves into a white ceramic teapot. She pulled two cups and saucers from the cupboard. As she turned to put them on the table, one of cups slid off the saucer. It smashed against the tile floor.

Ping jumped from her chair to help Helen. A door slammed. Heavy footsteps bounded down the hall to the kitchen. "What the hell's going on here?" a large middle-aged balding man with wide shoulders and a potbelly said gruffly.

"I'm sorry, Martin," Helen replied, hand shaking, eyes flitting nervously. "I was just making tea for my friend when the cup fell."

Seeing Ping, the man's stern expression softened. "I'm Martin, Helen's husband."

"This is Ping. She's in one of my classes."

"Hi," Ping said, standing up.

Martin nodded. "I'm going back to my room. Please keep it quiet. I'm trying to get some work done."

When the door clicked shut, Helen took a deep breath.

"I really should go," Ping said.

"No, please stay. It's OK. Martin isn't always like this. But he just had a paper rejected by a journal. He's terribly upset."

Ping threw the porcelain shards from the cup into a garbage can. Using a dustpan and brush, Helen picked up the remaining pieces. "There, that's done. I have to be careful. I don't want Nathan to cut himself."

"I think we got everything," Ping said, inspecting the floor.

Helen poured the water from the kettle into the teapot and placed it on the table. She pulled another cup from the cupboard to replace the broken one. "I met Martin at Beijing University," she began. "I was working as an assistant to the American professors who came to teach in a special master's in business program for Chinese students. My job was to be a sort of liaison between the students and the professor."

"Did you have to translate?" Ping asked.

"No, the students had to demonstrate proficiency in English before their acceptance into the program. But even though most were fluent, there were issues. For example, they complained because they couldn't read Martin's handwriting on the blackboard. At first he told me that was their problem, not his. He refused to change his writing. The students were not pleased."

Ping glanced toward the closed office door down the hallway. "Don't worry," Helen said. "Even if my husband could hear us, he only knows a few words in Mandarin."

"I finally convinced Martin," she continued, "to print on the board instead of using script. Once he started printing, the atmosphere in the class changed. The students felt their concerns were being addressed. After that, Martin listened when I made suggestions."

Helen glanced at the teapot. "The tea should be ready." She picked up the pot and poured the dark liquid into their cups.

As Ping sipped her tea, Helen related the rest of her story. At the time, Martin was married with two teenagers. He had wanted his family to accompany him for the three months he was in China. However, his wife, an attorney, wasn't able to leave for such an extended period. His children also complained that they couldn't miss so much school. More importantly, they didn't want to leave their friends. Martin and his wife settled for a one-week trip to China after he completed his teaching assignment.

"I guess he was lonely," Helen said. "He couldn't go to the movies or watch TV because he didn't understand Mandarin. There was a female professor from the United States he ate dinner with occasionally, but she only taught on weekends and traveled the rest of the time."

Helen paused, lifting the teacup to her lips. After returning it to its saucer, she continued. "One day, after the midterm exam, he asked me to help him correct the tests. He said I could do the multiple-choice questions. He would grade the problems. Although he had an office, he decided we'd do the correcting in his apartment. We—" Suddenly the doorbell rang.

"Oh, it's Nathan. I've got to let him in." When Helen returned she was holding the hand of a young dark-haired boy with eyes shaped like Helen's but a sharp chin and full lips like his father.

"Say hello to my friend Ping,"

"Hi, Nathan," Ping said, her smile doing nothing to erase the serious expression on the youngster's face.

Barely acknowledging her presence, Nathan turned to his mother. "Can I go to my room now?"

"As long as you are very, very quiet. Your father's home and needs to work."

"OK," Nathan said as he headed down the hall dragging his book bag.

"He's adorable," Ping said.

"Thank you," Helen replied, glowing.

"I'd better go now. It's getting late, and you probably have dinner to prepare. I'll see you in class on Thursday." Ping carefully placed her cup and saucer in the sink.

"I'm so glad we're in the same course," Helen said as she accompanied Ping to the front door.

"Me, too."

Walking home, Ping realized how lonely she had been. Although Mrs. Bennington was very kind, inviting her to attend functions at the club as her guest, Ping felt uncomfortable. She didn't fit in. She enjoyed her time with David, but he worked all week and occasionally on weekends. How nice it was to befriend someone who, like her, was a student married to an American, living almost seven thousand miles from home.

CHAPTER FIFTY

I n the weeks that followed, Ping and Helen were inseparable. They had the same classes. Most days, their courses finished at three. They would either go to the library to study, to the Saint Alps Teahouse for bubble tea, or to Helen's apartment. Ping was thrilled to find a compatriot, and someone interested in books and learning like she was.

"I have to go to the post office," Helen said one day after class. "Do you want to come with me? It's only a ten-minute walk from here."

Ping buttoned her wool coat and wrapped her plaid Burberry scarf around her neck. "What's at the post office?"

"Martin and his ex-wife are fighting again. He asked me to send this letter to her." Helen pulled out an envelope from her book bag. "It has to be sent certified with a postcard attached that she must sign to show she received it."

"What is the fight about?"

"Their son got accepted to graduate school. Doreen, his ex-wife, claims Martin is supposed to pay. This letter explains why he is no longer obligated."

"Does she often make trouble for you?"

Helen nodded. "But this is nothing compared to other things she's done."

As they turned the corner onto Broadway from Fourth Street, a sudden gust of wind caused Helen to pinch the collar of her jacket closed. Heads bent forward, they trudged along past Shakespeare & Co. bookstore, past the physics building, past the Student Health Center. As they approached the Tisch School of the Arts, the wind died down. With her gloved hand, Ping wiped watery eyes. "So, what terrible things did Doreen do?"

"Right after we were married, we received a letter from the INS—that's Immigration—suggesting that I married Martin just to obtain US citizenship."

"But you didn't."

"I know. But nonetheless we had to meet with what they called an adjudications officer to show this was not true. Martin was furious. He was right in the middle of a research project, and we spent days being quizzed in separate rooms to prove that our marriage wasn't—how did they say it? —a marriage of convenience."

"What did his ex-wife have to do with it?"

"Someone had told the INS that it was a marriage of convenience. Who else would be mean enough to do that?"

"And if the INS had decided it wasn't a real marriage?"

"I would have been on the next plane to China."

Ping's brow wrinkled. In spite of the cold, drops of perspiration formed on her upper lip. Shipped back to China. Would that be how her journey would end?

"We're here," Helen said. She stopped in front of a light-colored, semicircular, two-story brick building. Above the entry stood an eagle, wings outstretched and a sign that read *Cooper Station, New York City*. Inside, Helen turned to Ping. "We're lucky, the line's not too long. Wait here; I'll just be a few minutes."

Ping leaned against a display not too far from the entry and watched the steady flow of East Villagers—mostly young, wearing

215

oversize coats and jackets—waiting their turn in front of open service windows or withdrawing mail from boxes. A parade of people going about their business as if they belonged. There was an empty feeling in the pit of her stomach.

"What's the matter?" Helen asked walking toward Ping, her business finished. "You look worried."

"I need to tell you something."

"There's a Starbucks not too far from here."

In the coffee shop, they ordered hot chocolates and sat at a small, circular table. "I didn't tell you everything about David and me," Ping said, removing her coat and scarf. And with that she confessed to her marriage to Jianbo, his plan to obtain US citizenship, and how terrible she felt betraying David.

"Why did you let Jianbo talk you into something so...so vile?" Helen asked.

"I felt I had no choice. If I refused, who knows what Jianbo would have done to me?"

"Are you afraid of him?"

Ping lowered her eyes. She nodded.

"Has he struck you?"

"Yes."

"If he abused you, you could have left him or had the marriage annulled."

Ping frowned. "I didn't want to bring shame upon my family. And you know how it is in our country. Either the police don't believe the woman who says she was abused, or they feel domestic violence is not their concern."

"True," Helen said, clasping her hands together. "It would be your word against his."

"And we both know who would win in that situation," Ping responded, her shoulders slumped forward.

"How about your Baba and auntie? Do they know you're divorced and remarried?"

"No. They think the hotel where I worked sent me to America to improve my English." Ping picked up a spoon and stirred her drink. "I've really made a mess of things."

"I don't think you have. From what you've told me, your life with David sounds better than it was with Jianbo."

Ping bit her lower lip and sighed. "Perhaps, but only as long as David isn't aware that ours was a marriage of convenience. And I'm sure if I don't do as Jianbo asks, he will find some way to tell David the truth."

CHAPTER FIFTY-ONE

"Now wasn't that invigorating?" Helen asked Ping in Mandarin as the two exited the Jerome S. Coles Sports Center.

A cool late winter wind made Ping zip up her parka and pull a woolen cap down over her damp hair. "Even though I'm not crazy about swimming, it was refreshing. Does Martin ever come with you to the pool?"

"No, but Nathan and I swim on weekends. He's quite a good swimmer."

"He'd have to be to keep up with you."

Helen smiled at the compliment. "Martin may not do sports, but he is really smart," she added as if to compensate for his lack of athleticism. "He works hard and has very high standards. As his assistant in Beijing, sometimes I felt I did not live up to his expectations."

"You must have. He asked you to marry him."

A flush crept across Helen's face. "Not really."

"What do you mean?"

Helen shoved her hands into her pockets; her gait slowed. "Martin had to marry me. I was pregnant."

"When did you find out?"

"About a month after he returned to the United States."

"What did he say when you told him?"

Helen looked off into the distance. Finally, after inhaling deeply, she spoke again.

"Nothing."

She kicked a pebble that was in her path. "I was frantic. What would happen when I started to show? My parents would disown me. I would probably lose my job. I thought about an abortion, but I was too frightened. Plus, I didn't have enough money to do it."

Ping's lip curled; she wrinkled her nose and cast a disdainful look at Helen. How could she have gone to bed with a married man? Wincing, a flush crept across her cheeks. She recalled a saying of Auntie Yi Ma's— "A chicken can't see its own back." Who was she to think poorly of Helen? She, who had agreed to sleep with a man who was not her husband.

As they passed by a convenience store, Helen stopped. "I just want to run in and get some milk. I don't have any for Nathan." While Helen pulled a carton from the refrigerated section, Ping bought a package of nuts for each of them and a large chocolate chip cookie for Nathan.

"Thanks. He'll love that," Helen said when Ping handed her the bag with the cookie.

"Would you have had an abortion if you could have had one?"

"I don't think so, but I'm really glad I didn't. My life would be so incomplete without Nathan. But at the time I wasn't thinking too clearly. I was angry—very, very angry with Martin. He was safe in America; nothing would happen to him. And here I was left all alone to face the consequences of *our* act."

Sparks flashed in Helen's eyes. "One night I couldn't sleep. I looked at the alarm clock. It was 1:00 a.m. on a Saturday morning, so about 1:00 p.m. in New York. I had taken Martin's home phone number from the school files. It took all the courage I had to lift the receiver and dial."

Helen stared ahead, a pained expression on her face. "His wife answered. I heard her yell to him that some Chinese person was on the phone. I knew he was there, but when his wife returned she said he had gone out. I don't know what happened but I burst into tears. His wife told me to please calm down. If I had received a bad grade from her husband, it wasn't the end of the world. A bad grade? Did she really think I'd be hysterical because of that?"

Ping studied Helen's face, the pinched lips, the clenched jaw as she relived her ordeal. "Did you say anything else?"

"Yes. I told her everything—that I had been Professor Glauber's assistant in China, that I was pregnant, and that he was the father."

"What did she say?"

"Nothing. There was total silence on the other end of the phone. I heard the receiver drop. Then Martin came on. Six months later they were divorced, and I came to the United States to marry him."

"You were very brave," Ping said.

"I had no choice."

⚊⊰⊱⚊

That evening waiting for David to come home from a dinner with clients, Ping read her latest acquisition, *Wuthering Heights*. The story seemed to parallel her own. Jianbo was her Heathcliff; David her Edgar. If she refused to leave David, would Jianbo, like Heathcliff, try to destroy or seek vengeance on them? She leaned back against the sofa. Why worry? He was too far away to make any trouble.

Engrossed in the novel, Ping did not notice David until he flopped down beside her on the couch. She looked up, startled.

"I didn't mean to frighten you," David said.

"It's not your fault. I was really into this novel."

David picked up the book from the couch and glanced at the title. "I read this when I was a freshman in college. I didn't like it very much; I couldn't relate."

Ping smiled. Surely, he would think differently if he read it now.

"I have a surprise for you," David said.

"What is it?"

"Your birthday is this Friday."

Ping tilted her head expectantly. How sweet David was. She didn't have the heart to tell him that in China everyone celebrates their birthday on New Year's Day even if it's not the official date of their birth.

"I know how much you miss Jianbo."

At the mention of his name, Ping's pulse raced.

"He's coming tomorrow to help celebrate your birthday."

"To...tomorrow?"

David stared at Ping, who looked as if she had just received horrible news. He rubbed his chin. "I thought you'd be happy."

Ping's gaze wandered; her face went slack. "It's just that it's a bad time for me...with school and everything. I have papers and exams to prepare for." She paused. "What time will he arrive?"

"Around noon."

"I have classes until three. I won't be able to fetch him."

"I'll send a car."

David looked at Ping, a pained expression on his face. "I'm sorry. I thought I was doing a good thing. You haven't seen your brother since the wedding. I know how close the two of you were."

Ping gently touched the side of David's face, her eyes moist. "It's a very thoughtful present. Thank you."

CHAPTER FIFTY-TWO

After class the following day, Ping and Helen sat at a table in Saint Alp's Teahouse a few blocks off campus drinking bubble tea. Ping placed her straw over a pearl tapioca ball and sucked it into her mouth.

"What's the matter?" Helen asked in Mandarin. "You're frowning."

"Jianbo's here."

"What?"

"He came today. I told David I had classes, so he sent a car to pick him up at the airport."

"Why did you invite him?"

Ping stirred the tea with her straw, searching for another bottom-feeding tapioca ball. "I didn't invite him. It was David's idea—a surprise for my birthday."

Helen shook her head.

"Evidently Jianbo called a few weeks ago and told David he'd like to come to the United States. He claimed he was worried about me and wanted to make sure I was OK."

"Jianbo speaks English?"

"No. One of his friends interpreted—probably Feng, his best friend. I don't like him. He gives me the creeps."

After Ping successfully retrieved another tapioca ball, she told Helen that Jianbo was upset that it would take so long for her to become a US citizen. He wanted her to return to China immediately. "That's why he's coming, to drag me back."

"He can't make you go if you don't want to."

"He'll tell David the truth. I'll have no choice. David will make me leave. He's already asked me if I married him just to be a US citizen. If he finds out I married him to get my former husband citizenship..." Ping's voice trailed off.

Helen gave an understanding nod. "There is that possibility, but there's also another. You told me that David said the two of you had synergy, right?"

Ping nodded.

"That you have a special connection."

"Yes. But I betrayed him. I lied to him."

"Perhaps your connection will be strong enough to overcome what you did. After all, it was Jianbo's doing, not yours. Remember the invisible thread proverb?"

"Yes," Ping replied. "It says there's an invisible thread that connects those who are destined to meet, regardless of time, place, and circumstance. The thread may stretch or tangle. But it will never break." She sighed, a wistful look on her face. "If only that were true."

It was after five when Ping arrived home. As she slipped her key into the lock, her heart raced. She trembled at the thought of seeing Jianbo on the other side of the door. But it was David who greeted her. "Where have you been? I was getting worried."

"I had a study group after class."

"Did you forget Jianbo was coming?" David asked in a low voice. "Xavier told me he let him in about one o'clock. He's been here alone all afternoon."

"So sorry."

Ping dropped her book bag by the spiral staircase and followed David into the living room. She stopped abruptly, biting her lower lip, as she felt Jianbo's piercing stare. He sat on the couch, eyes narrowed, arms crossed. "So you finally decided to put in an appearance," he said in Mandarin.

"*Nie hao*," Ping responded, her stomach churning.

Jianbo got up, body rigid, clenching and unclenching his fists. "Why weren't you at the airport waiting for me?"

Ping said nothing. They stared at each other in an uncomfortable silence—former lovers unable to speak, former spouses unable to connect.

"What's the matter?" David asked Ping.

"Jianbo is upset that I did not pick him up at the airport."

"What did you say?" Jianbo asked in Mandarin.

Ping translated. Jianbo glared. "You could have at least warned me you wouldn't be there and to look for a driver holding a sign with my name on it. I wandered around the airport for a half hour before he found me. Where were you?"

"At the university."

"Where?"

"I'm finishing my degree."

"And that's more important than coming to get me?"

Ping lowered her eyes. David cleared his throat. "Can someone please tell me what you're talking about?"

"Jianbo is not happy."

"Tell him I have a treat for him. Tonight we're going to Per Se, one of the best restaurants in the city. That should cheer him up."

Two hours later, David, Ping, and Jianbo climbed out of a taxi in front of the Time Warner Center at Columbus Circle. An elevator took them to the fourth floor. In spite of his new suit, Jianbo felt out of place among the elegantly dressed diners at Per Se. He watched, a scowl on his face, as heads turned when Ping, her arm through David's, followed the maître d' to their table. Elegant in a slim-fitting emerald-green suit, she walked head high, chin lifted, seemingly oblivious to the admiring glances. The changes in her demeanor and level of self-confidence were even more dramatic than the last time Jianbo had seen her.

Feng had warned him. The longer Ping stayed married to the wealthy American, the less likely she would be to divorce him. He watched as the maître d' held the chair for her. She was obviously comfortable in her posh surroundings.

"I wanted to take you to one of the better dining establishments in Manhattan to give you an idea of what your competition would be if you opened a restaurant here," David said.

Jianbo's pulse quickened when Ping translated. The American hadn't forgotten.

"The menu changes daily here. I recommend the nine-course tasting menu."

Dressed in a dark suit and Armani tie, a waiter who had been hovering nearby rushed to describe each of the courses. Ping tried to translate, but she was unfamiliar with some of the food items. However, no translation was necessary to see Jianbo's enjoyment as he sampled coddled eggs laced with black-truffle puree and the chef's renowned "oysters and pearls"—Island Creek oysters, pearly tapioca, and Osetra caviar. He sat entranced, each course more exciting than the last. Even the very best offerings at the China Palace could not compete with these dishes. His mind raced. Perhaps he could come to the United States and work at a restaurant like this to improve his culinary skills.

"Is your brother enjoying the meal?"

From the expression on his face, the answer was obvious. But Ping's jaw dropped when Jianbo told her to ask David if he could arrange for him to come to New York to work at a restaurant like Per Se.

"I don't think that's possible," she replied.

"Ask the American."

"It wouldn't be a good idea for you to live here."

"I said, ask the American."

"What's the problem?" David said.

"Jianbo wants to know if you could get him a job in a New York restaurant like this one."

"I'm not sure. First he'd need to get a work permit."

Ping turned to Jianbo. "You would need a work permit," she said in Mandarin.

"How do I get this work permit?"

"Jianbo wants to know what he would need to do to get the work permit."

"He needs to formally apply to the immigration department. If you want, I'll have my lawyer check into it."

Ping turned to Jianbo. "He'll ask his lawyer to find out what needs to be done."

Eyes shining, Jianbo savored the four-story guinea hen that the waiter had placed before him. His old plan had morphed into a new one: come to America, live with Ping and David, and work at a top New York restaurant. Ping's marriage to the American would prove beneficial after all.

CHAPTER FIFTY-THREE

The next morning, Ping stood at the stove preparing breakfast when Jianbo snuck up behind her and put his arms around her waist. Ping jumped, nearly dropping the pan in which she was frying bacon. "What are you doing?"

Jianbo eyed Ping. "I heard David leave for work; we're alone now."

Ping cowered, holding the sizzling pan between them. Lunging forward, Jianbo grabbed the side of the pan. He screamed and pulled back. "My hand. I burned it."

"Wait here," Ping said, putting the pan back on the stove and shutting it off. Quickly she climbed the spiral stars to the bathroom, returning with a jar of *ching wan hung*.

Jianbo rocked back and forth cradling his hand. "Where did you get that?" he asked as Ping opened the burn ointment.

"Chinatown." She dipped her fingers into the salve. "Hold out your hand."

Jianbo did as instructed. Ping dabbed the ointment on the affected area. "There. That should help. Why don't you sit at the table and I'll finish making you breakfast?"

Ping held her breath as he walked to the dining room and took a seat, grateful for the accident. She shuddered, fearful that he would force her to be intimate.

"I've missed you so much," Jianbo said as Ping set two plates of scrambled eggs and bacon on the table. "I have not been with another woman since you left."

Ping lifted her hand as if to pat Jianbo's arm and then pulled it back.

"Do you and the American make love often?"

Ping lowered her eyes and said nothing.

"You're right. It's better if I don't know." Jianbo fiddled with the food on his plate. "I want to make love to you after we eat."

Ping flinched; she had a bitter taste in her mouth. "You can't ask that of me. While you are here, we are brother and sister."

Jianbo's dark eyes narrowed; he reached across the table and grabbed Ping's arm. She twisted free, bounded from her chair, and raced up the stairs. Once inside the bedroom she locked the door.

After showering and dressing, Ping crept silently down the steps. She could hear the TV from the living room. Jianbo was watching a cooking show. After placing a Mandarin guidebook to New York City and some money on the hallway table, she slipped out the front door.

⟞⟞ ⟝⟝

As she had the day before, Ping hung out with Helen after her last class. "Let's go to my apartment. Martin's at the university, and Nathan won't be home for another hour."

Grateful for any chance to avoid Jianbo, Ping readily agreed. They sauntered along the street, their faces warmed by the late winter sun. Trees awaiting spring finery lifted barren limbs skyward. Ping watched as a lone wrinkled leaf—a remnant from the previous fall—lost its grip and floated to the ground. A child wandered by with a nanny and stepped on the fallen leaf. He reminded Ping of Nathan.

"Does Nathan see Martin's older children?"

"No. His son and daughter were old enough to figure out what happened—why their parents divorced. I guess they blamed Nathan and me for breaking up their family. Martin sees them by himself about once a month."

"That's too bad."

"No, it's really for the best. Initially I tried. The children would stay with us on alternate weekends. Early on they adored Nathan— he was just a baby then—but they were very cold with me. One time his daughter Rebecca was going to a special dance at school. She saw a pearl necklace that had been my mother's and thought it would go nicely with her dress. Without hesitation, I loaned it to her. The next time I saw her, she gave me back a handful of pearls. 'It broke while I was dancing,' she said. 'It was probably a cheap necklace.'"

"How horrible," Ping replied.

"It was. She did this in front of Martin knowing I wouldn't do anything. You should have seen her; she was smirking when she handed me what remained of the necklace. She never apologized."

"What did Martin do?"

"He just looked disgusted. He didn't say anything to his daughter, but the next day he bought me a strand of pearls much more beautiful than my mother's. The few times I saw his daughter after that, I made sure I wore them."

Having reached the apartment, the two went inside. Helen checked the mailbox, pulling out several letters and a journal. "Martin will be pleased. An article he wrote is in this issue."

Upstairs, Helen removed the plastic from the *Journal of Finance* and opened it to show Ping Martin's article. "He'll be happy tonight."

Ping remembered the angry man who had rushed into the kitchen when Helen had broken the cup. She could not imagine him smiling.

After preparing and serving them each a cup of tea, Helen asked about Jianbo. Ping winced. "The minute David left this morning, he wanted to go to bed with me." Helen gave an understanding nod as Ping explained her morning ordeal and Jianbo's new plan to obtain a visa and work in the United States.

"Is David going to sponsor him?"

"I don't think so, why?"

"Then Jianbo will have a difficult time getting a visa."

A slow smile stretched across Ping's face. "That's good to know."

"How long is he staying?"

"He goes back the day after tomorrow. Fortunately, David will be at home this weekend, so I don't have to be alone with Jianbo."

They spent the rest of the afternoon discussing their classes and the courses they planned to take the following semester. Helen glanced at her watch. "Nathan will be home soon. Wait here. I'll be right back." She returned to the kitchen a few minutes later with two file folders.

"Here. Let me show you something. Martin's worried that if something happens to him, his first family will see that I get nothing. So he set things up to protect me and Nathan."

Helen opened the top file. In it was a financial statement from a brokerage firm. It had her son's name as the account holder and hers as the trustee.

"The money Martin puts into this account is for Nathan, for his education. I am in charge of the account." Helen opened the second file. "This is my account," she told Ping. "It is in my name with Nathan as beneficiary. There is not much in the accounts now, but every month Martin adds more. In this way, if anything happens to him, we will be taken care of."

Ping looked confused. "What is this word, *beneficiary?*"

"*Beneficiary* means if something happens to me, everything in the account goes to my son. It's all set up through an attorney. No one in his family can take this from me."

Ping's brow wrinkled. "Why are you showing me this?"

"You need to have David set up an account just for you. You told me he gives you money every week. You can add the money to the account. That way, if something happens you'll have more options."

"What do you mean?"

"You do want children, don't you?"

Ping nodded. "Of course."

"Right now you and David have a good marriage. But you don't know what the future will bring—especially with Jianbo in the picture. You know what they say: the rich man plans for tomorrow, the poor man for today."

Ping held the teacup in both hands and mulled over Helen's advice. "After Jianbo leaves, I'll talk to David about this account," she finally said. "Thanks for suggesting it."

CHAPTER FIFTY-FOUR

The remainder of the weekend passed without incident. Ping was able to avoid being alone with Jianbo. David appeared to enjoy, as he said, "tagging along." Early Saturday morning they walked to Chinatown. Clad in sweatshirts, pants, and sneakers, they joined a group composed mainly of Chinese who had co-opted a basketball court in Columbus Park to do tai chi. The group executed the forms in slow motion with a grace and ease that eluded David, one of the few Caucasians participating. In spite of his perceived clumsiness, he enjoyed the physical exercise but was eager to sample the offerings of nearby eateries from which tantalizing aromas perfumed the air.

Ping led David and Jianbo along the narrow, crowded streets to Mott Street and a restaurant recommended by Helen for breakfast. David found himself seated at a black table surrounded by Chinese men and women prattling on in Mandarin and Cantonese. The simply decorated eatery with the red tile floor was packed.

"We're lucky to get a table," Ping said to David. "Helen told me this place is jammed by local residents."

Jianbo perused the menu. "Tell the American, I'll order for us." Without waiting for a response, he told the waiter what they would have. The first dish to arrive was a congee with chopped beef. The waiter placed three bowls of the hot, thick, white porridge sprinkled with scallions and ginger in front of them. Next came plates of steamed rice crepes filled with fresh shrimp. Finally they sampled a seafood noodle soup served with a side of duck.

The patrons obviously enjoyed their breakfasts. From all sides came a symphony of lusty slurps as male diners picked up their bowls and downed the soup. A chorus of guttural burps provided the coda.

Ping winced as she watched the lack of manners based, of course, on American standards. What must David think? But instead of looking askance at those around him, he appeared to be enjoying himself. "I can't believe you eat all this for breakfast—and with such gusto."

"What did the American say?" Jianbo asked.

After Ping translated, he told her to tell David that the Chinese eat a big breakfast to give them energy for the whole day.

David grinned. "It's having the opposite effect on me. I feel like going home and taking a nap."

Before returning to the apartment, Jianbo insisted they stop at a market. He wanted to cook dinner that evening. "But David's made reservations at a restaurant for my birthday," Ping said in Mandarin.

"This will be my present to you," Jianbo announced. "But," he added, his hand extended. "You'll have to give me the money to buy the ingredients."

Dutifully, Ping translated Jianbo's request. David shrugged his shoulders. "If that'll make you happy, it's OK with me."

While Ping and David waited in a nearby tea shop, Jianbo walked up and down the aisles of the Hong Kong Supermarket, enthusiastically filling his shopping cart. When he emerged almost an hour later, arms laden with grocery bags, David hailed a cab to take them home. Ping was grateful for the change in dinner plans. With Jianbo preoccupied in the kitchen, she and David spent the afternoon reading and cuddled up together in their bedroom.

—<+ +>—

"This is terrific," David said as he savored the pear dessert. "What's in it?"

Ping explained how Jianbo was lucky enough to find Asian pears in the market. After steaming them, he filled the fruit with honey and Chinese dates.

"What did he say?" Jianbo asked.

"David really likes the dessert. I told him how you made it."

"Tell him in China we don't usually finish our meal with a sweet dessert. We prefer fruit. It's healthier."

David nodded. After taking a final sip of his wine, he continued. "Your brother is very talented. This meal was exceptional." Ping's translation produced a satisfied smile on Jianbo's lips.

Pushing back his chair from the table, David stood up. "Tell your brother I thoroughly enjoyed the dinner. But he'll have to excuse me. I'm going to the den to do a little work before bed." He bent down and kissed Ping on the cheek. Jianbo's face became sullen.

After David left the room, Ping picked up some dishes from the table and placed them in the sink. "I'll clean up," she said to Jianbo.

Jianbo remained in the dining room, elbows propped on the table, his head in his hands. Ping glanced up from putting the dishes in the dishwasher. "What's the matter?"

"I don't like seeing the American kiss you."

"I'm his wife."

Jianbo glared at Ping, a pinched expression on his face. "You look like you enjoyed it."

Ping rolled her eyes.

"Did you?"

Nothing good can come from this conversation, Ping thought. "It wasn't unpleasant."

"Humph."

"Can we talk about something else?"

"Are you riding with me to the airport tomorrow?"

"We both are."

"I only want to ride with you."

"David is coming, too," Ping said with finality.

That evening, Ping and David made love. At first, Jianbo's presence in their home had intimidated her. But tonight their lovemaking helped her cope with the anger she felt toward her ex-husband—anger that he acted like a puppeteer, pulling one string for her to marry David, pulling another to have David invite him into their home. And now he expected to come to New York and live with them?

Fingers around the necklace she wore as a talisman, Ping made a resolution. She would no longer remain passive; she would no longer play the puppet. No matter what Jianbo threatened, he would never again set foot in her home.

CHAPTER FIFTY-FIVE

The following evening Ping was cleaning up the kitchen after dinner. Jianbo was gone. For the first time in several days she felt she was no longer navigating a minefield. After turning on the dishwasher, she joined David, who was watching the evening news in the living room. He moved over on the couch and patted the vacated spot. Ping sat down next to him. David wrapped his arm around her, his head resting against hers.

"You're very pensive tonight," David said during the commercial break.

"I was thinking about some things."

"Like what?"

"In the taxi ride to the airport yesterday with Jianbo, we talked about him living with us while he possibly worked in a restaurant."

"We have a spare room..."

"I know." Ping fidgeted with a strand of her hair. "I'd rather he didn't come."

David pulled back, a puzzled look on his face. "I thought you wanted him to stay with us."

"I'm uncomfortable with him in the house. He still thinks of me as his...as his little sister and that I should do what he asks."

David raised an eyebrow. "Is my lovely wife developing an independent streak?"

"Perhaps. I don't like him telling me what I should do and feel. I think our house would be much happier without him living here."

"That's up to you. I'll do whatever you want."

David pulled Ping closer. "Is that all that's been bothering you?"

"I was also thinking about something Helen and I discussed a few days ago."

"Uh-oh," David said, feigning concern. "Whenever the two of you get together, it's usually trouble. What grand plan have you come up with this time?"

"There's no grand plan. She just thought I should ask you what I should do with the money I have in my checking account."

"How much is there?"

"Almost two thousand dollars."

"That much? Are you still sending some to your brother?"

Ping nodded.

"Your friend's right. If you're not going to spend it, you should be investing the money in something that earns a return."

The ring of the telephone interrupted their conversation. Ping walked to the kitchen to answer it.

"It's for you," Ping said handing the receiver to David. "It's your father." She listened to her husband's monosyllabic replies and watched as his face grew serious, his eyes avoiding hers.

"Is something the matter?" she asked after David hung up.

"No, it's some business matter my dad wants to discuss with me. I'm meeting him tomorrow for lunch."

"OK, so now can you tell me how to earn money with what I have in my account?"

"Let's talk about it another day. I have some work I need to do tonight."

Perplexed by his sudden change, Ping's eyes followed David as he left the room. Whatever his father had said to him on the phone had obviously upset him. His coolness made her wonder if the discussion had something to do with her.

CHAPTER FIFTY-SIX

"So, tell me again why I had to traipse all the way to midtown to have lunch?" David asked his father as the waiter pulled out the table to allow him access to the upholstered banquette.

"I'm meeting Christy around the corner at Lincoln Center for a play."

"Which one?"

"I don't remember the name. She's on this culture kick. She feels out of place when we're out with other couples and they talk about the theater or museums."

"I guess discussing *Project Runway* or *How to Become a Supermodel* doesn't cut it with your crowd."

David enjoyed his father's icy glare.

"Just joking, Dad. So, what do you recommend?" he asked as the waiter came over to their table. "It's been a while since I've eaten here."

"I'm having the New York strip. It's usually pretty good."

"I'll have the same," David said to the waiter. "Make mine rare."

Once their order was taken, David turned to his father. "So, what's this information you have about Ping that's so important?"

"You never did get the prenup, did you?"

David shook his head.

"Too bad, because I think she's out to get you." His father pulled an envelope from inside his vest pocket. "Sometimes you're too trusting. But I can see why you were taken in; your wife's a beautiful woman."

David folded his arms across his chest and looked at his father skeptically. Setting the envelope in front of his son, David Bennington Sr. said, "This is from a private eye I hired to find out about your wife—something you should have done before your marriage."

David's jaw tightened; his face flushed. "Dad, I told you not to do this. I don't want you interfering in my life. Do you understand?"

"You need to read the report," his father continued, ignoring David's protests. "The guy I hired was somewhat limited in what he could do. There are more restrictions on what's available on the Internet in China than here."

David pushed the envelope back to his father. "I'm not interested."

"Well, I can't force you to read it, but if I were you, I'd wonder why your wife wants two husbands."

David pulled back. "Are you crazy?"

"My investigator found something that shows Ping was married six months before your wedding."

David's mouth felt dry. "Let me see the envelope."

His father pushed it back to him. His palms moist, David opened it and pulled out the contents.

"It doesn't say who she married on that date."

"Like I said, it wasn't easy getting anything. The investigator said it takes sometimes a year or two before that type of information is made public."

"So, you're telling me my wife is a bigamist."

"I didn't say that; you did."

David placed the documents back in the envelope and handed it to his father. "I don't know how or where your private investigator got this information, but I don't believe it. It's either a misprint or a different Wang Ping. That's a popular Chinese name."

"Suit yourself, but I think you're making a mistake not following this up."

⊷ ⊶

Placing his briefcase on the floor, David transferred the bouquet of roses he was carrying to his left hand, searching for his keys with his right. Once inside the apartment, he picked up the briefcase and placed it by the stairs. David followed the aroma of sizzling pork to the kitchen, where Ping stood in front of the wok.

"For me?" she said, eyeing the roses. "What's the occasion?"

"No special occasion. I just want to thank my beautiful wife for being so wonderful."

Ping lowered the heat under the wok, wiped her hands on a kitchen towel, and took the flowers from her husband. "Thank you. They're lovely."

Taking a vase from the cupboard, she filled it with water. After carefully arranging the roses, she placed them in the center of the dining room table.

"Dinner will be ready in just a few minutes," Ping said, returning to the wok.

"Good, that will give me time to change out of this suit." David headed for the stairs.

Ping could hear her husband humming as he changed into sweatpants and a T-shirt and rejoined her in the kitchen.

"You sound happy," Ping said.

"I am. It's a gorgeous day, I'm with the woman I love, and I'm about to eat a wonderful meal."

"I hope it's not too much food. You had lunch with your father, didn't you?"

David took a seat at the table and debated whether or not to reveal to Ping his father's suspicions about her. In the end, he decided he needed to put his mind at rest; he needed to hear Ping refute the allegations. He told Ping about the private eye's claim that she had married someone before him. But rather than deny it, Ping began choking on the food she had just put in her mouth.

"What's the matter?" David asked anxiously, jumping from his chair and patting Ping on the back.

"I'm all right," Ping said, reaching for her water.

"Maybe I shouldn't have told you my father hired someone to check on you."

"No, that's all right. I'm just not hungry anymore." Nauseous and dizzy, Ping took her partially eaten meal into the kitchen. "I'm going upstairs to lie down for a few minutes."

David switched on the evening news and continued eating. Was Ping upset that her father-in-law distrusted her to the extent that he would hire a private investigator? Or were the investigator's findings true? After finishing his meal, David went upstairs. He found Ping lying on their bed, tears rolling down her cheeks. Sitting beside her, he hesitantly asked, "You aren't married to someone else, are you?"

Large tear-filled eyes stared at David in disbelief. "How can you ask me that? I am your wife, no one else's."

"Please forgive me," David said, taking Ping into his arms. "I was an insensitive jerk. I shouldn't have told you about what my father did." He slid his hand along her silken tresses as she sobbed uncontrollably on his shoulder.

"Look, Ping," David said when her crying subsided. "I don't care what anyone thinks. I trust you implicitly, and that's all that matters."

But instead of calming her, David's words had the opposite effect as Ping began to weep once again. Rocking her back and forth as they sat on the bed, she gradually calmed down.

"I was thinking about what we were discussing yesterday— about your visit with Helen," David said, avoiding the subject of his father. "We could set you up with a brokerage account. Then we could invest your money and make more money. We'd open the account with ten thousand dollars, and with your two thousand, you'd have enough to do some serious investing."

Ping wiped her eyes as David continued. "You could buy stocks, CDs—"

"CDs?" Ping interrupted. "I don't understand."

"Not compact discs," David smiled, realizing Ping's confusion. "CDs are certificates of deposit. I'll explain all this to you, and you can decide how you want to invest your money."

Ping lowered her head. *I am unworthy of such a kind and generous husband,* she thought.

CHAPTER FIFTY-SEVEN

May 2005

One evening as Ping and David sat at the dinner table, the phone rang. "Why do people call during dinner hour?" David asked, a pinched expression on his face. Ping's eyes followed him as he went into the kitchen to answer the phone.

"It's for you. The person is speaking Mandarin."

Ping jumped up. If the caller had been Jianbo, David would have recognized the voice. She rushed into the kitchen, a feeling of apprehension engulfing her.

"Who is this?" she asked in Mandarin.

"Feng."

Her palms began to sweat. "What do you want?"

"I am in New York City for a few days on business. I would like to see you."

"I'm afraid that's not possible. I am in school. I go to the university every day."

"Jianbo has given me a message to relay to you."

"What is it?"

"I don't want to tell you over the phone."

Beads of perspiration formed on Ping's forehead. Was this a ruse by Feng? Had Jianbo really sent a message?

"Perhaps I can come by your apartment?"

Ping swallowed hard. She had never trusted Feng. He might do something unconscionable if he came to the house, like reveal to David that Jianbo was not her brother. Jianbo had told her that Feng now spoke passable English. He would be able to talk with David.

"I'll come see you," Ping said. "Where and when should we meet?"

"How about tomorrow afternoon at three? I'm at the Four Seasons on Fifty-Seventh Street."

"I'll see you there."

Ping hoped her voice had not reflected the anxiety she felt. She turned to go back to the dining room and was startled to find David, arms folded, learning against the kitchen counter, staring at her. "Who was that?"

"A friend of Jianbo's. He's in New York and wants to see me. Jianbo has sent me a message."

"What does your brother want?"

She decided not to mention to David that Feng had not told her. "He wants to know if you have found him a job yet."

"What did you tell him?"

"That you hadn't."

David shook his head. "I really wish you'd tell your brother the truth...that you don't want him to come work in the United States."

CHAPTER FIFTY-EIGHT

The following afternoon, stylishly attired in a silk print dress with a matching sweater, Ping approached the receptionist at the Four Seasons Hotel. "Could you please call Mr. Li and tell him Mrs. Bennington is here?"

"Certainly."

The receptionist picked up the phone and dialed. "There's a Mrs. Bennington here to see you." After a pause, she hung up. "Mr. Li said to go right up to his room." She wrote down a room number on a slip of paper and handed it to Ping. "It's on the forty-ninth floor."

"Thank you," Ping said and walked over to the elevators, her high-heel slingbacks clicking on the marble floor.

She pressed the button to summon the elevator and waited, biting her lip. Entering the car, her stomach churned. Perhaps she should have met Feng in a public place, a restaurant, a teahouse. With each passing floor, Ping's anxiety increased. When the elevator stopped on the forty-ninth floor and the doors opened, she felt light-headed.

It was a short walk down the corridor to Feng's room. She rapped on the door. After a few minutes, Li Feng appeared, dressed in bathrobe and slippers. He was heavier than the last time she had seen him. His eyes almost disappeared beneath the folds of his eyelids. His round, puffy face resembled a full moon.

"So good to see you," Feng said bowing slightly. "Come in."

Ping sidestepped past him, clutching her pocketbook, keeping him in her gaze.

"Please take a seat," Feng said.

Entering the suite, Ping was struck by the view of Central Park visible through the large panoramic window. She crossed the room to better see the scene below. From this height, the horse-drawn carriages, cars, and pedestrians looked doll-like, children's toys with wheels that turned and limbs that walked.

"It's beautiful, isn't it?" Feng said, standing behind her. He was so close to Ping that she could feel his breath on her neck.

She stiffened and moved away. "Yes, it is." Taking a seat in a black leather chair next to a beige sofa and coffee table, Ping noticed French doors opened to reveal a large bed in the adjoining room.

"I've ordered some tea. It should be here shortly."

Feng plunked himself down on the sofa, which buckled under his weight. Patting the cushion beside him, he motioned to Ping to sit next to him.

"No, thank you. I'm comfortable here."

There was a knock at the door. Feng struggled to lift himself up, lumbered to the door, and opened it. Feng motioned to the waiter in the doorway to enter and put the food on the coffee table. After he arranged the silverware and the tea service, the waiter placed a plate of petit fours before Ping. Feng signed for the food.

"Close door, please," he instructed the waiter as he left.

Ping looked at her watch. "I don't have much time," she said in Mandarin, anxious to leave. "What did you want to see me about that was so important?"

"Jianbo is very concerned," Feng said, picking up the pot and slowly pouring the tea. "He hasn't received a letter from you in quite a while. He wants to know why the American has not yet found him a job."

"Finding a chef position is not easy...especially for a foreigner."

Feng handed a cup of tea to Ping. She reached for the saucer, but he didn't release it. "I hope you're not playing games because if you are, you'll regret it," he said, finally letting go of the plate. "Did you find out how long it will be before you become an American citizen?"

"I've already told Jianbo. Three years."

As Ping spoke, Feng's eyes wandered from her face to her chest. She shifted uncomfortably in the chair.

"Three years." Feng noisily sipped his tea. "So, effectively," he finally said. "Jianbo is screwed."

Ping lowered her eyes.

"Jianbo told me to tell you that if the American cannot find him a job, he refuses to wait more than one year. This wasn't the agreement you had."

Ping's jaw tightened. "The agreement we had? He should have found out all the rules for citizenship before he divorced me. As far as I'm concerned, we no longer have any agreement."

"Does that mean you plan on staying with the American?"

"I didn't say that." Ping pulled a handkerchief from her pocketbook and patted her brow. "But Jianbo and I are no longer married. He is not in a position to tell me what to do."

"He thinks otherwise. And he's willing to take you to court over this issue."

"To court? Doesn't he realize the foolishness of that action? It would be a Chinese court deciding a case involving a Chinese woman living in the United States married to an American citizen. A Chinese court has no jurisdiction here. And besides, Jianbo and I are officially divorced."

Feng was silent; he closed his eyes. Ping was uncertain whether the slight bob of his head indicated agreement or if he were dozing off. She picked up her teacup.

When Feng finally spoke, she jumped. "Well, then you give us no choice but to go to your American and tell him about your arrangement."

"You wouldn't…"

"I doubt whether the American would want to stay with a woman who only married him to gain citizenship for herself and her ex-husband."

"It would be your word against mine."

"Oh, really? Remind me again who the American thinks Jianbo is. Your brother. Isn't that right?" Feng's triumphant grin made Ping shudder.

She knew Feng was right. He had the upper hand. David would certainly leave her if he learned the truth.

"It doesn't sound like you're eager to divorce the American. Jianbo said he was very rich. I'm sure you live in a fine home."

The empty teacup rattled as Ping placed it on the coffee table.

"You've always been beautiful," Feng said, his eyes moving up and down her body. "But now you are also elegant. Wealth agrees with you."

Reaching across the coffee table, Feng grabbed Ping's left hand. He looked at the large solitaire diamond on her engagement ring, her diamond-studded platinum wedding band, and her Rolex watch. "These are very expensive," Feng said as if to prove his point.

"I wouldn't know. David bought them for me."

"Maybe he will let you keep them when you divorce."

Ping glared at Feng and pulled back her hand. Unfazed, he reached down for the pot and poured them each another cup of tea. Ping made no move toward the tea. She leaned back in her chair, arms folded across her chest.

"Personally," Feng continued, offering Ping a cigarette that she refused, "I feel Jianbo has not thought this thing through. Here's what might work to satisfy all parties involved. Why not pay him off?"

Ping tilted her head slightly. Feng lit a cigarette and exhaled, the smoke forming a circle as it exited his mouth.

"Jianbo wants to open a restaurant. I could convince him that it doesn't have to be in America. Why not Chongqing? With enough money, he could hire the best chefs. Success would be guaranteed."

Feng leaned back on the couch and pursed his lips, producing another smoke circle. "Why not give Jianbo, say $100,000. Certainly your wealthy American husband has that much available. I'm sure that I could make Jianbo see that this is a reasonable compromise. Then you could both get on with your lives."

"Are you blackmailing me?" Ping asked, eyebrows pinched together, lips curled.

"Not at all. I'm offering you a sensible solution to this dilemma."

"I would rather David learn the truth and leave me than do something so despicable."

"I hope you realize I'm only trying to help." Feng moved to the edge of the couch as he placed his cigarette in an ashtray on the table.

"I have one final offer," Feng said, his mouth twisting into a lascivious grin.

"And what is that?"

"I'll be coming to New York frequently over the next few months until this deal with my father-in-law's company is finalized. If we could have tea and talk like this when I come, I can make Jianbo see that he must be patient—that you and your husband are hopeful he will soon have a job in an American restaurant."

"What do you mean, have tea and talk like this?"

Without responding, Feng rose, grabbed Ping's arms, and pulled her to the couch.

"What are you doing?" she said, struggling to free herself.

"I've always been attracted to you. You are so beautiful," Feng said breathing heavily and shoving Ping down on the sofa. "I want to make love to you; I want you to be mine."

"You're crazy," Ping said pushing against his chest. "How can you betray your best friend?"

Feng forced himself on top of her, pinning Ping to the sofa. She felt one hand lift up her skirt and squeeze her thigh. He shoved the other down the front of her dress to fondle her breasts. Covering her lips with his, he forced his tongue into her mouth. Ping clamped down hard on the fat blob between her teeth. Feng jumped up from the couch in pain.

"Bitch," he said and slapped her face. He lunged toward her. She pulled away but not before he ripped her dress. Mustering all the strength within her, she pushed against his heavy-set frame. Caught off guard, Feng slid off the couch. Ping swung her legs around and thrust her high heels into her assailant's side, pushing him into the coffee table. She raced to the door and opened it. As she left the room, she heard the crash of the table overturning and the sound of shattering glass.

In the corridor, Ping glanced furtively behind her. Although Feng was still in his room, she could hear him cursing and threatening her. She ran toward the exit sign, fearful that if she waited for the elevator he would catch her. She bounded down two flights of stairs. When she realized Feng was not behind her, Ping left the stairwell and took the elevator. In the lobby, she fled toward the entrance, high heels echoing on the tiled floor. Outside, she asked the doorman to get her a cab.

"Ping?" said a voice behind her. Turning around, she was surprised to see Marjorie.

"Are you all right?"

Ping crossed her arms across her chest to hide the rip in her dress. "I'm fine," she responded, smiling wanly.

Marjorie lifted her sunglasses and leaned forward. "You have a red mark on your cheek, and you're trembling. Are you sure everything is OK?"

Ping backed away. "I'm fine."

Just then a cab pulled up. The doorman opened the taxi door. Ping tipped him and got in. "Give my best to David," Marjorie said as the cab sped off.

CHAPTER FIFTY-NINE

Mrs. Bennington's estate

Roger slumped into a chair by the side of the tennis court and wiped his face with a towel. "Whew, you really had me running today."

"That felt good," David said, placing his tennis racket inside its case and pulling up a chair next to his friend. "Got rid of a lot of tension."

"From what?"

"Work."

"Is everything OK?"

"Couldn't be better. But I'm spending a lot of time at the office. I'm working on another Chinese joint venture with a pretty big client. If it's successful, my boss is talking about sending me to Shanghai to head up the new office."

"I thought you were out of the running."

"I was, but after my boss and his wife went out to dinner with Ping and me, he changed his mind. She was absolutely charming. They were both taken with her."

"I'm glad things are working out so well. Is Ping finding enough to do?"

"She's doing quite a bit. In addition to her courses at NYU, she's taking art lessons. That's where she is this morning."

"Thanks, Ulrich," David said as the groundskeeper gave the two men large glasses of ice water.

Roger nodded appreciatively to Ulrich. He inhaled, breathing deeply, less it seemed from the strenuous workout than in preparation for what he was about to tell David.

"We've been friends for a long time," Roger began. "If not I wouldn't feel it was necessary to tell you this."

"Tell me what?"

"Something Marjorie mentioned."

"For God's sake, Roger, tell me already."

"Marjorie was walking by the Four Seasons last Wednesday when she saw Ping run out of the hotel."

David's body became tense. "Is she sure it was Ping?"

"Yes. She spoke with her. Marjorie said she looked like she had been in some sort of a tussle—there was a red blotch on her cheek. She thinks her dress was torn."

David clenched his jaw. He had seen the mark on Ping's face. She had told him she had walked into a closet door. What the hell was going on?

"Are you suggesting that my wife is doing something untoward in Manhattan hotels?"

"Of course not. I just thought you might want to know."

"I do. Thanks for telling me. I'll ask Ping about it when I get home."

"I'm sure it's nothing," Roger said.

David was silent for a moment, feeling an overwhelming need to confide in his friend. "Ping wasn't a virgin."

David's pronouncement seemed to surprise Roger. "So, what woman is these days?"

"I thought she was. She seemed so innocent. Her brother wouldn't let her out of his sight. He played the chaperone whenever we were together."

"Are you disappointed she wasn't?"

"Somewhat. I thought I was marrying someone with no baggage, no—"

"Sex life?" Roger asked.

"I guess I was naïve. My mom suggested we get tested before the wedding. I told her it wasn't necessary."

"Sorry to interrupt," Ulrich said, approaching the two men, "but Mrs. Bennington told me to tell you that lunch is ready."

"Thanks," David said. The two friends grabbed their tennis bags and towels and headed back to the house.

After lunch Roger excused himself. He and Marjorie had plans for the afternoon. David saw his friend to his car and then joined his mother for coffee on the patio.

"It's too bad Ping didn't come with you today."

"She takes an art class on Saturday morning."

"She's quite talented."

"Yes, she is."

Greta appeared briefly to refill their coffee cups. "No, thanks," David said. "I've got to go. I'll call you later this week, Mom."

CHAPTER SIXTY

The summer sun warmed David's face as he drove his Mercedes convertible across the George Washington Bridge toward Manhattan. The dark blue car cruised down the Henry Hudson Parkway, the breeze whipping through his hair. To observers, the driver would probably appear carefree and relaxed, the turmoil he felt inside well hidden. David had suppressed his concern that his wife probably had other lovers before they married. But after Roger's comments, he wondered if this was not the least of his worries. Was Ping having an affair? He had to confront her.

———

"How was your tennis game?" Ping asked, greeting her husband from the couch in the living room.

"Good."

Still in his tennis shorts, David sat next to her with his hands folded between his legs, eyes cast downward.

"What's the matter?"

"I need to ask you something," David said, turning toward Ping. "And you must be truthful with me."

Her heart pounded. Had Feng made good on his threat to tell David about Jianbo?

"Were you at the Four Seasons Hotel Wednesday afternoon?"

"Yes."

"You didn't mention going there."

"I went to see the friend of Jianbo's who called the other night."

"Who is he?"

"His name is Li Feng. His father-in-law runs a cement plant in Chongqing, where I grew up. Feng is in New York to meet with some Americans who want to invest in the plant."

"Why didn't you invite him here?"

"He doesn't speak much English. He would have felt uncomfortable."

"What did he want?"

"He had a message from Jianbo."

"What was it?" David sounded like a lawyer, pulling bits of information from his star witness.

"He wanted to know if you had found him a job yet."

"You must tell Jianbo the truth. As I said the other night, this is not fair. He thinks I'm the one who doesn't want him here, when it's you."

"I'm sorry."

Eyes closed, David rubbed his brow. After a few minutes, he turned toward Ping.

"I don't want you to take this the wrong way, but have you been intimate with other men before me?"

Ping looked confused. "What do you mean?"

"Have you gone to bed with other men?"

A pained expression crossed her face. "Well?" David said, raising an eyebrow.

"Yes."

"How many?"

Ping moved away from David, her face ashen, her lips trembling.

"One," she said as tears slid down her cheek.

"Only one?"

Ping nodded.

Although he asked no more questions, Ping knew that she had opened Pandora's box with her answer.

CHAPTER SIXTY-ONE

David slept fitfully for the next several nights. He had dreams of Ping with other men. In some, he would return home and she would be gone. When he awoke he was relieved to find her by his side. At work, he often found himself wondering about the circumstances involving Ping's former lover. Rationally, David knew he could not begrudge her one partner when he'd had so many. Yet the notion of Ping being intimate with someone else gnawed at him incessantly.

Three days after their discussion, David returned home from work to find Ping preparing dinner. Before his marriage, David would generally eat meals out. Now, except for business dinners and evenings with friends, he was happy to eat in. Ping was an excellent cook.

"Smells great. What is it?" David asked, peering into the covered casserole.

"Braised chicken with lemon. I got started late. It needs to simmer for about forty-five minutes more."

"Good. I wanted to talk to you."

"I have something to tell you, too."

David opened a bottle of wine and pulled two glasses from the cabinet.

"No wine for me," Ping said.

"That's not like you. Is something the matter?"

"No. Things couldn't be better."

David looked at his wife quizzically and then poured himself a glass. "Come; let's sit and talk."

"You start," Ping said, as she wiped her hands on a towel before joining David on the couch.

"I probably shouldn't ask you this, but I can't get it out of my mind."

Ping's cheerful expression disappeared. Trembling fingers rubbed the back of her neck.

"I want our marriage to be completely honest and open. I need to know about your lover—the man you slept with before me."

Ping sighed. "The man I slept with before you was my husband."

David's jaw dropped. He stared at Ping incredulously. "Did I hear correctly? Your husband?"

"Yes, it was a marriage arranged through a broker. It lasted only a few months."

"Didn't you think I deserved to know this before we were married?"

"I didn't think it was important."

David stood up and paced. "Not important? Are you serious?"

Her face flushed; Ping lowered her eyes.

"My God, Ping. This is major. How could you not tell me?"

"You never asked."

David held his head in his hands and slowly shook it from side to side. "This isn't the kind of question you ask your fiancée. This is something I would expect you to tell me."

Ping bit her lower lip and looked away.

"Are you divorced?"

She nodded.

"Did you have children?"

"No. We were married for only a few months."

"Why did you divorce?"

"My husband was unkind to me. He beat me. He asked me to do things that were not in keeping with my marriage vows."

"Such as?"

"Things I don't want to talk about now."

The two sat in silence on opposite ends of the couch.

"I need to finish cooking dinner," Ping said, getting up from the sofa.

David made no move to stop her as she walked into the kitchen. Checking the chicken, she watched David slowly climb the spiral staircase to the second floor.

When Ping announced that dinner was ready, David descended the stairs, his demeanor unchanged.

"Please talk to me," Ping said.

"I'm sorry; learning that you had been married is a real shock. What else don't I know? What other secrets are there? I don't ever want to be surprised like this again."

"There's only one thing that you don't know, and I just found out today. It was what I wanted to tell you when you came home."

"What?" David asked, preparing for the worst.

"I'm pregnant."

CHAPTER SIXTY-TWO

July 2005

"There's your baby," Dr. Robey said as he moved the transducer over Ping's swelled abdomen.

"I can see him," David said, watching the fetus on the monitor. "Look, there are his arms and legs."

Ping clasped her husband's hand tightly, overjoyed to see the tiny child forming within her. Transfixed by the image on the screen, she watched the positions the fetus assumed as Dr. Robey slid the scanner across her belly. There was a commonality among the fetal poses; they all resembled a question mark. And that's how Ping thought of her unborn child. Would the baby look Caucasian or Asian? Would her child be healthy? Was she carrying a boy or a girl?

As if reading her mind, Dr. Robey told the couple that everything looked fine. The baby was about twenty weeks old. "I can tell the gender of the child," he said. "Would you like to know whether you're having a son or a daughter?"

"Yes," said David enthusiastically.

"No," Ping said firmly.

David eyed Ping curiously. "Then I guess it's no."

"That's fine," Dr. Robey said as he shut off the machine. "I have many couples who wait until birth. They want to be surprised."

The doctor wrote some notes on a chart. "Have the receptionist schedule another appointment in about a month. If there's any problem before then, just give me a call."

After the doctor left, David helped Ping off the examination table. As she slipped on her clothes, he said, "I'm just curious. Why don't you want to know the baby's sex?"

"I just don't want to."

⊷ ⊶

"Ping, wake up; you're having a nightmare."

Opening her eyes, Ping stared at the man next to her; relieved to see it was David. "I had such a bad dream," Ping said. "I dreamed something happened to the baby."

David pulled her close to him, running his hands soothingly down her back. "It's OK. The doctor said everything's fine. Are you worried about something?"

"I don't know. Maybe it was the question about gender."

"I don't understand."

"Do you have a preference?"

"Honestly? No. I just want a healthy child."

"You wouldn't be upset if we had a daughter?"

"Absolutely not. I'd be delighted—especially if she looked like you."

The red glow from the numbers on the digital clock on the bedside table announced it was 2:30 a.m. David turned on the lamp.

"What's the matter?" Ping asked, eyes half-shut adjusting to the light.

"I don't know. You tell me. Something's been bothering you since the visit to the doctor."

Ping fluffed up the pillow and placed it behind her back. "I think you want a son. You kept referring to the baby as *he*."

"And if I did?"

"Would you ask me to abort if it wasn't a boy?"

David propped himself up, slowly shaking his head from side to side, a confused look on his face. "Don't you know me better than that?"

"I'm sorry," she said, lowering her eyes. "In my country, there is the one-child rule. Many husbands force their wives to abort or put their female child up for adoption."

"We're not in China, Ping. We don't do that here."

Eyes shining, Ping moved closer to David. "I guess I was being unreasonable. I'll call Dr. Robey in the morning to find out whether the baby is a boy or a girl."

"It is morning," David said, turning to switch off the lamp. His hand in midair, he suddenly changed his mind. "Wait a minute. If there's a one-child rule, how is it that you have a brother?"

Ping's face flushed. Hesitating briefly, she finally said, "The rule only applies to couples in the city. If you live in the country, two children are allowed to help with the work."

"But weren't you born in Chongqing?"

"I was," Ping stammered, "but Jianbo was born in the country. We moved to Chongqing when my mother was pregnant with me."

As David turned off the light, Ping slid under the covers. She felt like a clay figure in the rain being washed away by lies. Half truths begot more half truths; small falsehoods gave way to larger falsehoods. If only she could tell David the truth. She placed her hands flat on her stomach, and suddenly she felt it.

"David, the baby just kicked. Here, feel it." Grabbing David's hand, she pressed it against her abdomen.

"I can feel it," he said excitedly. "That's some kick. This baby's either going to be a place kicker for the New York Giants or a Rockette at Radio City."

Ping had no idea what David meant, but his enthusiasm convinced her he would be pleased with their child—son or daughter.

CHAPTER SIXTY-THREE

October 2005

The sudden gust of wind blowing through the partially open window caused the front door to slam shut. Helen had just said goodbye to the last of the shower guests. She wandered back into the living room, where Ping sat in the center of the couch surrounded by baby outfits, rattles, layette sets, pieces of pastel wrapping paper, pink ribbons and bows, paper plates with the remains of chocolate cake, and amber plastic cups, some empty, some half-filled with soda.

"Let me help you clean up," Ping said, trying unsuccessfully to hoist her rounded form up from the couch.

"Sit still. Relax. I have plenty of time to take care of this mess before Martin and Nathan come back from the movies." She removed a box from the couch and sat next to Ping.

"Thanks for giving me this shower."

"I was happy to do it. You received such nice gifts." As if to prove her point, Helen held up a tiny pink dress with matching booties.

"I hope I have a daughter one day," she sighed, putting the outfit back in its box. "Girls' clothes are so much cuter than boys'."

"Do you and Martin plan on having more children?"

"One day maybe, but not right now. He's stuck paying college tuition for his son's final year and for his daughter—she's only a sophomore. Plus there is the cost for Nathan's private school. Raising children in New York City is not cheap."

Ping shimmied to the edge of the couch. Placing her palms flat on each side, she managed to lift her body upright. "Jianbo used to say I moved like a gazelle. It's a good thing he can't see me now. With this belly, I look and walk like a hippopotamus."

"Have you told him you're pregnant?"

"No. But he's been telephoning from the hotel where he works and writing me threatening letters. He wants me to return home immediately. He told me he'd give me one more month to settle my affairs. After that, he would tell David everything."

"What will you do?"

"Nothing for the time being. I don't see how he can carry out his threat. Jianbo doesn't speak English. I usually bring in the mail, so if he tries to have something translated I can intercept it. As long as he's in China and I'm here, I'm safe."

"Why don't you just confess everything to David? Then you wouldn't have to worry about Jianbo."

"David would leave me."

"Are you sure?"

"He asked me if I had been intimate with anyone before I married him. I told him yes, with my first husband. I didn't say it was Jianbo. He was upset with me for not having told him before our wedding."

"Would he still have married you?"

"I doubt it. He had this image of me being pure, of him being my first lover. I don't think he would have married a divorced woman. I'm sure he would have questioned my motives."

"You mean he would have suspected it was a marriage of convenience?"

Ping nodded.

"And what about Jianbo's friend? What's his name?"

"Feng."

"Yes. Are you worried he'll tell David?"

"No. Same issue. According to Jianbo he speaks English. But he doesn't really. Since Jianbo can only ask, "How do you want your eggs?" anyone who can say more than that he thinks is fluent."

Helen giggled. "Plus," Ping continued. "Feng doesn't dare show his face to me."

She bit her lip. "He tried to rape me when I saw him at the hotel."

Helen gasped, fingers touching parted lips. "You never told me that."

"I was ashamed," Ping replied softly, lowering her eyes.

The telephone rang. "I'll be right back," Helen said as she squeezed Ping's shoulder on the way to the kitchen. Ping looked at the baby toys and clothes and patted her belly. She couldn't wait until her daughter's birth.

Picking up a paper plate from the coffee table Ping scraped the remains from one onto another. When she reached for a third plate, Helen, returning from the kitchen, grabbed her arm. "Please," she said. "I'll do that. Just sit and relax."

Slowly lowering her body, Ping sat down on one of the dining room chairs Helen had brought in for the guests. "It's easier for me to get up from this chair than from the sofa."

"Have you taken steps to protect you and your child in case David finds out?" Helen asked.

"David helped me open a brokerage account. Every week I add money to it."

"Good. Now, after the baby is born you need to change the beneficiary—the person who will inherit the money if you die,"

Helen said. "Right now the beneficiary is probably David. After the birth, change it to your daughter."

Ping took a pen from her handbag on the table and wrote on the back of a piece of wrapping paper. "Anything else I should do?"

"Yes. You need to have David set up an education fund for the baby with—and this is important—you as trustee. That way, if something happens to David or if you separate, you will be in charge of the funds in the account."

Ping finished writing the word *trustee* and put the scrap of paper and pen in her handbag.

"Who will help you when the baby comes?"

"David said we could hire a nurse. But what I really want is to have my Auntie Yi Ma come stay with us."

"Is David OK with that?"

"Yes, but Auntie Yi Ma knows nothing about my situation. She still thinks Jianbo and I are married."

"Tell her the truth."

"I'm afraid she won't come if I do. She and Baba would never forgive me for bringing shame on our family name. They would be upset that Jianbo and I divorced and especially that I married an American whom they've never met."

"Then don't tell your aunt why you want her to come—make up some reason that you need to see her. After the baby arrives, she won't leave."

"I'm so tired of lying and making up stories. It's like walking through thick brush where there are brambles waiting to scratch and rip my skin. So far I have remained relatively untouched, but one day I'll slip and fall and be covered with cuts and blood."

"Or," Helen said, "you might be lucky and come through unscathed."

CHAPTER SIXTY-FOUR

The taxi driver opened the trunk as Ping slid across the back-seat of the car, exiting with difficulty. A brisk autumnal wind whipped against her. She wrapped her scarf around her neck. "Good evening, Mrs. Bennington," the doorman said as he helped Ping out of the vehicle. "Should I have the porter take the packages up to your apartment?"

"Yes, thank you, Xavier." Ping walked to the rear of the cab to supervise the removal of the gifts from the car and to pay the driver.

"I'll have these sent right up." Xavier held the door open as Ping entered the building. The scent of burning wood greeted her as she walked into the apartment. She hung her coat in the closet and went into the living room, where David was sitting on the couch facing the fireplace.

"Hi," she said, kissing her husband.

"Hi, honey, how was the shower?"

"It was so nice. Wait until you see all the lovely things we received. Xavier's sending them up."

Plopping down on the couch, Ping leaned against David and shut her eyes, soothed by the warmth of the fire.

"There's the doorbell. Don't get up; you look tired. I'll take care of everything," David said.

Eyes still closed, hands resting on her protruding belly, Ping listened as David and the porter carried the gifts up the spiral staircase into the baby's room. Shortly after she heard the front door close, David reappeared by her side.

"Are you OK?" David asked as he brushed away a strand of hair from in front of her eyes.

"Just tired. It's been a long day."

"How many of your friends were at the shower?"

"Around ten or so."

"You should invite them here sometime."

"I'd feel funny," Ping said.

"Why?"

"Our home is so beautiful. Most of my friends from the program have part-time jobs. They struggle to get by. They live in dormitories or share apartments near campus. I'm uncomfortable having so much."

"Maybe someday you'll get used to having money," David said with a bemused smile.

"I doubt it." Ping placed her hand on her stomach. "The baby just kicked again. She's really active this evening." She turned to David. "She probably wants to see her gifts. Come, I'll show you what my friends gave us."

Slowly Ping led the way up the stairs to the nursery that had remained unfurnished until the previous month. When the doctor informed the couple they would be having a daughter, Ping and Mrs. Bennington worked together to prepare the vacant room. Mrs. Bennington wanted a sleigh crib in antique silver with matching changing table and dresser. Appalled at the price tag, Ping nixed the opulent furniture in favor of a standard white crib set.

Her only extravagance was a padded white wicker rocking chair and matching ottoman where she could sit and nurse the baby.

Ping glanced around the room, pleased with how it looked. A pink daisy valence stretched across the large bedroom window. Quilted nursery bedding and a rug repeated the daisy theme. The room was warm and welcoming, perfect for her daughter.

David and the porter had placed the pile of shower gifts on the rug. Ping moved some of the boxes and sat on the floor. David patiently watched as she opened each gift to show him. "It's so exciting," Ping said. "In just a few months she'll be here with us—wearing these clothes, playing with these toys."

"You know, we haven't picked out a name for our daughter. Any thoughts?"

"Yes. I would like to name her Lei Lei."

"Lei Lei?"

Ping fingered the *mother-daughter* necklace that rarely left her neck. "My mother's name."

Face beaming, David walked over to Ping and helped her up from the floor. He kissed her and held her closely. "Lei Lei. It's a lovely name. Does it have a special meaning?"

"Flower bud. My mother never had the chance to fully blossom. I'm hoping our daughter will."

Suddenly David's cell phone rang. "Damn, the phone," he said reaching into his pocket.

"Don't answer," Ping said, enjoying the embrace.

"It's my mother. She usually doesn't call unless it's important."

David sat down on the rocker while Ping began folding the gifts and putting them away.

"What's up?"

"Well, it's not your fault that the plumber went out of business." David winked at Ping. "After the mess he made repairing the pipes, the leaking ceiling, the ruined hardwood floors, we had to sue. That's what you said you wanted…We don't have our lawyers on retainer for nothing. You were really happy with the judgment and the settlement, don't you remember?...I know it was excessive, but it's nice to know our attorneys are worth what we're paying them...Look, the bankruptcy might be a ploy so he doesn't have to pay...Oh, he did pay most of it. Mom, it's not your fault. If he had done the job you had hired him to do, this never would have happened...Ping's fine. She just got back from a baby shower some of her friends from school threw for her. She's been showing me the gifts...No, we have everything we need and then some for your granddaughter's arrival...OK. I'll call you tomorrow."

David turned the cell phone off and put it back in his pocket. "There, no more disturbances this evening," he said getting out of the chair.

"What was the matter with your mother?"

"She had problems with the plumber who supposedly repaired the pipes in the master bath. The first time my mother took a shower, water leaked through the ceiling and ruined a good portion of the hardwood floors below. I thought she had told you the story."

"She did. She was very upset. Didn't the plumber claim the leakage came from—what do you call it?—the shower pan?"

"Yes. He refused to do anything. So we took him to court."

"And the judge ruled in favor of your mother?"

"The plumber had to pay my mother for the repairs, which were substantial. They were enough to put him out of business."

"Does the plumber have a family?"

"I don't know. What I do know is our lawyers did a helluva job."

"Why do you say that?"

"I don't think anyone ever checked to verify the plumber's story about the shower pan. His attorney wasn't very good."

"And yours was?"

"They're the best. You see, Ping, that's one advantage of having money. To win, especially in the courtroom, you have to pay top dollar for the best lawyers to represent you."

"I still think it's sad to put someone out of business. What if he has a wife who's pregnant? What if there are other children to support?"

"You're as bad as my mother. As I told her, if he had fixed the problem like he was supposed to, none of this would have happened. Let's go to bed."

As she shut off the pink daisy light on the dresser and felt the baby moving inside her, Ping grew somber. What if David found out she had deceived him? Would he use his powerful attorneys to send her back to China? Would he use them to keep Lei Lei with him? Sleep eluded her that night.

CHAPTER SIXTY-FIVE

"Damn, who could be calling at this hour?" David rolled over and checked the alarm clock. "It's two a.m."

"I'll get it," Ping said, jumping out of bed. She had no doubt who it was.

"*Nie hao*," Jianbo said as she picked up the phone in the baby's room.

"Please don't call at this time. It's two in the morning here. You woke David."

Ping heard a disgusted snort on the other end of the line. "So sorry. Will he ever forgive me?"

"What do you want?"

"It's been weeks since I've heard from you. I thought you'd be happy to hear my voice."

Ping shifted uncomfortably. "I've been busy with classes."

"Has the American found me a job in a restaurant like he promised?"

"He's asked around, but so far he hasn't found anything."

"I'm surprised. Feng had his secretary look for chef positions in New York City restaurants on the Internet, and there are many."

"Then why don't you apply?"

"It's a complicated procedure. It would be much easier with the American's help."

Ping sighed. "I'll see what I can do."

"You don't sound very enthusiastic. I thought you'd want me to come live with you."

Ping cringed and said nothing.

"Well?"

"I would be…I would be very uncomfortable if you lived with David and me."

"Why?"

"I cannot be a wife to two men."

"I wouldn't ask you to be."

Ping remained silent.

"I said, I wouldn't ask you to be."

"You wanted to sleep with me when you visited."

"It was wrong of me, I know." Jianbo's voice sounded sincere. "It was so hard to see you and not want you close to me. When I live with you and the American, I promise to act only as a brother."

Ping felt a thickness in her throat. Would it be so terrible if Jianbo lived with them? If she and David helped him with his career? After all, she was living well while Jianbo was struggling.

She shook her head. What was she thinking? Jianbo was born under the sign of the Monkey—the most manipulative of creatures. Lies and even tears are part of the Monkey's bag of tricks to get what it wants. Jianbo would do or say anything to work in a New York restaurant. She thought of the Chinese saying *Fool me once, shame on you; fool me twice, shame on me.* She had believed him when he had told her she would only be married to David for a few months. Although she had inadvertently benefited from Jianbo's lies and schemes, she could never trust him.

"So you will think of me only as a sister and not as a wife?" she asked sweetly, thinking two could play this game.

"Of course. As you have reminded me many times, we are no longer married."

"But that hasn't stopped you before from trying to sleep with me."

"I truly regret the way I behaved when we were alone in the apartment. I promise to respect your position as the American's wife when I come live with you."

"Then, I'll see what I can do."

━━┥┝ ┥┝━━

Ping slipped into bed trying not to wake David, but he wasn't asleep. "Who was that?"

"Jianbo."

"Was it about the restaurant job?"

Ping nodded.

"Did you finally tell him you didn't want me to find a job for him? That you didn't want him living with us?"

"Yes, I told him it was not a good idea."

"Did you tell him about the baby?"

Ping flinched and squeezed her eyes shut. "Yes," she murmured barely audibly.

"What did he say?"

"He was happy for us."

David put his arm around Ping. She snuggled closer. "Are arranged marriages common in China?"

"Why do you ask me that?"

"I was talking to a colleague who said they weren't done that often anymore."

"That is true."

"So why was yours arranged?"

"My father thought it was time for me to wed. He hired a marriage broker to find a suitable mate."

"Did he get a refund because it didn't work out?"

Ping stiffened. Why would he ask her such a question? Was he making a joke?

"You told me in addition to beating you, your former husband did something worse."

"Yes."

"What was it?"

Ping's chin quivered; her mouth felt dry. She had told enough lies tonight. Swallowing hard, she said softly, "He asked me to sleep in another man's bed."

"Why?"

"Please. I don't want to talk about it. It fills me with shame."

David wrapped his arms around Ping and drew her close. She sobbed as feelings of unworthiness engulfed her. "Please don't cry," David said. "Forgive me for probing."

Cradled in his arms, Ping felt safe. Like the tiger, David was powerful. Like the tiger, he would ward off evil and all that would bring her harm. Like the tiger, he would protect her—at least until he learned the truth about their marriage.

CHAPTER SIXTY-SIX

"Auntie Yi Ma, over here."

Ping waved her arm trying to attract the attention of the gray-haired Chinese woman, who appeared paralyzed by the frenetic scene that greeted her upon exiting international arrivals.

"Auntie Yi Ma. I'm here." Ping pushed her way through the waiting throng behind the chain barrier. She moved quickly around the crowd to the end of the walkway cordoned off for arriving passengers. Shuffling past her niece dressed in a cordovan brown maternity coat and matching leather boots, Yi Ma continued toward the exit.

"Auntie Yi Ma, it's me," Ping said in Mandarin, taking hold of her aunt's arm.

Yi Ma stared at her niece. "It is you," she said, sighing in relief. "I didn't recognize you. You look so different."

Ping bent over and kissed her aunt. When had she become so small and frail? Yi Ma's eyes became misty as she greeted her niece. "It's so good to see you. Baba and I have missed you."

"This is Ulrich," Ping said as he stepped forward to take Yi Ma's suitcase. She nodded but appeared confused as her gaze went from the middle-aged man dressed in jeans and a parka to the bulge under Ping's coat.

"It's all right," Ping said, smiling at her aunt's puzzled expression. "I'll explain everything on the drive home."

In the car, Ping told her aunt she was no longer married to Jianbo. They had divorced. Ulrich was not the father of the child as Yi Ma had first assumed. She was now the wife of an American and, if all went well, would soon be the mother of a baby girl.

"But I just saw Jianbo a few weeks ago. He told me that you were still studying English for the hotel."

Ping's face reddened as she revealed the plan devised by Jianbo to become an American citizen.

"Does your husband know?"

"He knows I've been married before, but he thinks Jianbo is my brother. If he finds out that I've deceived him, I'm afraid he will leave me."

Auntie Yi Ma's eyebrows pinched together; her lips curled.

"You are upset with me," Ping said.

"This is a terrible thing you have done. Why did you go along with Jianbo's plan?"

"I didn't know what else to do. I pleaded with him not to do this, but he insisted. In the end I was afraid—afraid to disobey him, afraid of what he might do."

"Do you plan on divorcing your husband once you're a US citizen and remarrying Jianbo?"

"I love my husband. We have been good for each other—we've both grown. I've been useful to David with his Chinese clients, and he has encouraged me to finish my university studies. And most importantly, we'll soon be parents." Ping patted her belly for emphasis.

Yi Ma studied her niece and frowned. "You are different. I didn't recognize you at first at the airport. But the change is deeper than your appearance. You're not the young woman that left Chongqing. You've become someone I don't know."

The two women rode in silence. Ping could sense her aunt's disappointment with her. She was filled with shame and sadness.

"How is Baba?" Ping finally asked.

"Unhappy that you are so far away."

"He will be angry with me when he hears that I'm divorced and married to a foreigner."

"Yes, he will. He was fond of Jianbo. When do you plan on telling him you are no longer married to Jianbo and are expecting a child fathered by another?"

Ping shrugged her shoulders and looked out the window. Was it a mistake to have Auntie Yi Ma come to the United States? She had let her family down—she had dishonored their good name. Why did she think a baby would make Auntie Yi Ma and Baba forgive her divorce and marriage to David?

Ping bit her lower lip. "You will stay with me as planned, won't you?"

"Of course I will," Auntie Yi Ma said, patting her niece's hand. "But I want you to do something for me."

"Whatever you want."

"When I call your father to let him know I've arrived safely, you must tell him the truth."

Ping felt a thickness in her throat; she breathed deeply. "Baba will be so upset with me. I wanted to wait until I could tell him in person."

"Paper can't wrap fire; lies cannot cover the truth. Eventually Baba will learn what has happened. It is important that he hears it from you first."

CHAPTER SIXTY-SEVEN

As Ulrich drove through Manhattan, Yi Ma's head turned repeatedly from left to right and back as Ping pointed out various monuments and famous streets.

"This is Tribeca, the area where David and I live. Not too far away is Chinatown. You'll like it. Most of the shopkeepers speak Mandarin. It reminds me of Chongqing."

The car pulled up to Ping's building. The doorman helped the two women out of the vehicle. He told Ulrich he could leave the car for a few minutes while he carried the luggage upstairs. Once inside the apartment, Ping took Yi Ma's worn winter coat and hung it in the entry hall closet. Ulrich carried her suitcase up the stairs to the guest room.

"I'll give you a tour of the house," Ping said after Ulrich left. Wide-eyed, Yi Ma padded after Ping into the living room. "You have a TV," she said. "It is so large."

In Chongqing there was no television. Ping smiled. This would be a treat for her aunt. In the dining room Yi Ma ran her hand along the solid oak table and paused to admire the contents of the china cabinet. Moving into the kitchen, Yi Ma gasped. Familiar with the refrigerator and the oven, she pointed to the microwave and the dishwasher. "What are these?"

Ping opened the door to the microwave. "This appliance cooks food very fast. I'll show you how it works later. And here's a dishwasher. It washes and dries the dishes for us."

Yi Ma shook her head and tut-tutted. "Americans must be very lazy if they have a machine to do the dishes."

Ping put her arm around Yi Ma's shoulders. "I thought the same thing when we first moved in. I refused to use it. One day David made me try it. Since then I haven't washed a dish."

With some difficulty Yi Ma negotiated the spiral staircase to the second floor. Sticking her head into the study, she stared at the contraptions on the credenza. "Computer, printer, fax machine," Ping said, brushing a hand over each.

Yi Ma trailed behind Ping into the master bedroom suite, the guest room and bath that she would use, and the baby's room.

"I've never seen such a beautiful home. I can't believe only two people live here. It's so large."

"Soon there will be three," Ping said, showing her aunt around the nursery.

"Your little girl is very lucky to have so much," Yi Ma said, admiring the white furniture, the stuffed animals, and the collection of baby clothes in the closet.

"I bought these in Chinatown." Ping pointed to two mobiles hanging from the ceiling. One held pandas in various poses. The other displayed the twelve Chinese signs of the zodiac.

"I hope I'm able to help you with the baby. I'm not as young as I used to be."

"You'll be fine. I'll only be gone to class a few hours each day. If it's too much, we'll get someone in to help."

Yi Ma sat in the white wicker rocking chair, a melancholy look on her face. "Your mother would be so happy for you. I wish she were here to see this."

Ping fingered her necklace. "I feel she is with me. Did I tell you the name we've chosen for our daughter?"

Yi Ma shook her head.

"Lei Lei."

"Your mother's name."

"Yes."

Yi Ma rocked in the chair, a wistful look on her face. "I am happy for you. Maybe this craziness—this divorce and marriage—is a good thing. A gem does not shine without rubbing; a person does not grow without trials."

"I hope Baba will feel the same way."

"That reminds me, I must call your father to tell him I've arrived."

Ping felt a sudden twinge of panic, remembering her promise to her aunt. "Follow me," she said. "There's a phone in the guest room."

The two walked back to the guest room and sat on the bed. Ping lifted the phone from its cradle and dialed her father's number in Chongqing.

"Baba, it's me, Ping. Guess who is sitting here next to me?"

She handed the phone to her aunt and lay back on the bed while Yi Ma described her first plane trip and impressions of Manhattan.

"Here," Yi Ma said, handing the phone to Ping. "It is time to tell your father the truth."

Ping reluctantly took the receiver; Yi Ma busied herself unpacking her suitcase and investigating the bathroom.

Sitting up, shoulders hunched forward, heart pounding, Ping told her father she and Jianbo were no longer husband and wife; they had divorced.

"I don't understand," Baba said. "I saw Jianbo a few weeks ago. He did not mention this."

"He didn't want you to know. He thought we'd be remarried by the time I came home."

"I don't understand this—married, divorced, remarried."

Ping told her father Jianbo's plan to become a US citizen through her marriage to an American.

"So now you are married to an American?"

"Yes. His name is David Bennington."

There was silence.

"What you have done is dishonorable, but facing your shame is close to bravery."

"I did not want to do this terrible thing, but Jianbo insisted."

"Wang Jianbo has violated the vows of your marriage. He has disgraced both our families."

"I do have some good news."

"That's a relief. What is it?"

"I am pregnant. You will soon have a granddaughter."

"Who is the father?"

Baba's question brought a lump to Ping's throat. This was a question a father should not have to ask of a daughter. "David."

"And when will I meet my son-in-law and my granddaughter?"

"When the baby is old enough, we will visit you."

"Are you happy with your new husband?"

"Very."

"Then I am happy, too."

Ping inhaled deeply. "Thank you."

"I will say good-bye now."

"If you see Jianbo, please don't mention that I'm pregnant."

"If I see him, I will cross to the other side of the street."

CHAPTER SIXTY-EIGHT

Heads turned in the dining room as the maître d' led Katherine Bennington, Ping, David, and Auntie Yi Ma to their table.

Grinning broadly, Ping whispered to David, "The club members probably think we're part of an Eastern invasion."

David laughed as he turned to see the staring faces. His mother seemed oblivious to the attention the group was attracting.

"Has Ping been showing you Manhattan?" Mrs. Bennington asked Yi Ma after the waiter had taken their orders.

Yi Ma nodded as Ping noted all the places they had been.

"Auntie Yi Ma has been learning English," David said. "Ping is teaching her."

"That's wonderful," Katherine replied acknowledging her efforts with a smile. "And what does the doctor say about my granddaughter?"

"Everything seems to be fine. Auntie Yi Ma and I saw him last week. The baby was in a position to drop. He told me it wouldn't be long."

"You're carrying the baby low," Mrs. Bennington said. "It looks like she's already dropped."

"We're prepared, Mom," David replied. "We have a suitcase in the trunk of the car, just in case."

Ping looked up as the maître d' sat a rather large and noisy group at several round tables. She recognized Alexis in the center of the crowd.

"Look, David, there's Alexis," Ping said.

"It's her engagement party. She got engaged last week."

"Please tell Mrs. Bennington how thankful I am to be included in this dinner," Yi Ma said to her niece in Mandarin.

Ping relayed the message. Encouraged by Mrs. Bennington's appreciative nod, Yi Ma attempted a sentence she had prepared for the occasion in English. "Ping father send greetings."

Mrs. Bennington frowned. David looked confused. Ping, who had just put a forkful of salad into her mouth, choked on the food. Regaining her composure, she interpreted her aunt's comment. "What Auntie Yi Ma means is that my father, had he been alive, would have given us his blessing."

"How sweet," Mrs. Bennington said picking up her fork.

Pretending to translate David's mother's remark, Ping asked her aunt not to say anything else about Baba. She would explain later.

The rest of the meal proved uneventful. Ping translated faithfully between English and Mandarin. Suddenly, about to order dessert, Ping doubled over and moaned.

"What's the matter?" David asked, a frantic look on his face.

"It's time," Ping replied.

"Instead of dessert," David said to the waiter. "Could you bring us a wheelchair?"

"I can walk," Ping said.

"We've attracted enough attention, tonight," David replied, eyes twinkling. "Giving birth in the dining room would probably get my mom kicked out of the club."

CHAPTER SIXTY-NINE

"Push," the doctor said to Ping, who lay on her back on the bed in the birthing room, legs lifted, feet ensconced in stirrups. Face twisted in pain, Ping screamed. "It hurts so much."

"You're doing great," David replied. "Hold my hand; breathe hard and fast."

"A few more pushes and she'll be out," Dr. Robey announced, hands at the ready.

Ping used all her force for her next push.

"I can see the top of my granddaughter's head," Mrs. Bennington said. "Look at her full head of hair."

Yi Ma stood alongside Ping holding her other hand.

"Very good," the doctor said. "I need another push just like that."

Once again, fighting the pain, Ping pushed down hard. The baby slid out. The doctor lifted up the howling, wrinkled newborn.

"She's got great lungs," he said carrying the baby to her mother.

Ping stared in awe and wonderment at the tiny creature she had just produced. Except for her small hands and feet that remained blue, her daughter's body became redder with each cry.

The doctor handed David a scissors. "Here, cut the umbilical cord."

David looked uncomfortable as he took the instrument in his hand.

"Is this spot OK?"

"That's fine."

With a snip of the scissors accompanied by a splattering of blood, mother and child were separated. The nurse took the infant to weigh, measure, and wipe clean. Moments later she returned and placed the baby, swaddled in a blanket, in Ping's outstretched arms. Ping was radiant. David came over and sat on the edge of the bed admiring his wife and daughter.

"I don't think I've ever been so happy," he said, as the baby wrapped her tiny hand around his finger.

"May I?" David took the baby from his wife and lovingly held his daughter for the first time.

Ping gazed at the child in her husband's arms. Turning to Yi Ma, who stood next to her at the side of the bed, she said in Mandarin, "Lei Lei will be strong like my mother. No one will tell her who to marry. She will make her own decisions. She will obey only what is in her head and in her heart."

"What did you say?" David asked.

"I said Lei Lei is beautiful—just like her namesake."

PART THREE

"Out of the ashes rises the phoenix."

—Chinese saying

CHAPTER SEVENTY

February 2006

The early afternoon sun slithered in through the partially open window, crept across the plush carpet and settled on the white crib in which Lei Lei slept. Nearby, Auntie Yi Ma had nodded off in the rocker, feet propped up on the ottoman. She exhaled; a sonorous din escaping from her mouth.

The telephone rang. Startled, she sat up abruptly. Lei Lei responded to the continuous ringing with a loud wail. Yi Ma picked her up, tried to quiet her, and padded over to the telephone. "Hello, Bennington residence," she said in heavily accented English.

A voice on the other end responded in Mandarin. "Auntie Yi Ma?"

"Jianbo, is that you?"

"What are you doing in the United States?"

Yi Ma cast a furtive look at Lei Lei, her face crimson, her mouth readying for another cry. Holding the telephone in one hand, Yi Ma bounced the baby with the other, but to no avail. Lei Lei released a series of yowls.

"Is that a baby?" Jianbo asked.

"No."

"C'mon, Auntie Yi Ma. I know a baby's cry."

Yi Ma said nothing.

"That's why you're there, isn't it? To help Ping with her baby."

Yi Ma did not respond.

"How could Ping not tell me she was pregnant? This is something a wife shares with her husband."

"You are no longer her husband."

Jianbo remained silent. Then in a menacing tone he said, "Tell Ping I will telephone this evening. We need to talk. This has changed everything."

⟫⟪

"Auntie Yi Ma," Ping called out as she entered the apartment.

"In the kitchen," Yi Ma said in Mandarin.

Ping hung her jacket in the hall closet and put her book bag by the spiral staircase. She would take it to her bedroom on her next trip upstairs. Auntie Yi Ma stood at the counter chopping vegetables for dinner. Nearby, Lei Lei lay on her back in a mesh-sided portable play yard, eyes fixed on an animal mobile rotating to "Rock-a-bye Baby."

"How is my little pumpkin?" Ping said, lifting her up.

Lei Lei squirmed with pleasure in her mother's arms. "Has she been fed?" Ping asked.

"No, I waited for you. She prefers the breast to the pumped milk."

Sitting on the sofa, Ping lifted her T-shirt and undid her bra. She closed her eyes and let her head fall back against the couch, enjoying the tiny pulls on her nipple. She loved everything about her daughter, eyes that never ceased to explore, tiny fingers that encircled hers, heart-shaped lips that cooed and gurgled.

Face solemn, Auntie Yi Ma took a seat next to Ping on the couch. "Something happened today."

The ominous tone caused Ping to jerk forward, almost dislodging Lei Lei from her breast. "What?"

"Jianbo called."

Ping's heart raced.

"The phone woke Lei Lei. I held her in my arms when I picked up the receiver but couldn't keep her from crying."

"Didn't you turn the ringer off when you put her down for her nap?"

Yi Ma swallowed hard. "I forgot."

"What did Jianbo say?"

"After hearing the baby and realizing I was here with you, he put two and two together. He knew the child was yours."

Ping switched Lei Lei to her other breast. She couldn't be angry with Auntie Yi Ma. Jianbo would have found out eventually. Initially, she feared Feng would follow through on his threat to reveal everything to David. But over a year had gone by since their meeting at the hotel, and she had not heard from or seen her detractor. On the other hand, Jianbo wrote almost daily. At first the letters begged her to divorce David. Jianbo wanted her to return to China and become his wife again. He no longer cared about finding a job and becoming a US citizen. He missed her too much. Ping answered, always finding a reason to delay her return.

Recently, the tone of Jianbo's letters had changed. They were threatening and hostile. Although disturbed by the anger that spewed from the pages, Ping was not afraid. Almost seven thousand miles, a continent, and an ocean separated them. In addition, Jianbo did not have the money to come to the United States. Since Ping felt responding to Jianbo's diatribes would serve no purpose, she no longer answered or even opened his letters. She used David's shredder and discarded the severed strips in the garbage. Even though David could not read Mandarin, Ping wanted no evidence to implicate her in Jianbo's scheme.

She looked down at Lei Lei asleep at her breast. Gently she lifted her and placed her against her shoulder. Ping shuddered. What would Jianbo do now that he knew about Lei Lei?

CHAPTER SEVENTY-ONE

The alarm clock on the bedside table flashed 3:00 a.m. Unable to sleep, Ping put on her robe, picked up the copy of *The Scarlet Letter* she had just purchased at a secondhand bookstore, and quietly descended the spiral staircase. She sat on the living room couch to read, but she couldn't concentrate on the words. Her stomach churned. She waited for Jianbo's inevitable call.

The sudden shrill ring of the phone shattered the silence of the house. Jumping up from the couch, Ping ran to the kitchen hoping to lift the receiver before the second ring. She and David both said hello at the same time.

"I'll take it, David. It's Jianbo."

"*Nie hao,*" she heard David say. "Is anything the matter?"

"I'll let you know after I finish talking to him."

Before continuing, she listened for the click of the receiver indicating David had hung up.

"Why are you calling at this time of night?"

"I wanted to be sure you'd be home, that you'd answer the phone."

"What do you want?" Ping asked knowing full well why Jianbo had called.

"I have not received a letter from you in over two months."

"Your letters are filled with threats and hateful words. I have nothing to say."

"I was angry with you. You act as if our marriage, our agreement, means nothing. I wanted to know when you would divorce the American. I am alone in Beijing, waiting for you to return. All I have to look forward to are your letters. And then I call and find out you have a child."

"I was going to tell you."

"When? When the child was grown?"

"I wanted to tell you when I found out I was pregnant, but I was afraid you'd be angry."

"I am angry. Why didn't you wear protection? You did this on purpose to sabotage our agreement. And then you didn't have the guts to inform me so I could get on with my life. I have been faithful to you. I have not been with another woman since you left."

Ping swallowed hard. Her throat was dry. "I'm sorry. I never intended to hurt you."

"How old is your child?"

"She's almost four months."

"So it's a girl. I suppose the American still doesn't know that you were my wife. I'm sure that's one secret you didn't reveal."

Ping did not answer.

"You've dishonored our marriage with your deceit and your broken promises," Jianbo said.

"My only shame was to obey rather than challenge you. I did not dishonor our marriage. It is you who asked me to share another's bed. You are the reason we are no longer together."

"You are yelling. Have you forgotten how to talk to your husband?"

Taking a deep breath, Ping said slowly and deliberately, "You are no longer and will never again be my husband."

"What are you saying?"

"I am not going to divorce David. He is the father of my child."

"You will not get away with this," Jianbo said.

She heard the click of the broken connection. Hand shaking, Ping hung up the receiver. She lay back on the couch, curled up, facing the rear cushions. She had awakened a sleeping tiger.

"What's wrong?" David asked as he descended the staircase and moved toward her.

"Nothing."

"You're trembling. What did your brother say to you?"

"He asked me several months ago to see if you would send him money to open a restaurant in Chongqing."

"Why didn't you ask me?"

"I didn't think it was right."

"But if it's something you'd…"

"Please, I'm tired. Could we just go to bed?"

"OK, we'll talk about the restaurant tomorrow."

Wearily, Ping climbed the spiral stairs to the bedroom. She fell asleep and dreamed she saw David with Lei Lei in his arms walking ahead of her. The distance between them increased. She tried to run, but something was holding her back. Struggling against an invisible force, she finally freed herself and chased after them. She called out, but they continued walking. She ran faster. The distance between them narrowed. Now she could see Lei Lei smiling at her over David's shoulder. She reached out to touch her daughter but suddenly felt herself banging into an impenetrable wall of glass. The impact knocked her backward. She struggled to her knees. Pounding on the glass, screaming their names, she watched helplessly as her husband and daughter disappeared from view.

CHAPTER SEVENTY-TWO

"Time to hand in your exams," Professor Hwang said. "Your grades will be posted on Blackboard by the end of the week."

As the students filed out of the classroom, Ping caught up with Helen. "What did you think of the test?" she asked in Mandarin.

"It was harder than I thought it would be, but overall I think I did all right. How about you?"

"I think I did OK, too."

Helen glanced at Ping. "You look worried. Is everything all right?"

"I'm just concerned about what Jianbo might do."

"Has he called since the other night?"

"No. But his silence is worse than if he did something. Every time the phone or the doorbell rings, I expect it to be him or Feng."

Helen smiled. "My phone is vibrating. Did you give Jianbo my number?"

"Very funny."

"Excuse me a moment while I take the call."

Helen moved to a less crowded hallway to escape the noise of the main corridor. Ping waited, saying good-bye to her classmates as they filed past. Suddenly, Helen came running toward her.

"What's the matter?" Ping asked, seeing the anxious look on her face.

"Martin's had a heart attack. They've taken him to Mount Sinai Hospital."

"Do you want me to come with you?"

"Would you?"

Ping sprinted down the hallway trying to keep up with Helen. The two women bounded down the stairs. Once outside, Helen hailed a cab.

"Mount Sinai Hospital. Madison and Fifth," she said to the driver. "Please hurry, it's an emergency."

Twenty minutes later, the taxi pulled up to the Fifth Avenue entrance of the hospital. Helen handed the driver some bills. Without waiting for change, she and Ping jumped out of the cab and raced inside. At the information desk, an aide asked the two women to sign in. Once they received passes, they followed the aide's directions to the surgery area. Leaving the elevator, they entered a waiting room where a handful of visitors sat or paced nervously. Ping took a seat as Helen rushed to a desk where a dark-haired woman sat.

"He's still in surgery," Helen said, returning to Ping. "They won't tell me any more than that. As soon as everything is over, I can talk with the surgeon."

Helen collapsed on the chair next to Ping, her face ashen.

"What about Nathan?" Ping asked. "Will anyone be there when he comes home from school?"

"Oh my God. I forgot about Nathan." Helen pulled out her cell phone. "Please, let my neighbor be there," she said, holding the phone to her ear.

"Mrs. Worth? Thank goodness you're home. I'm at the hospital. My husband had a heart attack. Could Nathan stay at your place until I come home?"

Helen sighed, relieved. "Thanks so much. Yes, I'll let you know as soon as I hear anything. Please don't tell Nathan about his father."

Ping and Helen said little, flipping through old issues of magazines randomly strewn on chairs and tables. Periodically, Helen would ask the woman behind the desk about her husband. Each time she returned to where Ping sat, shaking her head. Ping understood Helen's anxiety. How horrible she would feel if suddenly, without warning, David was no longer a part of her life.

An hour passed. They were the only people left in the waiting room. "Mrs. Glauber?" said a male voice. Helen's head shot up. A doctor dressed in green scrubs had just walked through the double doors of the surgery ward. Helen leaped from her seat and raced to the surgeon. He put his hand on her shoulder. As he spoke, Ping watched as the hopeful look on Helen's face disappeared. She stood erect, her slim form quivering, her face covered by her hands. The woman behind the desk motioned Ping to go over to Helen.

"Martin…Martin's dead," Helen said to Ping, tears streaming down her face.

"I'm sorry. We did all we could," the surgeon said, tired eyes staring sympathetically from his drawn face. He stood beside Helen watching her body shake in response to her anguished cries. He held out his hand to touch her shoulders but pulled back, turned, and disappeared through the double doors.

The woman from behind the desk helped Ping move Helen to a sofa. She left and returned with a bottle of water and a plastic cup. "See if she'll drink some water," she said to Ping.

Helen waved the cup away. The woman went back to her desk. Leaving Helen huddled on the couch, knees pulled up to her chin, Ping went over to the receptionist. "What happens now?" she asked.

"We take the body to the hospital morgue. Once arrangements are made, it's transported to the funeral home. Would Mrs. Glauber like to see her husband before he's moved?"

Ping walked back to Helen. When she nodded, the woman at the desk picked up her phone. After a couple of minutes, a nurse appeared to escort her to where Martin lay. Ping stayed behind. She did not want to intrude as Helen said a final good-bye to her husband.

Alone in the waiting room, Ping reflected on how quickly situations change—a wife was now a widow; a child was fatherless. Ping's heart was heavy, not only for Helen's loss but for what fate might have in store for her.

CHAPTER SEVENTY-THREE

A soft spring rain fell as Ping rang the bell marked *Glauber.* "It's me," she said in Mandarin in response to a voice over the intercom.

A buzzer sounded. Ping opened the door and climbed the two stories to Helen's apartment. Her friend stood in the doorway to greet her.

"Come in," Helen said. "Sorry, but there's no place to sit."

The living room was stripped of its furnishings, replaced by a mountain of sealed cardboard boxes. Little remained to identify the inhabitants of the apartment—beige rectangles where book-cases and sofas had stood, holes in the wall where paintings had once hung. Ping recalled how warm and welcoming the apartment was for her baby shower. The living room was decorated with pink streamers and balloons. All that remained of the family who lived here was a forgotten teddy bear with one eye missing lying in a corner of the room.

"I wish you weren't going," Ping said.

"I have no choice. Martin knew his former wife well. She saw to it that Nathan and I received almost nothing from the estate."

"Aren't there laws that protect you? You're a US citizen now."

"His ex-wife's an attorney. She locked up most of their assets when they divorced. Martin felt so guilty about our relationship that he gave her almost everything she asked for—even his life insurance policy."

"But didn't he set things up so you'd be OK?"

"He tried. There wouldn't have been a problem if he had passed away ten or fifteen years from now. Without his salary, I can't afford the rent for the apartment or Nathan's tuition. Even if I found a job, I couldn't earn enough."

"You're so close to getting your degree."

"I know," Helen said gloomily. "But without Martin's income, there's no way I can continue. The only thing I can do is go back to my parents' home in Yichang. I have no other option."

Ping shivered. Would this be what happened to her if Jianbo made good on his threats? Without David's support, she would be forced to return to China as well.

Helen stared at Ping, her eyes dark and serious. "Make sure you put money away in your name or Lei Lei's. If you do, you'll have choices if your situation suddenly changes—unlike me."

"I'll really miss you. I feel so bad about what's happened," Ping looped her arm around Helen's shoulders to comfort her.

"Don't worry. I'll be all right. I still have what's most important to me—my son."

Ping looked around. "Where is he?"

"With my neighbor. She's taking care of him so I can get things ready. The movers come tomorrow. The university has been very kind. They're paying the cost of transporting the few things I'm taking to China. Most of these boxes are filled with books and journals that I'm giving to the university library."

"I know you're busy. I just wanted to say good-bye and give you this." Ping pulled a small box from her handbag.

"Thank you," Helen said as she opened the gift. Inside was a pendant in shou chow jade on a leather cord.

"It's the *fu* symbol, so you will have good fortune," Ping said.

"Thank you. I will treasure this gift." Helen put the pendant around her neck and smiled warmly at Ping. "As soon as I get an e-mail address, I'll contact you. You've been such a good friend. Without your help with the funeral arrangements I don't know what I would have done. Although an ocean will separate us, we will never be far from each other's thoughts."

Her heart heavy, Ping bade Helen farewell. She slowly made her way down the dark stairwell. Outside, she looked up to the third floor. Helen stood at the curtainless window and waved. With a lump in her throat, Ping turned to walk home, indifferent to the rain falling on her face.

❈

Xavier rushed to open the door for Ping as she approached the building. She glanced at her watch. Two thirty.

"Has the mail been delivered?" she asked the doorman.

"Yes," he nodded. "It came early today."

Her rain-soaked jacket dripped on the parquet floor as Ping walked into the mail area and opened her box. She thumbed through the mail and discarded advertisements and flyers. Inside the elevator, she examined what remained. Her eyes grew wide. There was a letter sent from China to David. It was from Jianbo.

Auntie Yi Ma greeted Ping at the door. "Shush. I just put Lei Lei down for a nap," she said in Mandarin.

"Did anyone call?" Ping asked as she removed her wet jacket and placed it over a chair to dry.

Auntie Yi Ma shook her head.

"I'm going to go upstairs and get out of these wet clothes. I'll only be a few minutes."

After peeking into the nursery to assure herself that Lei Lei was asleep, Ping went into her bedroom and shut the door. She ripped open the envelope and read the letter from Jianbo to David—a letter that had been translated into very strange English.

Dear Honorable Mister Bennington:

I beg your forgiveness for myself and Ping. We have committed a dishonorable deed for which we have much regret. I am sad to inform you that your marriage to Ping was not a love marriage, but a convenient marriage. When we met in China, we were not brother and sister as you had imagined, but husband and wife. We thought you could help us obtain US citizenship.

I see you have two options. First option is to send Ping back to China. Second option is to pay me 100,000 American dollars to have Ping continue to be your wife. Then I will no longer demand her return as is my right as husband.

If I do not receive response by May 1, I go see a lawyer to assure my legal rights.

Yours with respect,
Wang Jianbo

Ping's head ached; she felt nauseous. If she had not intercepted the letter, what would have happened? She changed her clothes and slowly descended the spiral staircase. Over a cup of tea, she translated the letter from English back to Mandarin for Auntie Yi Ma.

"The letter makes it seem like you are still married to Jianbo."

Ping reread the letter. Her brow furrowed; she bit her lower lip. "You're right. He even refers to his right as husband."

"You did divorce, didn't you?"

"Of course. I made it clear to Jianbo that I would not marry another while we were still man and wife."

"Who handled the divorce?"

Ping ran her fingers through her hair. "A lawyer, a friend of Feng's."

Yi Ma's eyes narrowed. "Did you sign papers?"

304

"Yes. We went before a judge in Beijing. After he agreed to our divorce, he had us sign papers."

"And you have copies of these papers?"

Ping's heart dropped. "No. Jianbo took them."

"He didn't give you a copy?"

Covering her face with her hands, Ping shook her head. "How foolish I was. I have nothing to prove we are divorced."

Yi Ma poured them each another cup of tea. Ping held the cup in her hand. "What should I do?"

"We need to get a copy of the divorce agreement. I will do what I can when I get back to Chongqing. Until then, you must not visit China."

"Why not?"

"Under the new marriage laws, bigamy is now a crime in China. Several wealthy men have been sent to jail because they had two wives."

"Why would they want two wives?"

"It was an attempt to get around the one-child mandate. Having more than one wife enabled these men to have more children."

Ping got up and placed her teacup in the sink. "I can't believe Jianbo would still claim we are husband and wife."

"Jianbo is not an honorable man. As they say: 'Do good, reap good; do evil, reap evil.' Rest assured, he will be punished."

CHAPTER SEVENTY-FOUR

Yi Ma stayed with Ping until the end of the semester. She took care of Lei Lei while Ping was at the university, prepared most of the meals, and tidied up the house. Ping watched her aunt lovingly coddle and cradle her daughter. *This is the way she must have cared for me when I was an infant,* she thought.

The bond between the two women was strong. Only one issue tarnished the relationship. "You must tell David that he has a father-in-law," Yi Ma would say. "You dishonor your father by denying his existence."

"But Auntie, I've told you. I cannot tell David about Baba. My husband thinks my father is dead. If I tell him the truth, he will probably leave me."

"You don't know that. He's very much in love with you."

"Yes, but learning that Jianbo is my ex-husband is too great a deception, even for someone who loves me. Especially if I'm unable to prove I'm divorced."

"But what about your father? You need to think about him. When I spoke to him last night he asked me why his daughter had not introduced him to his new son-in-law, why you have not invited him to

America, why he has never seen his granddaughter. He thinks that you are ashamed of him now that you are living so grandly."

"You know that's not true."

"Yes, but he doesn't."

Yi Ma's words saddened Ping.

"And what if your father becomes ill?" Yi Ma continued. "He is not a young man. Would you go to him?"

"Of course. I would think of something to tell David."

"Be careful. You think you are the spider building this web of lies. But one day, just like the fly, you will find yourself trapped."

A chill went through Ping's body. She feared that Auntie Yi Ma's prophecy might come to pass.

⊷⊷

A semblance of routine gradually took shape after the school year ended and Yi Ma returned to Chongqing. Sundays were the most predictable. Somewhere between 5:00 and 6:00 a.m., Lei Lei's first whimpers were transmitted over the intercom from the nursery to Ping and David's room. David was the first responder. Gently, he would pick up the hungry infant and carry her to Ping. She held the child while David propped up the pillows behind her so she could nurse Lei Lei. As the infant suckled, the two would admire their creation—the tiny hands that lay open on Ping's breast, the slight bob of the head as Lei Lei suckled, the dark, luminous eyes that lingered on her mother's face. When the baby had her fill and she let the nipple slide from her lips, her attention focused on the rotating blades of the fan above the bed. Ping would lift her up to her shoulder to be burped. If Lei Lei were still sleepy, Ping would place her daughter on her chest as she lay on the bed, and the three of them would nap. If the baby was awake, David would put her on her back between them on the king-size bed. They would tickle Lei Lei's feet, play with her toes, and offer her rattles, stuffed animals and other toys kept on the nightstand for her amusement.

CHAPTER SEVENTY-FIVE

On a Sunday late in May, invited to Mrs. Bennington's for lunch, Ping dressed Lei Lei in a yellow floral and white eyelet dress with matching bonnet. The outfit was a recent gift from her grandmother. Uncertain about the temperature outdoors, Ping put on a white sweater trimmed with the same floral design over the dress. On her feet, Lei Lei wore white socks with a ruffled border and leather Mary Janes.

"What do you think of your daughter?" Ping asked David, who had just entered the nursery.

"A beauty, just like her mother."

David had arranged with Ulrich to pick the family up at Port Imperial. The day was perfect for the short ferry ride across the Hudson River. Ulrich was waiting when they arrived. During the drive to Mrs. Bennington's, the caretaker discussed repairs he had made and those that still needed to be taken care of.

Ping realized how fortunate her mother-in-law was to have Ulrich and Greta living with her. She thought of her father and Auntie Yi Ma so far away. Several times David had suggested that Auntie Yi Ma could come live with them. But if she came, Baba would be alone. Not having them with her was the price she paid for having deceived David.

When they arrived at Mrs. Bennington's, Greta greeted them at the door. Her eyes glowed as she took Lei Lei and held her for the brief walk down the entry hall to the backyard patio.

"Here she is," Mrs. Bennington said, eagerly rising to hold her granddaughter. Lei Lei looked apprehensively from one admiring face to the other before she began to cry.

"Here, let me take her, Mom." David reached over for his daughter. "She's not used to all this attention."

Once in her father's arms, Lei Lei's sobs ceased. When he held her over his shoulder she grinned at her fans now a safe distance away. "She's a real charmer," Mrs. Bennington said.

"I think my mother's forgotten that Lei Lei's not her only guest," David declared to Ping.

"I'm sorry. How are the two of you?"

"We're fine, Mom. Ping just got some good news."

"What is it?"

"She's made the dean's list again."

"Congratulations. Well done."

Ping blushed and lowered her eyes as Katherine gave her a hug.

"Not only is my wife beautiful, but she's smart, too," David said.

"Please stop, David; you're embarrassing me."

"Well, on that piece of good news, let's go inside and have lunch." Mrs. Bennington led the way into the house.

Ping placed Lei Lei in an automatic swing in the dining room area before she joined the others. She looked around the table, at her husband and her mother-in-law. How fortunate she was to be part of this kind and generous family.

A cell phone rang. "Sorry," David said, reaching into his pocket.

"Please turn it off. I hate those things; they're so disruptive," Mrs. Bennington said. She glanced at Lei Lei asleep in the swing. "Besides, you're going to wake your daughter."

"I would turn it off, except it's my boss. I'll take it in the library. I'll just be a second."

After a few minutes David returned to the dining room, his eyes shining. "What is it?" his mother asked.

"Tomorrow morning, I have an eight a.m. meeting with the top brass of the firm. They want me to head up the new office in Shanghai. It's a big promotion with a major salary increase."

Awakened by the noise, Lei Lei began to cry. No one noticed the look of terror on Ping's face as she got up from the table to tend to her daughter.

CHAPTER SEVENTY-SIX

"What do you want to do?" Ping asked David after putting Lei Lei down for the night.

"About what?"

"About Shanghai?"

"We'll go, of course. It's perfect. A big promotion for me and a chance for you to see your brother and Auntie Yi Ma."

David could tell by his wife's expression that she did not share his enthusiasm.

"What's the matter? I thought you'd be happy about spending time in China."

"It means postponing my studies," Ping said, searching for an excuse.

"I guess it does. Would you rather we didn't go?"

Ping walked over to the couch where David was sitting and slid next to him.

"You would stay here for me?"

"I'd consider it if you were that concerned about your degree."

Ping put her arms around David's neck and hugged him. "You would?" she said. "No one has ever put my preferences above their own."

"I didn't say I wouldn't go. But we might be able to come up with a compromise."

"Like what?"

"Maybe I could arrange to spend two weeks a month in Shanghai and two weeks here."

"Then we'd be apart fifty percent of the time. Wouldn't you miss Lei Lei?"

"Of course I would. I'd miss you even more."

"That would mean so much traveling for you."

"If you really don't want to interrupt your studies, I'd do that for you. You and Lei Lei could join me on your vacations."

"You are so different from the men I knew in China. In my country, the wife's wishes are not often considered."

David took Ping's hands in his. "You mean everything to me. If you really feel strongly about staying behind, I'd understand. We have to do what's best for both of us."

Ping squeezed her husband's hands. At that moment she felt anything was possible. Their love was strong. Nothing would come between them, not even the truth.

"You really want to go, don't you?" Ping asked.

"Yes. If I'm successful, I'll be well on my way to making partner. Plus, living in Shanghai would give us the opportunity to visit places I've only read about."

"What about your mother? She wouldn't want to see us go so far away."

"She'd be able to visit whenever she wanted. I think she'd enjoy China."

"And Lei Lei?"

"This would be a great experience for her. She'll learn about her mother's country. She'll probably end up bilingual. Plus, she'll get to spend time with her uncle Jianbo and great aunt Yi Ma."

The mention of Jianbo's name caused Ping's stomach to churn. She rested her head on David's shoulder. She knew he wanted them to go to Shanghai as a family. Living there would also make it possible for her to visit Baba and Auntie Yi Ma while David was working. Her father could finally meet his granddaughter.

Returning to China was not without risk. She could run into Jianbo in Chongqing on trips to see her father. But he lived and worked in Beijing. With a little luck, they might be able to spend a year or two in China without Jianbo discovering they were there.

"Forgive me," Ping said. "I'm being selfish. It would be best for our family to go to Shanghai."

"This could delay your studies for two years or more."

"I'll survive. Besides, I'll be useful to you in China. You can hire me as your interpreter and guide."

"And my mistress," David said with a grin, sliding his hands up under Ping's skirt and stroking her thighs.

Various scenarios of returning to China played out in Ping's mind as she waited for David to return from a dinner with clients the following evening. She sat on the living room couch trying to finish *The Scarlet Letter.* Two years in Shanghai. A chill ran through her body. The trip presented some serious risks. Her father would insist upon meeting his son-in-law. She thought about introducing him to David as her uncle, but Baba was a proud man. He would never consent to assuming any other role than that of her father. And what if Jianbo found out she was there? He would tell David theirs was a marriage of convenience and deny ever divorcing her. Would she be shamed and the object of scorn like Hester Prynne? Would they try to take Lei Lei from her as they did Pearl from Hester?

David said they wouldn't leave until the fall. She would call Auntie Yi Ma. Hopefully she would have tracked down a record of her divorce before then.

CHAPTER SEVENTY-SEVEN

Shanghai, September 2006

Sliding back the drapes covering the windowed wall of the hotel suite, Ping stared at the hodgepodge of buildings on the western bank of the Huangpu River. From her vantage point on one of the highest floors of the world's tallest hotel, the Grand Hyatt Pudong, she saw vestiges of the history as well as the panorama of Shanghai. Skyscrapers alternated with colonial and art-deco structures. Across the river was the Bund with its succession of grandiose neoclassical buildings. Her grade-school teacher had praised the takeover in 1949 of Shanghai by the Communists. They successfully rid the city of the British, French, American, and Japanese colonists. But she neglected to tell the class that in the process, they destroyed the city as a major economic power.

From the window, Ping saw signs of Shanghai's revival. She counted no fewer than eighteen cranes—cranes constructing office buildings and multiunit residences. To her right was the new symbol of the city, the 457-meter-high Oriental Pearl TV Tower. Its bulbous top and spire resembled an ornament similar to one she had seen on Mrs. Bennington's tree at Christmas.

"Mama."

Summoned by Lei Lei's call, Ping lifted her daughter from where she had been playing on the floor and carried her to the window. "Look at the big city. See the boats on the river."

"Bo," Lei Lei said, pointing to a ship.

"This is my country. Chi-na," she said slowly. "Chi-na."

But Lei Lei had lost interest. Struggling to get down she crawled back to her toys.

"My country," Ping repeated, a note of pride and wistfulness in her voice. She marveled at the transformation taking place in China. There was a vitality, an energy that engulfed Shanghai. That energy propelled the populace. People moved purposely through the streets, eager to work, eager to be part of this new momentum that would transform their lives. For the first time, she understood Jianbo.

Jianbo. What would happen if he found out she was in China? Ping shuddered at what he might do. She gazed out the window again. When they had arrived yesterday at the Pudong airport, she thought she had seen him. Her heart raced; chills coursed through her body; she felt faint. David had made her sit down, blaming her panic attack on the hordes of passengers pushing and shoving them in the crowded terminal building. In a more rational mood, Ping realized she probably wouldn't run into Jianbo in Shanghai. Beijing or Chongqing, yes. But there was no reason for him to come here. Plus, she was only in Shanghai for a brief visit. Two weeks while David set up his office and they found a place to live. Nonetheless, she knew she wouldn't relax until she was back in the United States and an ocean away from Jianbo.

Ping closed the drapes and picked up Lei Lei. She pulled down the covers and lay down, cuddling her child. "Mommy is going to take a nap with you," she said in Mandarin.

━◁┼▷━

"OK, up and at 'em. Can't spend the day in bed." David rushed into the suite and over to the bed where Lei Lei snuggled against Ping.

"What are you doing back from work so early?"

"I wanted to take my two favorite girls on a river tour."

"What?"

"The boat leaves in thirty minutes. You get dressed, and I'll change Lei Lei." Picking up his daughter to sounds of *Dada, Dada,* David searched for a clean diaper.

Fifteen minutes later, the three were in a taxi en route to Shiliupu Wharf. Wheeling Lei Lei in her stroller, Ping shadowed David as he hurried up the gangplank. Once on deck, they slowed their pace. Surrounded by boisterous passengers, they pushed their way through the unruly crowd of tourists on the main deck. Ping searched in vain for an empty wooden bench.

"There's no place to sit."

"This isn't where we're going," David said, making his way through the horde of passengers and opening a path for Ping and Lei Lei. Lifting his daughter in her stroller, he climbed up a set of stairs that led to a large, almost deserted lounge.

"This is more civilized," David said as they settled into overstuffed armchairs. Lei Lei's outstretched arms signaled she wanted to get out of the carriage. Ping lifted her daughter onto her lap while a hostess brought over hot tea and sweets.

The hard seats on the lower-class deck reminded Ping of the train ride she and Jianbo had taken from Chongqing to Beijing following Feng's wedding. She did not want to make such a trip again, sitting for hours on hard wooden planks in crowded cars, passengers inadvertently hitting her with packages and backpacks as they walked by searching for seats. Yet, ensconced in the plush chairs of first class sipping tea and eating cake, she was ashamed—ashamed that she could no longer tolerate hard seats.

Looking at her daughter, Ping felt a pang of regret. Lei Lei sat on her lap smearing her face with the sweet she was trying to eat, looking at her mother smug and satisfied. Her daughter would never realize how fortunate she was. She would always travel in comfort, pampered and waited on like her father. *Sometimes, it is good to ride on hard seats.*

The loud blasts signaling the departure of the ship frightened Lei Lei.

"Mama, Mama," she cried.

Ping wiped her daughter's hands and lifted her up. The boat slowly made its way up the yellow waters of the Huangpu River passing sampans, rusty freighters, and several shining Chinese navy ships.

"Did you know that this river is the main supply of drinking water for the people in Shanghai?" Ping said.

David grimaced at the sight of the yellow liquid, flavored with the grease and oil of the many vessels gliding over its surface. "We'll drink only bottled water while we're here."

The waitress removed the plates and brought another pot of tea to set on the table between the two chairs. An emcee appeared and announced in Mandarin and English a performance by a world-famous juggler. To polite applause from the sparse audience, a young man appeared dressed in black slacks and shirt. His attractive assistant in a traditional long, form-fitting scarlet silk dress with a high side slit entered next, pushing a cart. She handed the juggler five colorful hoops about one and a half feet in diameter. He gradually introduced a new hoop into his routine until all five were in play—three in the air and one in each hand. Transfixed, Lei Lei stared at the whirling objects.

At the conclusion of the show, the lounge passengers were served more tea and cake. Ping wrapped her arm around Lei Lei's chubby legs as she stood and peered over the back of her mother's chair. Suddenly, she burst into shrieks of laughter. Ping turned around. A woman seated at the table behind her was playing peek-a-boo with Lei Lei. Ping's smile at the woman turned into a gasp. Seated at the same table were two men, one of whom was Li Feng.

Feng rose and walked over to her table. David looked up as he approached. "What a coincidence," Ping said, forcing a smile, her heart pounding. "David, this is Li Feng. He's from Chongqing."

"Pleased to meet you," David said, shaking his hand. "How do you know Ping?"

"I friend with husband."

Ping's eyes narrowed. She placed her hand on David's arm. "David is my husband."

"So sorry," Feng said with a sneer. "I mean her brother, her brother Jianbo. My English not so good."

A red flush crept up Ping's neck and face; she could scarcely breathe. What game was Feng playing with her? He stood, arms clasped behind his back, rocking back on his heels. The addition of a wide grin anchored by two gold teeth informed Ping he was in control.

Perhaps sensing her mother's anxiousness, Lei Lei started to cry. David got up, took her from Ping, and paced back and forth in an attempt to quiet her.

"What are you doing here?" Ping asked Feng in Mandarin.

"I should ask the same question of you. Jianbo didn't tell me you were here."

Ping glared at Feng. She understood his message. He would inform Jianbo that she had returned to China. Any further conversation with Feng was cut short. David had returned with Lei Lei.

"This your daughter?" Feng asked in English. "She is beautiful like mother."

By this time, the couple from the neighboring table had joined them. "Hi, I'm Ronald Winston, and this is my wife Margaret. We're from the United States."

"So are we," David said. "Are you here for pleasure or business?"

"Business. My company's setting up a joint venture with Mr. Guo, Li Feng's father-in-law, to build a cement facility a few miles north of Shanghai. Mr. Li thought we might enjoy the boat trip."

"And we have," Margaret said, "especially with this adorable child to charm us. How old is she?"

"Eleven months," David replied.

"What's her name?"

"Lei Lei."

While the American couple and David talked, Feng turned to Ping. "How long are you staying in Shanghai?" he whispered in Mandarin.

"Not long."

"Where are you staying?"

"Not far from here."

"Talkative, aren't we?"

Ping glowered at him. "I have nothing to say to you."

With a smirk, Feng sidled up to David. "How long do you stay in Shanghai?"

"I was just telling Margaret and Ronald that we're only here for two weeks. But we'll be back for a longer stay in a few months."

A smug smile on his face, Feng turned to Ping and then back to David. "And where do you stay now?"

"The Grand Hyatt."

"What a coincidence. That's where we're staying, too," Ronald said. "I'd suggest we have dinner together, but we're heading back to the States early tomorrow morning, and we need to pack."

A blast from the steam whistle signaled the ship was turning around. The juggler reappeared onstage on a unicycle accompanied by his assistant, now in a gold gown. Margaret grabbed Ronald's arm. "We'd better sit down. The show is about to start." She turned to David and Ping. "So nice meeting you."

Feng and the couple returned to their table. The assistant handed the juggler several bowls and a teapot that he balanced on his head. As the crowd applauded, the young woman gave the performer two dinner-size plates that he twirled on the index finger of each hand. Lei Lei slept through the performance, lying limply against her father's shoulder. Ping sat rigidly, hands clutching the arms of the chair. It was a mistake to have come back to China.

CHAPTER SEVENTY-EIGHT

If you don't scale the mountain, you cannot view the plain. In the taxi ride back to the hotel, this refrain repeated itself in Ping's mind. She fingered her necklace and thought of her mother. She had had the courage to confront her husband. Ping must do the same with her ex, Jianbo.

"I'd like to fly up to Beijing with Lei Lei the day after tomorrow to see Jianbo," Ping told David that evening after they had put their daughter down to sleep.

"This is rather sudden."

"He's never seen his niece."

"What about if we fly him down here?"

"It would be easier if I go there. I'm not sure he could get off from work. Lei Lei and I could leave the day after tomorrow and return the next day."

David frowned. "I'll miss you."

Ping felt a thickness in her throat. "I'll miss you, too, but it's something I must do."

"I'll have the company's travel agent get the plane tickets and a car and driver for you while you're there."

"I really don't need a car and driver. I know Beijing well."

"I don't doubt that you do. But now you'll be taking Lei Lei and all her paraphernalia. Please, it will make things much easier."

"You're right."

"I'll request the driver I had in Beijing." David pulled a small black address book from his pocket. "What was his name again? He had been a boxer..."

Ping recalled the night she and Jianbo had had dinner with David and Alexis. The driver, broad-shouldered and hefty, had helped Alexis exit the car.

"Here it is," David said. "Zheng Bai. I'll feel better knowing he'll be driving you around."

Closing her eyes, Ping drew a deep breath. It would be wise to have someone strong at her side.

"Will you stay with Jianbo?"

"Of course not." Ping's face reddened. "I mean there won't be enough room for both me and Lei Lei."

"I'll have the travel agent make a reservation for you at the China Palace."

"I don't know if that would be a good idea," Ping replied. "After all, Jianbo's an employee there. It might make him feel uncomfortable."

"Please. It would ease my mind. I'd know you and Lei Lei would be well taken care of."

Ping bit her lip. If she and Lei Lei avoided the dining room and had only room service, it might work. After all, it would be for only one night. "Fine, if it would make you feel better."

⊷⊷ ⊶⊶

Two days later David waved good-bye as Ping and Lei Lei pulled away in a cab headed for Pudong airport. Although this was a trip she had to make by herself she missed her husband. It was not easy traveling alone with Lei Lei, an overnight case, a diaper bag, and a stroller.

Upon her arrival at the Beijing airport, Ping was relieved to see a tall, familiar-looking man holding a sign with her name on it. "*Nie hao*," Ping said in Mandarin. "I'm Mrs. Bennington."

"Welcome. I'm Zheng Bai, at your service, Madame." He bowed and took Ping's overnight case and the diaper bag while she followed pushing Lei Lei in the stroller.

In the car, holding her daughter on her lap, Ping instructed Zheng Bai to go to the apartment she had once shared with Jianbo. When they arrived, she asked him if he wouldn't mind waiting. "I have been hired to stay with you all day. I am fine waiting."

Zheng Bai helped Ping and Lei Lei out of the car and unfolded the stroller. He remained behind as she pushed the carriage over the cobblestones toward the apartment. The courtyard was empty. Ping knocked at the door and called out Jianbo's name. Satisfied that he wasn't home, she pulled a key from her purse. Hand shaking, she unlocked the door and turned the knob.

Shoving the stroller inside, Ping's heart beat rapidly. She glanced around the room. She walked over and touched the sofa, the sofa where she and Jianbo had shared jasmine tea and chatted at the end of the day. Life had been joyful and simple in the early months of their marriage. It had not yet been darkened by schemes and lies.

Nothing of her remained in the apartment. It was not as she had left it. Dishes were piled high in the sink; clothes were strewn about; the bed was unmade. Ping opened the window and left the door slightly ajar, hopeful that the stench of cigarettes and other unsavory odors would dissipate.

Lei Lei arched her body against the straps that contained her, crying to get out. After lifting Lei Lei from the stroller, Ping sat on the bed, cradled her, and gave her a bottle. She drank, sighing contentedly. Soon her eyes closed; her lips released the nipple. She was asleep.

Ping had to work quickly. She wanted to be gone before Jianbo returned. If he worked only the lunch shift, he would be home soon. She spread one of Lei Lei's blankets on the dirty bedsheet and placed her in the center, protected on each side by pillows. Assured that she wouldn't fall off the bed, Ping looked around. The divorce decree had to be somewhere in the apartment, but where?

The armoire was her first guess. Crouching on the floor, she emptied the contents of the first two drawers just below the closet space. Surrounded by a ring of white briefs, mismatched socks, and grayish undershirts, she pulled out the drawer completely. Maybe it was taped to the bottom. She pressed her lips tightly together. There was nothing there. Replacing the drawer, she returned the contents and began emptying the second drawer.

Suddenly someone grabbed her by her hair. She screamed as Jianbo yanked back her head. Lei Lei awoke. Her cries rang out.

"Stop, you're hurting me."

"What are you doing snooping through my drawers?"

Rubbing her head, Ping rose, picked up Lei Lei, and stood inches from Jianbo, eyes smoldering.

There was a knock on the door. Zheng Bai stuck his head inside. "Is everything all right, Mrs. Bennington?" he asked in Mandarin.

Jianbo glared. "Who's he?"

"My driver." Putting Lei Lei in her stroller, Ping wheeled her to the door. "Could you please take the baby for a walk? She's very tired. She'll fall asleep."

Zheng Bai hesitated, tossing a sideward glance at Jianbo. "Are you sure you'll be all right if I leave?"

"I'll be fine."

"When should I come back?"

"In about fifteen minutes."

The stroller bounced over the cobblestones. Peering around, Lei Lei's eyes widened as they moved farther from Ping, arms outstretched toward her mother, tears streaming down chubby cheeks.

Ping felt a tightness in her chest as she shut the door. She walked toward Jianbo, who stood in the center of the room clenching and unclenching his fists.

"So what were you looking for?"

"Our divorce certificate."

He crossed his arms over his chest and stood, legs apart, staring at Ping. "I thought so."

"Where is it?"

"Why would I tell you?"

"Because I have a right to a copy."

"I have no idea what I did with it," Jianbo said, smirking.

Ping drew in steady, controlled breaths. She had to remain calm; she couldn't show Jianbo her anger. "What would it take for you to provide me with a copy?"

"Why would I want to do that?"

"It's the right thing to do."

Jianbo's face reddened; his lips curled. "The right thing to do? The right thing to do is for you to honor your commitment, to divorce the American and remarry me."

"I have a child."

"Leave her with the American."

Ping's eyes hardened. "I will never give up my daughter."

Jianbo moved closer, chest thrust out, an ugly twist to his mouth. "When the American learns the truth, he will cast you into the street. Then you will come begging me to take you back."

"I would never stoop that low."

Grabbing Ping by the arm, he flung her onto the couch. She gasped, her eyes blinking rapidly. "We had an agreement," he repeated, his voice rising. "We promised each other eternal love. I have been faithful to you."

"What kind of agreement is it when you send your wife to sleep with another man? You disrespected our marriage vows and brought shame on both our families."

Jianbo stood and began pacing. "How long will you be here?"

"Until tomorrow."

"Where are you staying?"

"At the China Palace."

"What? Are you trying to make me lose face? I've told every-one—including your former boss—that you had a scholarship to study English in the United States. No one knows we're divorced. When they see you with a child, I will be humiliated."

"I'm sorry."

"I don't believe you. You probably plan on having me make your breakfast tomorrow morning in front of all the other cooks and waiters."

"No. I'll have room service."

Jianbo continued to walk back and forth, his face contorted, his eyes smoldering.

"You know it's only a matter of time before I obtain proof of our divorce. What purpose does it serve to not give me the docu-ment now?"

Jianbo stopped pacing and stared at Ping. "You are not the same person I married. The woman I married did what I asked."

"You were my husband. I wanted to please you."

"What changed?"

Eyes wide, Ping stared in disbelief. Did Jianbo really have no idea of what he had done? "You are a very ambitious man, which is a good thing. But I became a victim of your dreams and aspira-tions. You treated me like a prostitute to obtain US citizenship. As the proverb says: 'He who sacrifices his conscience to ambition burns a picture to obtain the ashes.' I am those ashes," Ping con-tinued. "And like the Phoenix, I have risen. I can never go back to you."

"Feng was right," Jianbo said, walking toward her as she cow-ered on the couch. "He saw you in New York with your fine clothes and jewelry. He said you would never leave the American to re-marry me."

"Did Feng also tell you he tried to rape me in his hotel room?"

Eyes ablaze, Jianbo stood inches from Ping. "You're a lying bitch."

Trembling, her heart racing, she cringed before him. "I'm not lying," she said barely audibly.

Muscles and veins strained against his skin. Jianbo pulled back his hand and slapped Ping in the face. "Liar," he yelled. "You lied about loving me. You lied about remarrying me. Now you're lying about Feng."

Lifting his fist, he struck Ping again in the face with such force that she fell off the couch. As she tried to get up, Jianbo kicked her. She screamed in pain.

The door swung open. Zheng Bai appeared. He grabbed Jianbo from behind and held him in an armlock. When Jianbo struggled, Zheng Bai forced him to the floor and placed his knee on his back.

"Get off me," Jianbo said.

"Only if you sit on that couch and don't move."

Jianbo grunted his assent. Zheng Bai released him, and he crawled over to the sofa.

"Make one wrong move," Zheng Bai said shaking his fist in Jianbo's face, "and I'll break every bone in your body."

Ping pulled herself up, face battered, eyes frantic. "Where is Lei Lei?"

Zheng Bai rushed to the door and rolled in the stroller. Lei Lei looked curiously at her mother. "You need to put ice on your face," Zheng Bai said.

Glancing at herself in the broken mirror of the armoire, she gasped. Her cheeks were red and swollen. One eye was half-closed, the area around it already turning a deep violet.

Darting to the kitchen, she threw cold water on her face. From the small refrigerator she pulled out a tray of ice, wrapped the cubes in a towel, and applied it to her eye.

Jianbo made a move to stand up. Zheng Bai pushed him back down. "I told you not to move." Turning to Ping he asked, "What do you want me to do with this guy?"

Squirming on the couch, beads of sweat formed on Jianbo's forehead. Lei Lei whimpered. Ping lifted her out of the stroller and propped her on one hip while she continued to ice her face with her other hand. She glared at Jianbo, who averted her gaze.

"I'm sorry. I didn't mean to hit you," Jianbo said.

Lips curled, Ping responded. "You are a bully—just like your friend Feng."

"What are you going to do?"

Squinting at Jianbo, Ping tilted her head. "You have a choice: give me the divorce certificate, or I'll let Zheng Bai decide your fate."

Jianbo sat for a minute as if debating the choices. Slowly he rose and made his way to the armoire. He opened a side drawer. Shuffling through the contents, he pulled out an envelope on which was written in Mandarin "Divorce Decree–Wang Jianbo and Zhao Ping." He walked over to Ping and handed it to her. She grabbed the document. "*Xie, xie.*"

"You shouldn't thank me just yet."

"Why not?"

"Feng is on his way to see the American. He is going to tell him everything tonight."

Ping's heart raced; she had a heavy feeling in her stomach. She strapped Lei Lei back into her stroller. "I must go back to Shanghai immediately," she said to Zheng Bai.

CHAPTER SEVENTY-NINE

Some enchanted evening, you will see a stranger. Walking from the elevator to his room, David hummed the song he had heard the pianist play when he first met Ping. He couldn't remember ever having such a feeling of well-being. Work was going well; setting up the new office proved exciting. He was married to a wonderful woman. And then there was Lei Lei. Words could not describe the joy his daughter brought him.

When he entered the room, he noticed the button on the telephone blinking. *Probably Ping,* he thought. Picking up the receiver, he called the front desk for his messages.

"Good evening, Mr. Bennington. There is a gentleman waiting to see you. He has been here almost an hour. His name is Li Feng."

"Li what?"

"Li Feng. He said he met you on a boat trip a few days ago. That he's a friend of Jianbo."

"Do you know what he wants?"

"He didn't say."

"Tell him I'll be down in a few minutes."

David really didn't want to go downstairs. It had been a long day at work. He had been looking forward to relaxing with room service. Ping had also bought him a copy of Pearl Buck's *The Good Earth* that he planned on reading. Nonetheless, he didn't want to be rude.

Ten minutes later, David stepped out of the elevator into the lobby. The hotel occupied the top thirty-five floors of the eighty-eight-story Jin Mao Tower. As such, the lobby offered a spectacular view of Shanghai. A gleaming circular marble walkway separated an interior area of registration and concierge desks from a sunken lounge furnished with ecru sofas and armchairs. From anywhere in the two-story lobby, a guest looking through the floor-to-ceiling windows had an unobstructed view of the city. David recognized Li Feng seated in one of the armchairs. "*Nie hao,*" he said as he approached his visitor.

"*Nie hao.*" Feng stood, displaying his wide gold-toothed grin.

"What can I do for you?"

Feng hesitated before speaking as if weighing his words. "I have something of—how do you say it? —a delicate nature to talk to you about."

"I haven't had dinner yet. Would you like to join me? We could eat in the café."

Feng nodded.

At the restaurant, the maître d' led them to a table by the window. The nocturnal haze that often surrounded the tower had not yet made its appearance. From this height, twinkling lights appeared starlike, delineating the Bund on the other side of the Huang Pu and outlining the barges and other boats gliding up the river.

Tearing his eyes from the view, David perused the menu. "I'll have the fried pork with laurel," he told the waiter. "And just water to drink."

"Beer, please," Feng said. "Tsingtao if available."

"Are you sure you won't have anything to eat?"

Feng patted his protruding belly. "No, I ate when I wait for you. Filled up."

After the waiter departed David asked Feng why he had come to see him. "Actually," Feng replied. "It is Jianbo who wished to talk with you, but his English is not so good. I come in place." Feng pulled out a package of cigarettes and offered one to David who shook his head. After lighting up, he continued. "Jianbo and I best friends. I know him since little." Feng put his arm out to illustrate the size.

"So, you have known Ping and him for many years."

"Not true. Only Jianbo."

"How is that?" David asked.

"I know only from when Ping marries Jianbo."

David's eyes narrowed; he sat back in his chair. "I don't understand."

Feng was silent as the waiter returned with their order. After he had placed David's dinner and his beer on the table, Feng extinguished his cigarette. "Ping and Jianbo are husband and wife." He reached into his jacket pocket and pulled out an envelope containing photos. "These pictures of marriage."

David studied each photo: Ping dressed in red standing between her bridesmaids, Jianbo and Ping kneeling at an altar, dancing in a restaurant. What the hell was going on? Was this a joke? David glared at Feng. "Why are you showing me this?"

"Jianbo feels great guilt. He and Ping deceived you; he and Ping were not honest. He wants you to know the truth."

David felt lightheaded. He was at a loss for words. He listened as Feng outlined Jianbo's plan to obtain citizenship, in which, he claimed, Ping was an enthusiastic participant. When he finished, Feng sat back, a self-satisfied expression on his face.

What a scumbag, David thought, *taking such delight in another's misfortune.* David stared at Feng, eyes hard and cold. Apparently surprised by David's reaction, Feng glanced out the window. Dark clouds had rolled in and extinguished the lights of the city, just as Feng's words had smothered the conversation at the table.

Now David understood Ping's reluctance to identify her first husband. "He made me do things a husband should never ask a wife to do," she had said. How humiliating it must have been to be pimped by your husband. No wonder she refused his suggestions to invite Jianbo to the United States. The only thing he didn't understand was Ping's urgency to see Jianbo now.

The waiter returned to the table and asked David if they wanted anything else. "No, I think we're finished here. Unless," he said turning to Feng. "You'd care for something else."

Feng shook his head. After the waiter left, he cleared his throat. "I have something else to say."

"I'm listening." David leaned back in his chair, arms crossed over his chest.

Averting David's steady gaze, beads of perspiration glistening on his forehead, Feng shifted uncomfortably. "Ping bigamist. Crime in China."

"Really," David said calmly. "Should I call the police?"

Feng's jaw dropped. "I not say that."

"What are you trying to tell me? That Ping and Jianbo are still married?"

"I...I think yes."

David rubbed his forehead. "And wait. Let me guess what's coming next. You won't tell the authorities..."

"Tell the authorities?"

"Tell the police if I give you...what? Ten thousand dollars? Fifteen thousand dollars?"

"One hundred thousand. That is fair wife price."

"Afraid not," David said, getting up. "I don't deal with scumbags."

"I don't understand this word—*scumbags.*"

"Look it up in the dictionary," David replied, as he walked out of the restaurant.

CHAPTER EIGHTY

Like a wilted flower, Ping collapsed into the window seat of the plane with Lei Lei asleep in her lap. After waiting for hours in the airport on standby, they were finally on their way back to Shanghai. As the plane rumbled down the runway, she glanced at her watch. They wouldn't arrive back at the hotel until almost midnight.

She removed her sunglasses and felt her face, which was red and raw like meat in a butcher's shop. Her fingers touched the slit that was her right eye. She wore the scars of battle, a battle in which she had emerged victorious. But would it be like that American saying? She had won the battle but lost the war.

By now David knew everything. What would he do? Would he leave her? Kick her out of their home? Or worse yet, would he use his powerful lawyers to take Lei Lei from her? Her stomach churned. She glanced out the window. The plane was wrapped in a shroud of dark clouds headed toward disaster—the blowup of her marriage.

⟞⊹ ⊹⟝

David ran his hands through his hair as he paced about the hotel room. He lay on the bed to read only to close the book and turn on the TV. A few minutes later he got up and strode back and forth, stopping to grab nuts or a soft drink from the minibar or to pull back the drapes to stare at the miasma of pollution outside the window. He looked at his watch, picked up the telephone, shook his head, and replaced it in its cradle.

He'd already called the China Palace four times—most recently about fifteen minutes earlier. Ping had not yet checked in. It was past eleven. Where the hell was she?

Sitting on the bed, pajama top unbuttoned, he clasped his hands between his legs. Feng's words rang in his head. *Ping and Jianbo are husband and wife. Ping only married you to get US citizenship. Once a citizen, she will divorce you and remarry Jianbo.*

David had not been totally surprised to find out that Jianbo was Ping's abusive first husband. There had been indications. Instead of being happy when he had invited Jianbo to help celebrate her birthday, Ping appeared anxious. Whenever Jianbo visited, she avoided him. She claimed to be busy with wedding preparations, schoolwork, study groups. David shook his head. How had he missed the signs? Ping was terrified of Jianbo.

And Feng's claim that they were still married? Ping had told him that she had divorced her first husband. Was this another of her lies?

Unable to sit still any longer, he picked up the phone and dialed the China Palace. "Are you sure she hasn't checked in? Did she call to leave any messages for me?"

A pained look crossed his face as he listened to the response.

"Please have her call me immediately when she arrives. Let me give you the number. Oh, you have it. Well, thank you."

Slowly, he hung up the phone, reluctant to give up his only possible connection to Ping. He had tried to get hold of Jianbo at the hotel, but he wasn't working the dinner shift. And he had no phone where he lived. He had called the car service agency but received only a taped message in Mandarin. He had never felt so helpless.

CHAPTER EIGHTY-ONE

Ping adjusted her sunglasses as she left the elevator and headed toward the hotel room. A feeling of dread overwhelmed her. Perhaps she should have returned the next day as scheduled. A confrontation with both her husbands in one day was like leaving a bear's den to enter a lion's cage.

With Lei Lei dozing on her shoulder, Ping fumbled in her purse for the key card. "Can I help you?" the porter asked in Mandarin.

"Thank you."

Inhaling deeply, Ping entered the room. David stood gazing out the window. The fog had lifted, unveiling pinpoints of city lights. Upon hearing the door open he turned. "Thank God," he said, running over to embrace Ping. "I've been worried sick about you. Where have you been?"

"At the airport in Beijing trying to get on a flight."

"I wish you had called me."

David stepped aside. "Please bring everything in," he said to the porter.

The porter placed the suitcase, diaper bag, and collapsed stroller inside the room. As he left, David handed him a tip.

"I'm going to put Lei Lei in her crib," Ping said, avoiding David's glance.

The baby whimpered at the loss of her mother's warmth but quickly fell back to sleep once in her bed. Ping turned around and walked to where David stood, her head lowered.

David placed his hand under Ping's chin and lifted her face. He removed the sunglasses. His head jerked back when he saw the half-closed black eye and the bruises. "Who did this to you? Tell me, I'll tear him apart."

Tears squeezed through the slit that was her eye and glided down her swollen face. "Jianbo."

"I'm calling the police. I'll have him arrested," David said, livid with rage. "No one treats my wife like this."

"Shh," Ping replied, a finger over her lips. "You'll wake Lei Lei. Can we sit down?"

Nodding, David followed Ping to the bed where they sat side by side. "It won't do any good to call the police. In China, they don't get involved in domestic squabbles."

"Something must be done. Look what he did to you."

Ping shifted uncomfortably on the bed. "I am not concerned about Jianbo. He can no longer hurt me. What is more important," she continued, tears welling in her eyes. "Is what are you going to do now that you know the truth about our marriage."

"First I need some answers from you. Was ours a marriage of convenience?"

Eyes focused on her hands folded in her lap, she hesitated, reaching deep inside herself for the answer. "Initially, I was following Jianbo's orders. That is true."

She looked up into David's anxious eyes. "But when I think about our situation, I believe my marriage to Jianbo had to occur in order for us to be together. If I had not married him, I would not have gone to Beijing, and we would never have met. It was destiny that arranged our meeting, even though thousands of miles separated us. Now, I am linked to you forever. Our hearts beat as one."

David wrapped his arms around Ping and pulled her close. She felt protected and safe in his embrace. Her body relaxed for the first time that day.

"Are you going to leave me?" Ping asked softly, knowing but wanting to hear David's response.

"Never. To lose you would be to lose a part of my soul. Like you said, the Gods had to move mountains so that a businessman from New York could meet a beautiful Chinese woman named Ping. We are destined to be together forever."

Tears of joy cascaded down Ping's cheeks. "I have felt your love. It has helped me accomplish what I thought was impossible. As they say in my country, being deeply loved by someone gives you strength while loving someone deeply gives you courage. You gave me the strength and courage today to confront Jianbo."

As Ping recounted her visit to Jianbo's, his abusive behavior and Zheng Bai's intervention, David appeared more and more remorseful. "You shouldn't have gone by yourself. Jianbo is dangerous."

"I had to go. He had our divorce decree. Without it I could not prove we were no longer married."

"Aren't divorces recorded somewhere?"

"Eventually, but the government is very slow. It would take two to three years before it would reach the official records. Auntie Yi Ma checked. My wedding to Jianbo is still not recorded."

Ping shut her eyes trying to rid her mind of the horrible moment when she lay on the floor helpless, and Jianbo started kicking her. "I don't know what would have happened if Zheng Bai hadn't been there."

David held her hands. "Thank God he was."

"I am so ashamed. Many times I wanted to tell you Jianbo wasn't my brother. But then he threatened me. He said he would tell you we weren't divorced. I asked him for the divorce papers, but he wouldn't give them to me."

"And that's the reason you went to Beijing?"

Getting up from the bed, Ping padded over to the table where her pocketbook was lying and pulled out an envelope. She handed it to David.

David opened it and removed the papers inside. "It's in Mandarin. What does it say?"

"It says that Wang Jianbo and Zhao Ping are officially divorced."

Ping sat down again next to David. "I was so afraid you wouldn't want me anymore when you found out I had deceived you."

"I want you, and I always will. But I'm going to ask you again. Is there anything else I should know about you that you haven't told me?"

"No." Ping thought for a moment. "Wait. Yes."

David sighed. "What is it? Please don't tell me there's a third husband. You're not a trigamist, are you?"

"What's a trigamist?"

"A word I made up for a woman with three husbands."

"Nothing like that. What I want to tell you is that you have a father-in-law in Chongqing who is anxious to meet you."

CHAPTER EIGHTY-TWO

The taxi stopped in front of a row of attached nondescript houses. The light rain and clouds added to the squalidness of the dwellings. "Which is your father's home?" David asked, helping Ping and Lei Lei from the cab.

"The one with the yellow door."

Raindrops fell upon them as they made their way to the house. Before they reached it, the door opened, and Yi Ma appeared. "Welcome, welcome. We so happy you here."

David appeared struck by the shabbiness of the home. The living room was dark and somber. The carpet was worn, faded colors indicating the path of greatest traffic. An effort had been made to spruce up the room. A scented candle burned on a chipped coffee table, losing the battle to replace the musty odor that filled the dwelling, an odor redolent with age and tobacco.

Ping followed her aunt through the familiar entrance. Clad in traditional garb, Zhao Jiang sat in his faded green armchair, barely discernible in the dim light emanating from the single lamp on the other side of the room. He rose from the chair with difficulty, hair and beard now almost entirely white. Ping watched, eyes troubled, as her father shuffled toward them. His wrinkled face lit up as he approached his granddaughter.

"So this is little Lei Lei," he said in Mandarin, seeming to savor each syllable of a name he knew so well. "And today is your American birthday."

Ping held her breath, fearful that Lei Lei might cry before this unfamiliar face. But she simply stared at her *nai nai*. Fascinated by the long white beard, she reached out to touch it. Ping grabbed Lei Lei's hand. Zhao Jiang shook his head. "It is OK," he said, eyes twinkling. "The tugs do not hurt."

Lei Lei twisted the long, coarse hairs around her fingers, just as she had her grandfather's heart.

Ping felt a tap on her shoulder. David moved beside her. "And this is my husband, David Bennington."

"*Nie hao*," David said, bowing in the Chinese way. Earlier, Ping had taught him the correct way to greet elders. As Ping watched smiling her approval, David made a fist with his right hand. He held it in the palm of his left at stomach level and bowed deeply. "*Hen gaoxing renshi ni*. So pleased to meet you."

"*Hen gaoxing jiandao ni.*" Zhao Jiang responded, dropping his head slightly.

David handed his father-in-law a gift in a suede-covered case. Placing it on the coffee table, Zhao Jiang opened it. Inside was a second box made of cork. Shaking his head, Zhao Jiang glanced at Ping and David seeming uncertain as to what to do.

"The gift is inside the second box," David said.

Ping translated whereupon Zhao Jiang opened it and removed a black silk bag with gold decorations. Inside the bag was a bottle of Merlot from one of China's best wine producers. Smiling broadly, Zhao Jiang held up the wine for all to see.

There had been something else in the box, a scroll with the producer's official seal. The note informed the recipient in both

English and Mandarin of the high quality of the wine and its cost—$580. Earlier, Ping had removed the scroll. She knew her father would be uncomfortable with such an expensive gift.

Bottle in hand, Zhao Jiang moved backward to his chair, bowing in appreciation as he went. David and Ping sat on the couch with Lei Lei, who squirmed from her mother's arms. She stood by the sofa for a while with one tiny hand clenching her mother's knee, the other on the coffee table. Wobbling back and forth on chubby, unsteady legs, Lei Lei let go of Ping and stood with both hands on the table, doe eyes sparkling, heart-shaped mouth open just enough to reveal two baby teeth.

"Look," Yi Ma said in Mandarin, "Lei Lei is trying to walk."

As if she understood, Lei Lei took tiny tentative steps clinging to the table. Yi Ma knelt a few feet from her and held out her hands. "Come to me, my precious."

Her audience watched, captivated as Lei Lei let go of the coffee table and took two steps toward Yi Ma before falling. Seated on the floor, she looked ready to burst into tears. But her mouth reversed itself into a grin when Baba, Auntie Yi Ma, and her parents applauded.

"Isn't this wonderful?" Ping said. "We are all here for Lei Lei's first steps. She should be rewarded. Let's open her birthday gifts."

Auntie Yi Ma excused herself to get the presents. A pungent odor escaped from Lei Lei. "I think our daughter needs to be changed," Ping said, lifting her up.

"I'll do it," David said. "This will give you a chance to talk to your father."

"Are you sure?"

"Yes. Just point me in the direction of where it should be done."

Ping pointed to her old room. David took Lei Lei, picked up the diaper bag, and headed toward the bedroom.

"Is your husband going to change Lei Lei's diaper?" Zhao Jiang asked in Mandarin.

Ping nodded.

"He is a good husband. Most men I know would refuse such a task."

"I am fortunate. David is very considerate."

Zhao Jiang pulled himself out of his chair to sit next to Ping on the couch. "You've told me only bits and pieces of why you and Jianbo divorced. I want you to tell me the entire story."

"It is a story that fills me with shame and regret," Ping began, hands folded in her lap, face flushed, eyes tearful. She told her father about Jianbo's plan to go to America and become very wealthy, a plan for which he sacrificed her dignity and self-respect.

Zhao Jiang flinched when he heard what his daughter had endured, the beatings, a marriage of convenience to a foreigner, the accusations of bigamy. "With each indignation inflicted by Wang Jianbo, I felt like the cormorant diving deeper and deeper into an ocean of sorrow," Ping said.

Zhao Jiang's eyes filled with tears. "Can you ever forgive me for arranging such an ill-fated union?"

"It was not your fault. You did everything you could to assure a good marriage."

Zhao Jiang wiped away his tears with the back of his hand. "I am fortunate to have a daughter who forgives. I am also fortunate to have a daughter who can overcome difficult situations. Like they say, our greatest glory is not in never falling but in rising every time we do. I am very proud of you."

They turned as Auntie Yi Ma, David, and a freshly diapered Lei Lei entered the room. Yi Ma placed the birthday gifts on the coffee table. She handed Lei Lei the smallest box. Looking at it quizzically, Lei Lei appeared uncertain as to what to do. She glanced up at Ping, who showed her how to rip off the wrapping paper. Rather than open the gift, Lei Lei amused herself for some time tearing the colorful paper into small pieces. When she put some of the confetti into her mouth, David pulled it out. Then he helped her open the box. Inside was a small, brightly colored ball. Yi Ma showed Lei Lei how to roll the ball on the floor. Zhao Jiang watched, eyes glowing, as his granddaughter played with his gift.

Lei Lei tore off the wrapping paper and opened the second box herself. It was a panda bear hand puppet from Auntie Yi Ma. David put the puppet on his hand and grabbed his daughter's nose with its paws. Lei Lei brought her fingers to her face and shrieked with laughter.

Ping handed Lei Lei the third box. "This is from my friend Helen and her son Nathan. You remember them, don't you David?"

"Wasn't she the one married to the finance professor who died?"

Ping nodded.

"What is she doing now?"

"She's teaching English in a high school in her hometown. In fact, it's not too far from here. Maybe on another trip we can visit her."

Reaching inside, Lei Lei pulled out a colorful stuffed rag doll with a large head and a protruding button nose, ink-drawn eyes and mouth, and red hair made of yarn. "*Bu wa wa*, rag doll," Ping said.

"*Wa wa*," Lei Lei repeated, hugging the doll.

"Lei Lei lucky, many presents," Yi Ma said to David in English. Ping thought of the birthdays he must have had. He would have felt deprived receiving only three gifts.

"Come, time for lunch," Yi Ma announced. "I prepare special food for birthday."

The kitchen had barely enough room for the table. The back of Yi Ma's chair was pressed against the stove. A dim light emanated from a small fixture hung overhead. Yi Ma had decorated the kitchen earlier for the occasion with colorful streamers.

Plates were passed to Yi Ma, who filled them with freshly cooked delicacies. "This reunion," Yi Ma said, pointing to a mound of shredded meats.

In response to David's questioning look, Ping explained. "The shredded meat dish is a combination of pork, ham, and chicken with cooked bamboo shoots. As you can see, the meats are packed closely together—like a reunion. It's a perfect dish for today with the whole family together for the first time."

Having lost interest in her birthday gifts, Lei Lei crawled over to her mother, pulled herself to a standing position, and stretched her arms upward. Ping lifted her onto her lap. Lei Lei took bits and pieces of food from her mother's plate.

For dessert, Yi Ma placed a large dish on the table. "Eight-jewel rice," she said.

"What's this?" David asked.

"This is a traditional birthday sweet," Ping replied. "It's a mound of steamed sticky rice, mixed with sugar and bits of dried fruit. The pieces of fruit are the jewels."

"No birthday cake?" David asked.

"Too expensive," Yi Ma replied.

"Lei Lei doesn't know what she's missing."

Ping glanced at her daughter. "She doesn't seem to mind. She looks happy." As if to support her mother's claim, Lei Lei looked up smiling, grains of rice encircling her mouth and sticking to chubby fingers.

Zhao Jiang said little during the birthday celebration. He sat hunched over, staring at his hands. "Baba, what's the matter?"

"I wish your mother were here to share in our joy," he said in Mandarin.

Ping touched her necklace with one hand and squeezed her father's hand with the other. "She is here now. She will always be with us."

The overhead light flickered briefly as if it would go out. Zhao Jiang looked at his granddaughter, his wife's namesake. His expression told Ping he knew she was right.